THE WEB OF DESTINY
THE COMPLETE CABALISTIC CASES
OF SEMI DUAL, VOLUME 4

BOOKS IN THE ARGOSY LIBRARY:

SATAN'S MARK: THE COMPLETE CASES
OF SATAN HALL, VOLUME 2
CARROLL JOHN DALY

INTO AND OUT OF THE PRIMITIVE
ROBERT AMES BENNET

THE WEB OF DESTINY: THE COMPLETE
CABALISTIC CASES OF SEMI DUAL, VOLUME 4
J.U. GIESY & JUNIUS B. SMITH

MIDNIGHT TAXI: THE COMPLETE CASES
OF SMOOTH KYLE, VOLUME 1
BORDEN CHASE

THE JADE SERPENT: THE COMPLETE CHINATOWN
CASES OF JIMMY WENTWORTH, VOLUME 2
SIDNEY HERSCHEL SMALL

THE SAPPHIRE DEATH: THE ADVENTURES
OF PETER THE BRAZEN, VOLUME 7
LORING BRENT

THE SWAMP ANGEL: THE COMPLETE
CASES OF CALHOUN, VOLUME 2
EDWARD PARRISH WARE

STUNT MAN
EUSTACE L. ADAMS

THE DARK PERIL
MAX BRAND

THE SNOW GIRL
RAY CUMMINGS

THE WEB OF DESTINY

THE COMPLETE CABALISTIC CASES OF SEMI DUAL, VOLUME 4

J.U. GIESY & JUNIUS B. SMITH

POPULAR PUBLICATIONS · 2024

TABLE OF CONTENTS

The Curse of Quetzal 1

The Web of Destiny 127

About the Author: Dr. J.U. Giesy 291

About the Author: Junius B. Smith 293

THE CURSE OF QUETZAL

1

AT THE GRAND CAÑON

IT WAS IN the billiard-room of the Grand Cañon Hotel that I first met Laredo, Evelyn and Dayton.

I remember that it was ten-thirty by my watch, which I had just consulted at my wife's request; and she had gone up to our suite. Dual also had decided on going up, and I was the only member of our party who did not feel like turning in.

Some of my old habits of the days when I was a newspaper reporter still clung to me, and made me always hate to hunt my bed before midnight.

Dual offered to see Connie to our suite, and I strolled into the billiard-room to watch a game, if there happened to be a good one in progress. I always loved billiards and pool.

But there was little doing. A couple of college boys were waging a noisy contest in one end of the place, with a great deal of boasting and acclaim when one of them chanced to pocket a ball. The rest of the room was empty save for myself and three persons—a woman and two men.

It was the woman who at first attracted my attention. She was a beauty of the pure Saxon-Norman type, if you know what I mean. She was blond, with straight, regular features, a pink-and-white skin which looked firm, vividly red lips, blue eyes, and actually golden hair. In height she was about five feet four; and just as I came in she was bending over the table to execute a shot, so that her lithe figure was thrown into a strikingly alluring outline by her posture.

As I took a seat not too close for a tactful inspection, she made a successful essay on her ball, and straightened up with a smile, dropping her cue to the floor with a little thud of the butt.

"Bravo!" exclaimed one of the men. "Señor Dayton, we must look to our laurels or we lose them. Behold a still further argument in favor of votes for women, is it not? That was a truly masculine shot."

The girl laughed. "How you men always compare everything to the masculine standard," she retorted. "Your shot, Spencer, I think."

The third member of the party squinted at the cue ball. "Sewed me up, what?" he remarked in deep bass.

He was a brown-haired chap, with eyes of the same color, and a ruddy, British skin, a good chin and a firm-lipped but pleasant mouth. Plainly, the girl and the one she addressed as Spencer were English. The other member of their table was not easy to place.

He was swarthy, slender, supple, yet with a good breadth of shoulder and a thinness of flank almost suggesting an Indian type.

As to face, his was an elongated oval, high in the cheek bones, with a sharply bridged nose. His hair, worn rather long, was straight, black, and brushed directly back from his high and narrow forehead. His lips were thin, and lay firmly together in a way which indicated a strong voluntary habit of control.

Withal, there was a hint of a high Spanish type in his features, and I finally decided that he might be a Mexican of the better sort—one of those families which have maintained their integrity ever since the Spanish invasion of the country to the south.

Spencer, or Dayton, as man and girl had called him, made his shot and missed. Laredo bared his teeth and lifted his cue. "An' now, Mees Wingarde, behold!" he exclaimed.

I have seen good playing. I have even thought myself a good shot at times, but never have I seen a finer exhibition of skill than followed. Ball after ball dropped into the pockets in swift, unerring succession. The fellow literally swept the table, and stopped only when there was nothing more to accomplish. He set down his cue and bowed.

"Ungallant," said Miss Wingarde, pouting her lips. "You might have left me one little chance at the end."

"My dear lady," he retorted. "A thousand pardons. But I forgot."

He spread out his hands, which I had watched throughout his playing. Long, supple, nervously tense they were. As they had held his accurate cue on ball after ball, I had found a pleasure in regarding their calculated adroitness. I watched them again now, as he swept them wide in a gesture of apologetic deprecation.

"No matter," the girl was saying. "I've had enough. Take me up now, Spencer; I think I'm a trifle tired."

"No more?" queried Laredo, trifling with the cue.

She shook her head. "Thanks, no; it is useless. Good night."

Laredo bowed deeply from his hips.

Miss Wingarde and Dayton moved off. The other

followed them with his eyes until they left the room and, I confess, I did not like the momentary expression which swept over his face.

But it lasted only for a moment. With a shrug he turned his glance from the girl's retreating figure, and I felt it fall on me. In fact, our eyes met in a way which would have made it awkward without speech.

"You play a strong cue," I remarked.

He smiled in a purely mechanical way. "And you, *señor?*" He paused. "Would you give me the pleasure?"

"Small pleasure, I fear," I returned. "My fate would be similar to Dayton's and Miss Wingarde's." However, I arose and picked up the Englishman's cue.

Laredo's face became interrogatory in expression. "You know them?" he questioned quickly.

I shook my head and picked up a cube of chalk. "Only from hearing you mention their names."

"Delightful people." He racked up the balls. "Mees Wingarde is the daughter of Professor Mathias Wingarde, an English archaeologist. The Hon. Spencer Dayton is the secon' son of a British title. Your break, *señor—*"

"Glace," I bent and drove into the massed balls, getting one on the rebound.

"Pleasure," said Laredo. "Myself—Señor Rodriguez Laredo, of Mexico, *señor.* Ah!"—as I got my second ball—" be generous, *señor.*"

"I think I'd better take what I can at the start, after watching you play," I retorted, and dropped the two ball into a corner.

His teeth flashed.

"Take fortune by the forelock? 'Tis a motto of mine also,

Señor Glace. No time like the present. Precisely, the three is yours. But you will not be so fortunate with the four."

I wasn't. Laredo lifted his cue.

I watched him. Save for a faint accent at times, he spoke perfect English, and he had a splendid poise. Beyond doubt, he was a man of the world. I wondered as to his mission in life.

And, no doubt, you who have followed the course of my somewhat erratic honeymoon, which succeeded my marriage to Connie Baird, will wonder how Dual and myself and my wife chanced to be at the Grand Cañon Hotel.

It came about in a very natural way, yet, perhaps, I had better explain briefly, none the less, for some may not know my friend Semi Dual, that strange, latter-day metaphysician of whom I have written from time to time.

I first met him when a reporter on the *Record,* long before I myself took to detection as a profession. In fact, it was Dual's association which put me into the latter game.

In my earlier accounts, of our friendship I have told of his wonderful exploits in bringing wrongdoers to justice and freeing the innocent from suspicion, and I have described his use of the higher universal laws, the so-called occult powers, in bringing this about.

The man was an ardent student of astrology, telepathy, chirography, psychometry, and the higher psychology of life on a purely scientific plane.

I think he knew more of such subjects than any man I have ever met. It was his canny ability to unveil the truth from a mass of misleading seeming which first made them dub him the "occult detector" in the city where we both lived.

Wherever he went he seemed always to be drawn into tangles of human affairs, which his wonderfully sympathetic nature made him seek to unravel. He was the most altruistically sympathetic soul I have ever known.

And it was this readiness to help which had left Connie waiting at the Goldfield home of Colonel McDonahue Sheldon, while Sheldon and Semi and I went on to San Francisco to save the life and welfare of two women before we were done.

Our original destination, when we became Dual's guests for a honeymoon trip immediately after our wedding, had been the home of his mining partner, John Curzon, in Goldfield, and it was here we returned after the San Francisco matter was ended. Dual spent several days looking over the properties he and Curzon owned, and then quite without warning, suggested a stop at the Grand Cañon on our way back home.

We were sitting on the veranda of Curzon's home when he brought up the matter.

"Mrs. Glace," he said to Connie, with a faint smile on his firm lips and lighting his gray eyes; "this has been a sadly irregular honeymoon for a little new bride, I fear. As your host, I should like to atone in a measure for taking Gordon away from you, as circumstances compelled me to do. How would you like to return by way of the Cañon of the Colorado? It is one of the Great Builder's masterpieces, you know."

Connie's eyes began to shine in anticipation.

"How would I like it?" she cried in a tone which was an

answer. "I should love it. I have always wanted to see it. But, Mr. Dual, you are a sort of fairy godfather, it seems. All one has to do is to wish for a thing, and you produce it. I fear you are too kind."

Dual smiled. "Then it is settled. I think I *have* sensed your wish, Mrs. Glace. But do not trouble about the matter. Kindness is one of the few things which gives pleasure both to the recipient and to the giver."

It was a reply typical of our masterful friend. He had a way of offering something and taking your breath the next minute, by making you feel that you gave him a pleasure commensurate with your own in accepting.

Such then was the apparently simple manner in which we came to arrive on the scene of the Wingarde affair and become involved in the series of rapid events which revolved about the strange little Aztec idol of Quetzal as about a pivot. But I am sure that not even Semi himself suspected at the time that he was once more to be called upon to apply his peculiar gifts to the solution of a problem of human passions when he made the suggestion.

In fact, if he had I am sure there would be a far different story to tell about the whole affair.

We left Goldfield and went by a roundabout way to reach the great tourist hotel on the lip of the gorge the restless Colorado has dug for its way to the sea.

Wholly like other sightseers, we arrived and registered and were shown to a suite of three rooms, with a common sitting-room between two bedrooms. And like others we went out the next day and viewed the wonderful works of nature and came back.

We dined and sat for a time on the veranda of the hotel,

and then Connie said she felt like retiring, and Dual said he would take her to the suite. Commonplace enough in all conscience surely, with no hint of what was to come.

Laredo lifted his cue.

The four sought refuge in a pocket as though tied to an elastic string. He smiled slightly and took the five with equal ease from an exceedingly poor position.

"You live up to your motto," I observed. "I had decided that you were from Mexico, but you remind me more of the Castilian type."

He nodded. "I believe we have kept it pretty pure—the blood. A slight Aztec admixture, I am told; but long ago, *señor*—long ago."

"One learns to judge of type in my line," I threw out.

"Ah!" He squinted at his next shot. "And that, *señor?*"

"Detection," I said.

He missed his ball, shrugged, and put down his cue with an apologetic smile, as it seemed. "We all study mankind, *señor,*" he returned. "You in the living example, the Señor Wingarde in those who have died and left but their bones and their records. Some one has said truly that the chief study of mankind is man. Myself, I am more in the English *señor's* line.

"I have traveled and studied somewhat myself, but mainly am I interested in the ancient races of our own Mexico. There was a wonderful civilization, *señor*—wonderful indeed. Save that my ancestors conquered that people, who can tell to what they might not have risen?"

I shook my head. "I don't know much about it," I told him. "You ought to meet my friend Dual. He's up on all that sort of thing."

"Dual?" he repeated. "Ah, you mean the large man I have seen with you about the hotel? He is of a striking appearance. So what you call—composed. One feels him a man of power at a glance."

"He is," I said, and made my shot. "He's helped me with more than one of my cases. In fact, he's cleared them up when all the rest of us failed."

"Is he also a detective, then?" questioned Laredo.

"Not in the ordinary sense," I returned. I went on and gave him a more or less rapid account of Semi's methods, to the accompaniment of the clicking of the balls, as he swiftly accomplished my defeat. "But perhaps, like many others, you do not believe in such things," I made an ending.

Laredo frowned as the last ball dropped slowly into a pocket. "I'm afraid, *señor,* that the admixture of Indian blood in my veins has carried a proportion of superstition with it," he said. "Or *should* we call it superstition? All races of man so far as we can learn have had their belief in such things, have they not?

"Where all have believed, is it not perhaps true that there is some ground for that belief? Myself, I think that in every age of man there are some who are able to sense things more acutely than others. No. I confess you interest me ver' much in this friend of yours.

"Take astrology, for instance. When we are learning each day of so many wonderful things in science—the wireless, the X-ray, and such things—why should we refuse to believe in the influence of equally invisible but none the less potent effects of the magnetic emanations from the stars? Myself I do not know. I have always depen' on my own intelligence, as you say; but because I know not is no reason to laugh."

I was rather surprised at his response. More, his dark face had taken on a sort of introspective expression. In a moment he shrugged and flashed his teeth as though throwing the subject aside. "Shall we have another game?" he suggested.

I glanced at my watch. It was a quarter past eleven. However, I still felt wakeful, and nodded as I reached for the triangle to frame up the balls, which Laredo was now scooping out of the pockets.

I set them up, hung the frame back beneath the table; and my opponent was just drawing back his hand to make the break, when young Dayton appeared in the door of the room, glanced quickly in our direction, and then hastily approached.

It was evident that he sought a word with Laredo, and the Mexican held back his shot until the Englishman had reached the table.

He spoke at once. "Ah, I say, Laredo, you haven't seen Wingarde anywheres about, have you?"

"But, no, Señor Dayton. Eef you remember, I was in this room when you an' Mees Wingarde came in, an' we made up the game." He rested his cue on the floor and regarded Dayton squarely. "Is it that something is wrong?"

"Oh, no!" said Dayton lightly. "I don't fancy it's anything of importance, only when we went up just now the professor was not in their suite, and Miss Evelyn was a bit worried. He went off with one of his guides this evening to see some other chap about something, and he hasn't got back. I dare say he'll turn up after a bit, but I told Evelyn

I'd inquire and have a look about. Thought he might have looked in here if he'd come in lately."

Laredo smiled.

"No. Señor Glace an' I have been here since you left. We have seen no one. But there is no cause for alarm, I would imagine."

"No," said Dayton. "It just seems a bit funny he'd stay out with those guide chaps till this hour of the night. If you see him tell him his daughter is worried about him."

He nodded shortly to Laredo and myself and walked off.

Laredo made his break and took down several balls. I got a couple, and he missed completely on his second turn. He came back on the next round, however, and scored neatly.

I said I'd had enough. Declining an invitation at the bar, I went out and ascended to our suite.

I entered to find Connie and Dual both sitting in the parlor, and she opened on me at once: "I was just considering the advisability of asking Mr. Dual to go down and see if this running away from your bride had grown to be a habit."

I laughed.

"I wasn't lost; I was playing pool. If Dual had come down it would have been an epidemic. There was *one* man inquiring for a missing guest just before I came up."

"A missing guest?" Connie repeated.

"Not present at roll-call," I retorted. "Professor Mathias Wingarde's daughter says her father hasn't come in. Shocking hours for an old man, even if he is an archaeologist, eh? She's set a young chap named Dayton on to the old boy's trail."

"Mathias Wingarde?" said Dual.

"Yes," I nodded. "Know him?"

"I know of him," said Semi. He drew a small pad of paper from a pocket and began to write rapidly.

"But where has he gone?" queried Connie with a woman's curiosity in such matters. "He hasn't wandered off or gotten lost, has he? Is he old or childish?"

"I don't know," I returned as I took a chair. "I never saw him or heard of him before. I was playing pool with an ancient Aztec, when Dayton inquired for the professor."

"An Aztec?" said Dual quickly.

"Not really," I responded. "Mexican chap named Laredo, who said he had Aztec blood in him from away back." I went on and told what had happened.

Dual made no comment. He continued with his writing on the pad. He seemed to be putting down figures in a column and adding them up. For an instant I felt strange.

I had seen him do things like that before at the beginning of one of his odd adventures.

He would take a name, write it down, put a figure for each letter, and add them up, calculate a bit and calmly announce that something would or had happened. He called it the astrology of letters and numbers, and it gave results in his hands, as I knew.

Now I watched him in silence. By and by it grew oppressive. I turned to Connie. "I thought you were going to bed," I remarked.

"I was, but Mr. Dual and I got to talking. I think I will now."

"Wait one moment," Semi begged.

We both turned toward him. He finished his work with the paper and pencil, put the pad away, and sat staring across the room for a time. "Rather, I would suggest that you change your clothing for something free of restraint, yet warm enough to avoid feeling chill in the night," he went on.

Something gripped me by the throat. "Dual—" I began. "What—"

"Because," he continued in a voice of subdued sorrow, "there is a woman in this house to-night who will need the support of a woman. Knowing you as I do, Mrs. Glace, I know you will go to her comfort and support."

He turned his strange, calm eyes in my direction. "Gordon," said he. "Miss Wingarde has suffered the loss of her father. The professor when found, will be dead!"

2

THE EYE OF QUETZAL

"DEAD!" I SPRANG to my feet.

"Dead," repeated Dual.

Connie sank back in her chair. She was suddenly pale. "Not really?" she gasped. "Oh, the poor girl! I must go to her at once. Gordon—"

I shook my head. "Not yet, sweetheart."

I turned to Dual. "You set up the figure of his name?" I declared.

He nodded. "It shows that Mathias Wingarde will die on July 19. This is the 19th of July. From the figure death should have occurred before this, as it is now a quarter to twelve."

I shivered. Often as I had seen and heard him calmly announce the action of fate, it never ceased to affect me strangely.

"I'm going back down and find out," I said in a moment. "Connie, do as Dual suggests. If the worst has happened, that girl will surely need somebody to help her. It will be a terrible shock."

Semi straightened. "Go down," he said quickly. "Lay little and keep your wits about you. Forget all save that you are a detective, Gordon. With your permission I shall tell Mrs. Glace what to do."

I turned to the door. Connie came to my side. "Be careful," she whispered. "Something terrible has happened. I feel it. Look at Mr. Dual. He looks as he always does when he is ready to drag something evil to light."

I nodded. I, too, had seen the strange, intent expression which had settled on Semi's face. I took her into my arms and kissed her and went out of the room.

It was midnight. What is there about the hour which always makes the unseen draw closer, the heart beat slow, the breath catch, the impossible become but the possible for the time? You have felt it, and I felt it that night as I passed down the hall of the hotel toward the stairs to the ground floor.

Our rooms were on the second floor, and but a short distance from the main staircase. The lights were on. Even some of the transoms still showed light within rooms.

Yet as I went with soft-footed tread along the hall I felt a cold wind which seemed to play upon the full length of my spine till the scalp on my head appeared to tighten.

Dead!

I could not doubt it. Too often had Semi Dual foretold the thing I was to find. I reached the staircase and turned to descend. I became aware of a group of men standing near the desk in the lobby of the hotel.

Before I was half-way down I saw that two of them held lanterns already lighted, and sensed that they were cañon guides attached to the hotel staff. Another of the party was Dayton, who seemed to be directing the others or giving them information. Still another was the clerk, who had come out from the desk and was shaking a vigorous head as I reached the lobby floor. A couple of bell-boys hung wide-eyed on the edge of the circle of men.

I advanced to the group quickly.

"That's all," Dayton was saying as I came up. "Miss Wingarde and I were sitting on the veranda about eight-thirty as near as I can recall. One of the guides we had with us on our trip came to the foot of the steps and spoke to the professor.

"He went down and talked to the chap. We didn't hear what they said. After a bit Wingarde turned and called up that he was going a ways with the guide and would be back shortly. They walked off, and I haven't seen him since. Of course I can't speak from a deep knowledge of your aborigines around here, but it looks funny."

"Nonsense," the clerk cut in. "Those fellows the professor took on his trip are perfectly reliable men. There's no chance of their having done anything to him."

The two guides shook their heads in agreement with the clerk's pronouncement.

"Then he must have sustained a fall or something and been hurt," said Dayton. "Here it's after twelve and he wouldn't be apt to stay around the Indian village till any such hour. I fancy we'd best start a search. That's why I sent for you chaps," he addressed the guides.

"Then let's get at it," suggested one.

Dayton nodded. "One minute. I'll inform Miss Wingarde and go with you." He started for the stairs.

I followed and touched him on the arm. He turned with an impatient manner. "Go on," I said, speaking softly. "I'm Glace. You saw me in the poolroom this evening."

"Oh, yes!" he acknowledged. "Well?"

We began to mount the stairs. "Just this," I returned. "Miss Wingarde is worried about her father. She'll have a dreary time waiting the results of this search alone. My wife would be glad to stay with her, and I'd be glad to help in the search, if you like."

"Jolly good of you," said Dayton. "If you'll wait a bit till I can ask Evelyn about it—"

I nodded.

We went on up and turned down the same hall on which our own suite was placed. Passing its door, we went on a few numbers farther and Dayton rapped. Almost at once the girl I had seen earlier in the evening drew it open and he stepped inside. I waited. In a few minutes he was out.

"I have advised Miss Wingarde to accept, if you will be so kind," he advised me.

I led him back to our suite and inside. Connie, dressed in a soft, loose gown, was sitting in the chair where I had left her. Dual, at a writing-table, bent forward, and I knew that already he was at work upon those abstruse calculations which had so often served to point the way for suspicion to follow in the past.

He rose and I presented Dayton.

Without delay Connie and I followed the Englishman back to the Wingardes' rooms. There I met the young girl who, if Dual was right, as I knew him too well to doubt, was already an orphan. With a word and a glance Dayton told her to keep up her courage.

He swung open the door.

A man stood there—a tall, slender, swarthy man, clad in soft flannels. His hand was half lifted as though he had been on the point of rapping. Even before he spoke I saw it was Laredo.

"Ah, Señor Dayton," he said in a manner totally free from embarrassment or restraint, "I was passing and noticed the light. I was about to rap, oh, so lightly, if perchance you were awake, to inquire about the professor. Has he perhaps return'?"

Well, it was plausible enough. Dayton had asked him about Wingarde, and what more natural than, knowing them, he should stop to inquire when he saw the light. Before Dayton could answer, however, I got in a question. "Your room along here, Laredo?"

I spoke shortly, I fear, for he lifted his brows slightly. "But yes, *señor.*"

"The professor has not yet been found," said Dayton in an undertone as he quickly closed the door behind him. "We are on the point of organizing a searching party. They are waiting for me below stairs now. Come on, Glace."

"One moment," said a voice I knew.

Dual had drawn open the door of our suite and now stepped into the hall. Clad in his soft, gray suit, with tie to match, soft, gray shirt, and gray canvas shoes, he made a striking appearance as he approached us along the passage. We had all turned at his words and stood waiting. His strong face was quite calm and his voice was impersonal in tone as he went on:

"In my estimation, Mr. Dayton and Mr. Glace can do more good by remaining here than they possibly can by joining the searchers. They, of course, will be led by the professional guides who are quite familiar with the region and can give it a thorough beating even at night. I am sure they can do quite all which will be essential for Professor Wingarde."

I saw at a glance that he had plainly overheard our remarks to Laredo. My heart leaped, for I knew that his action could mean but one thing, and that already his masterful hands had caught up the reins and would drive to the end of the venture. Dayton on the contrary seemed inclined to resent his interruption.

"But I say," he objected. "As Wingarde's friend and his partner on this trip, and all that, I can't turn the search over to a lot of disinterested nobodies, you know."

"It is precisely because you were his friend and partner on this trip that I wish you to remain here," said Dual. "Shall we not go down and see that the search is started promptly? After that I would desire to ask you some questions."

"You know, I can't just see what gives you the right to interfere in this, my good man," Dayton began.

Dual's eyes came up and rested steadily upon him.

"There are so many things you have not time to see now, Mr. Dayton. For instance, you do not appear to know that Professor Wingarde is already beyond the need of any friendship—"

"Is what? I say now—what do you—" Dayton stammered, and his voice rose.

"Softly," said Semi. "The news will be hard enough for the daughter, no matter how gently broken. The professor, you see, is dead."

"Dios!" It came in a gasp from my elbow.

I saw Laredo start a pace backward, a momentary expression of shocked surprise on his dusky face.

"My God!" chimed Dayton like an echo. "How do you know that? Has somebody found him?"

"Not that I know of," said Semi. "In fact I think not yet."

"Then how do you know?" Dayton's face, which had paled, went suddenly red. "I don't understand all this."

"Not yet," said Dual. "Later. Come, let us go below."

I took Dayton's arm and led him along. I was conscious of Laredo behind us. So we went down again to the lobby and found the guides and several more of the guests who had been sitting up over a card game and had volunteered to join in the search.

They stood or sat in a close little group in the otherwise deserted lobby. The guides had set down their lanterns, and they shone sickly in the electric glare. All eyes turned toward us as we approached. As I half expected, Dual took control. He spoke directly to the clerk:

"I have suggested to Mr. Dayton that he place the search in the hands of the guides as the best parties to conduct it quickly."

Both the guides nodded and the clerk rubbed his hands. "Exactly, sir. It would avoid delay and unnecessary excitement. I agree with you completely."

Semi turned on the two men. "Then select your parties from these gentlemen here and proceed. Continue till you find Professor Wingarde."

One of the two men spoke to his companion. "You take half of 'em, Bill, an' we'll get on the job." He stooped to pick up his lantern.

"But I say," Dayton again protested. "I don't think Evelyn would wish me to stay about here when her father may be in danger or injured—or—or worse. Wait a bit, you chaps."

I took him again by the arm. "Do as Dual says," I whispered. "He knows what he's doing. I think he's the only one of us who does."

"But who gave him the authority to take hold?" he retorted, growing more and more flushed. "Who is the chap? What—"

"He's a detective," I said, choosing the word for what I hoped would be its impression.

He shot me a sharp glance. "Eh? Oh, by Jove—"

"Well, do we go or do we stand around and chew the rag?" Bill's tone was one of palpable disgust.

Dayton turned toward him. "Go on," he said with sudden decision. "I'll wait here. Stay till you find the professor. You'll be well paid."

At once they moved off.

They left the hotel, went down the steps, and we followed them to the veranda. Through the night we could see their lanterns separate and go bobbing off in two different directions. With them went the bell-boys, who had joined the search while the clerk had turned his eyes for a moment.

Dual, Dayton, Laredo, and myself remained standing at the head of the veranda stairs.

"Sit down, if you please," said Semi, taking a chair against the side of the house. "Gordon, bring up some chairs."

Both Dayton and I took one. I set mine so as to face Semi, and Dayton placed his at my side.

"I fancy I may intrude, is it not?" spoke Laredo softly.

"Not at all," Dual took him up. "I believe you knew the man who is missing. I should like you to remain."

The Mexican shrugged.

He dragged a chair over and sat down beyond me in the

shadow. Seated as we were, both Dayton and I were in the light from a lobby window. I found myself wondering if perhaps Dual had intended to place us all in such a position that our faces would be readily seen. I glanced about me just as he spoke.

"Draw in closer, gentlemen, if you please. We shall speak softly of this matter."

Dayton and I complied. Laredo, as a matter of course, followed. Dayton cleared his throat. "And now I fancy I'd better ask you to explain, Mr. Dual. You know I can't just see by what right you are taking your stand in this matter. It was jolly good of Glace to send his wife in to Evelyn and all that, but—"

"I told him to," said Semi.

"Eh?" Dayton fairly gasped.

"You see," Dual went on, "I knew Miss Wingarde would need a woman's support when her father was found, and during the waiting. Permit me now to add, that if you are really interested in the young woman's welfare, as I feel sure you are—"

"Rather. We're to be married, you know," said Dayton quickly.

"You will offer me all the assistance you can in clearing up this matter of his death." Dual paused.

"But that's what I can't understand," the Englishman rushed on. "You say he is dead, but I can't believe it. How is one to know that till he is found?"

"That," said Dual, "is a matter for later explanation. What you must do now is to tell me all about the last few weeks of your association with Miss Wingarde and her father."

"Why?"

Dayton was not inclined to a quiet surrender.

"Mr. Dayton," said Semi, "it is a truth that at times the most trivial things in their seeming lead up to the tragedies of life. For years I have made a study of such matters. If there should, by any chance, be more in this man's death than an accident, perhaps some fact you might mention in your narration would serve to point out the real cause.

"If you are unwilling, I shall not insist, but as we have some time to wait for the searchers' return, I think we may as well employ it in gaining all the facts of the past few weeks which you can recall."

"Let me ask you this," Dayton returned. "Are you and Glace detectives?"

"In a sense, yes. In Glace's case, unequivocally so."

"Very well then." Dayton lowered his voice still further and began: "I have known Professor Wingarde and his daughter for years. Possibly you may have heard of his name, for he has been known of late as an authority on archeology of no little weight.

"For a long time he has desired to make a trip to the cliff dwellings in this part of your country, in order to prove or disprove a theory of his in regard to those vanished people. Briefly, he believed that in them would be found the progenitors of the later Maya and Aztec civilizations, and some months ago he announced that he was about to make the trip.

"As I just told you, I am engaged to Miss Wingarde. For years, ever since her mother died, in fact, she has been in the habit of accompanying her father on his various journeys about the world. She declared that she would come over here with him, and I suggested that I come along.

"That was the way we arranged it. We crossed and went on to Mexico, where the professor made some investigations of the various ruins he could reach, as a preliminary step, toward his investigations up here. It was in the City of Mexico itself that we met Mr. Laredo, and from him the professor received no little help in his work."

Dual's eyes sought Laredo's. "You are interested in archeology?" he inquired.

"Not in the same way as the Señor Professor," the Mexican returned. "Always, however, have I felt an interest in the people of Montezuma. I have studied their history no little."

"The call of the blood?" said Semi.

It seemed to me that Laredo's eyelids narrowed. They left Dual's and turned on me as though to judge how much I had told him. "Perhaps," he replied at length.

Dayton nodded.

"That's right. Laredo here told us he was a descendant of Montezuma. He's up on their past records. Well, after we'd poked about a bit we came on up, outfitted, and got guides from the Indian camp a bit over here. We employed two brothers who said they knew the region where the cliff dwellings were to be found, and as it was beastly rough going, we left Evelyn at the hotel, and the professor and I made it alone.

"And on my word it was a trip. Any man but one as deeply interested in the subject as Wingarde would have chucked it, I assure you. But not he. Seems he'd picked up a bit of something I hadn't heard about—something about a place up there where some sort of idol or image was stored. I don't know where he'd dug up the information, and I never asked him, but he was as eager about it as a dog on a hot trail. You didn't put him on, did you, Laredo?"

"No," Laredo answered shortly and shook his head.

"After a bit," Dayton went on, "we got up there, however. Rotten country. One can see why the original inhabitants moved out. Regular tumble of hills and draws—or cañons, as you folks call 'em.

"Not much water, and what there was pretty poor stuff. We fogged along, though, getting deeper and deeper into the jumble of hills, and the guides seemed to know where they were going, though I'm blessed if I could have told from one day to another.

"Then one day we came to a place where there was a ruin, 'way up in the side wall of a cliff. It looked like a rather poor spot to have taken so much effort to reach, but Wingarde was delighted to get there. The next morning we tried to get up to the thing. There'd been a sort of road along the cliff once, but it was pretty well gone to pieces, and we had the deuce of a time from the start.

"After a bit, though, what with the Indians' help and a good bit of work with ropes and some grapples we'd brought, I managed to get up on the ledge where the ruin stood and pull the professor up on a sling. Then we had a look at the place.

"It wasn't much but a jumble of stones. They must have built without mortar, just piling the stones up in a thick wall and chinking them up with mud maybe. Anyway, the thing was pretty much fallen to pieces, though we did find a sort of central space, which might once have been a big room.

"And right in the center of that there was a blackish sort of stone, about six feet long and three feet wide and maybe three feet high. It looked just like a big piece of cut stone to me, but when Wingarde saw it he let out a whoop, and ran over and stood leaning his hands on its top. 'The altar, Spencer,' he said. 'Here, we have it—the old sacrificial altar.'

"I know I made some remark about having sacrificed a lot to reach it, and being glad if it was up to specifications, for he grinned, and began counting the number of hand-spans in the thing's length. A bit after he was down on his hands and knees, digging alongside it.

"I guess there must have been a good deal of sand and dirt blown up there in the years since the old place had been falling down, because he scooped out quite a hole before he called me to come and help him pull out a stone.

"I went over and found he'd uncovered what looked like a loose slab of rock set on edge just below the bottom of the big stone. Between us we got it loosened up and it came away, leaving a sort of hole under what Wingarde called the altar.

"He thrust in his hand and began to fumble around, frowning and twisting his face, and then after a bit he uttered an exclamation and pulled out something about as big as a hen's egg. He gave it a squint and yelled till I jumped.

"Then he handed it over, and I jumped again. The thing he held was an emerald. That's right, really. It was an emer-ald with one side flattened and a sort of rough picture of a face, with a lot of lines raying off from it, cut into the smoothed-off surface."

A sort of sigh escaped the man at my elbow. "So large as a hen's egg, *señor*," he said in a voice of the deepest interest. "They had such intaglio stones—but so large as a hen's egg!"

"The Eye of Quetzal," said Dual.

"Dios!" hissed Laredo. "Señor—you mean—"

"That there was such a stone. The *conquistadores* sought to find it, but it was never found. Proceed, Mr. Dayton."

Laredo was breathing audibly as Dayton resumed:

"That wasn't all Wingarde found. There was a bally little idol in the hole under the altar. It was made out of bronze, with a round sort of face, a flat nose, and thick lips. Rotten looking old god. It had a sort of handle attached to it, too, which, I reckon, the priests must have held it by when they were doing their mumming."

"Did it," said Semi, "seem to have long hair falling to its shoulders and a sort of draped head-dress, something like the pictures you have seen of Egyptians at times?"

"Precisely," nodded Dayton. "I remember Wingarde said it reminded him of some Egyptian images he had found."

"It was an image of Quetzal," said Semi Dual.

3

THE END OF THE SEARCH

DUAL TURNED DIRECTLY toward Laredo.

"I fancy your friend Wingarde made a very interesting discovery up here, from what Mr. Dayton says. By the way, Mr. Dayton, did the Indian guides appear to find anything of unusual interest in these objects?"

Dayton shook his head.

"No, I hardly think so. They were stoical brutes, you know. One couldn't tell what they thought half the time. I know Wingarde showed them the idol and the stone, and asked them if their people ever had anything like them, and all they did was grunt something about their god living ' 'way up in the sky.' Struck me they rather looked down on the stuff."

Once more Dual addressed Laredo.

"Of course, you know the history of what this stone may have been. At the time of the Mexican conquest by Cortez the worship of Quetzal, the earlier Aztec god, had largely fallen before that of Huitzil. Montezuma, the so-called child of the sun, worshiped the war god.

"At the same time the priesthood of Quetzal still existed, and among the temple ornaments was an immense emerald worn during the religious rites. Quetzal, translated into English, means shining with green gold fire. Quetzal himself was the god of agriculture rather than violence and war. Unlike the other Aztec deities he was said to be of totally different physiognomy from them, and to have long hair falling to his shoulders.

"The *conquistadores* looted the various temples, but they did not find the great 'Eye of Quetzal.' It disappeared. That brings us to the legend itself. The priests have always declared that Quetzal would be reestablished as the national god.

"As a result, when his temple jewel disappeared, a story started that not until it was recovered could the now enslaved Indians be freed; but should it be brought back, then Quetzal would lead his children out of bondage.

"Even yet, so great is the power of suggestion and superstition, that I fancy should one appear with the jewel in his possession, he might find a fanatical following waiting to follow his leadership in an attempt to overthrow the present government of the country. Now, I do not pretend to say upon what data the professor stumbled, but in some way he must have learned that the great stone had been carried into the north. Have you ever heard of such a thing, Señor Laredo?"

"I have heard, yes. To such a story I give no credence," said Laredo. "Yet, when you named the stone but now, it startled me at first. You appear to be well informed concerning the ancient peoples, Señor Dual."

"I have read somewhat," returned Semi.

We lapsed silent. A soft breeze fanned along the veranda. The great stars winked out of the night sky like a thousand eyes. From where we sat we could see the dark outline of the great gorge of the Colorado.

None of us spoke for a time. Each was busy with his own thoughts. Somewhere out there under the night a man was lying dead, if Dual was right. Other men went to and fro searching for his body.

Up-stairs his daughter was waiting, hoping, counting, doubtless the slow drag of an eternity of minutes, until she should hear of his finding. And she did not know!

I glanced at Dual. He sat silent, his face in the shadow, inscrutable, calm, apparently unmoved by the emotions which stirred in the breasts of us other, less impassive mortals. My gaze rested lingeringly on his strong, shadowed features; and as though he sensed all I was feeling, yet keeping from voicing, he began to speak:

"The stars—silent monitors of the earth." His voice was low, soft, brooding as the darkness beyond us. "How much they have seen in all the ages they have looked out of the void at man. Harbingers of destiny, the stars! Through all ages mankind has looked up and questioned, and in each age a few have learned to read an answer from the fiery numerals set down on the Master's blackboard."

I sensed rather than heard Laredo catch his breath. Dayton turned his head slowly and regarded Dual as though half comprehending. I waited, knowing full well that he would go on.

"Those old people, the Aztecs, read them; they believed in their voices, gave heed to their predictions. So well they knew them that when Cortez came they showed him a calendar more nearly perfect in its fine calculation than the one he used. In a natural crisis of affairs, their priests not only inspected the augury of the sacrifices, but they stood on the top of the temple and questioned the stars.

"And if the priest were sincere in his question, desiring the truth and only the truth, then the stars answered him truly. For he who seeks the truth for truth's sake shall ever find it, though he ask of a stone in the fields, or of a little child, or of a star in the sky.

"Mr. Dayton," Semi Dual went on, "an hour ago, perhaps, you asked me how I was able to make a certain statement; where I had gained my knowledge. What would you say should I tell you I, too, questioned the stars and but voiced their answer to you."

Dayton's head came up with a jerk. "I say—" he began and paused. "You wouldn't joke now, would you? You mean you believe in—"

"Astrology, Mr. Dayton? Yes."

"Wingarde spoke to me about it on one or two occasions," said Dayton. "He mentioned that all the old races believed in the thing. But I thought it had been given over by every one except fortune-tellers and that sort of chaps. I never thought there was anything in it. It seems a bit foolish, you know, to imagine the stars can have anything to do with our lives."

"How?" came a voice from the lips in the shadow.

"Why—why—how could they?" Dayton failed to marshal an argument to his need.

"Why could they not?" said Dual. "For ages mankind believed it—through ages of enlightened civilization, before the dark ages put out the light of achievement. They worked out a wonderful system of calculation by which to read their answers in the stars.

"And as the truth never dies, Mr. Dayton, so what truth was theirs has come down through the years to mankind; and those who wish may use it, as I did to-night, by taking the name of the man who was missing and questioning as to his fate."

Dayton's eyes were wide and staring in the light from the lobby. "I—er—if you'll pardon me, just what are you?" he stammered.

"A student of life," said Dual.

"And you really believe in this thing?"

"Why not? We send an invisible ray across a thousand miles of ether and believe the thing which it says to the man who sits there, the detector at his ears. Why not believe the invisible message the Omnipotent sends from a star?

"Why deny their magnetic influence on life on this planet? Why accept the wireless and deny telepathy, Mr. Dayton? A thought is a thing generated by the cell action of a brain. It is no less real than a Hertzian wave. Once set into motion, it lives until it comes into contact with another brain sufficiently sensitive to translate it.

"Does not that suggest another means to you of my learning Professor Wingarde's fate? Can you not see that when I learned from my astrological calculation that his probable fate was death, I, who have studied life forces, would seek for the wave of some other who knew? Presuppose for a moment that he had died of murder. The one who struck him down would, beyond any power of his own volition, project the thought of his deed. Could I intercept it, then my certainty would grow."

"My God!" said Dayton.

Laredo had turned his chair so that he sat facing directly off the veranda and was staring out into the night.

"You believe, then, in telepathy, *señor*," he remarked at length.

"Having proven it, yes." Dual leaned yet farther back in his chair. "If you will maintain silence a moment, perhaps I can give you an example. There are a series of thought-waves charging this atmosphere at present. I shall see if I can receive and translate them."

He deliberately closed his eyes, letting his hands lie relaxed on the arms of his chair. His chest rose and fell slowly, while we watched him. I felt Dayton's eyes upon me, and nodded.

Too often had I seen Dual lapse thus into concentrated attention on one point. Something like awe had come into the ruddy face of the Briton, and I saw he was holding his breath as he waited. Laredo, on the contrary, was sitting staring out into the night and not moving a muscle.

Suddenly Dual rose, stepped forward and stood by the veranda rail. "Your pardon," he addressed Laredo. "You are breaking the waves with your thoughts, as a wireless may be broken up."

He swung round and faced toward the night. For perhaps three minutes he stood there before he dropped his arms and turned round.

"They have found the body of Wingarde, and of one other," he said. "The second is an Indian guide. Both are dead."

"A thousand curses! Are you going to kill off the entire hotel, with your predictions, *señor?*" cried Laredo, springing to his feet.

Dual smiled, yet as I recall it now, there was no humor in that smile.

Dayton, too, had risen. "The Indian," he rasped. "I never did trust that fellow. He attacked the professor, and Wingarde killed him. What a beastly mess!"

"Hah!" Laredo turned toward him. "But *señor,* that might be. If the fellow knew the emerald's worth. Wingarde would fight for the possession most surely.

"But—" he paused and his lips drew back. "Are we not like the children who believe and cry out at the nurse's story? What proof have we really that these things are so? The Señor Dual's remarks have interest' us deeply, so that for the moment we are carried away an' forget that we are not children of Nature to tremble at thunder, but civilized men."

Dual returned to his seat.

"And civilized man must ever have proof," he remarked. "Material proof for material man. Perhaps it is as well. These higher forces of life are like high potential currents; improperly used, they would work incalculable harm."

"Just the same," said Dayton, "if Wingarde is dead, I believe that Indian killed him. I know he used to listen a lot when Wingarde and I talked. I told the professor he wasn't up to any good. I don't know how much of all you have said I really believe, but just now you certainly did something rather odd to my way of thinking. How did you know he had that guide with him? I didn't mention it in your hearing?"

"Suppose you tell me just what happened?" suggested Dual. "How did the professor come to go out tonight?"

Dayton complied.

Dual nodded. "And you do not know what the man said which made Wingarde go with him?"

"No. I didn't try to listen. I was talking with Miss Wingarde. Fact is I didn't consider it important until the professor said he was going off with the fellow."

"You must not confuse the real with the unreal, Mr. Dayton," said Semi. "My means of knowing of the guide was extremely simple. When you asked of Señor Laredo for the professor, you mentioned his having gone with the guide.

"Mr. Glace heard you. He mentioned the affair to me, and of course I recalled it. Much of so-called mind reading and such is but merely getting your subject to tell you something and repeating it to him in a different manner, or using information concerning him, already in your possession. There is a very close mixture of the false and the true. A great many people have pretended to powers they did not possess and so have thrown the genuine occult into disrepute."

"Exactly," agreed Laredo. "Having known of the guide, and drawn out the information that he knew of the Señor Wingarde's finding the emerald, and been shown it, and assuming to hold it in contempt, you deduce that he sought to take it, and that Wingarde resisted.

"Therefore you assume that each killed the other an' hazard the statement on the probability that it is correct. *Señor*, you are clever. For one leetle minute, you stirred in me a latent superstition. But now I see, how you have arrive' at the conclusion."

"Yours is the obvious conclusion, I fancy," said Dual.

"You mean this was mumming—at such a time?" Dayton's voice grew hoarse. "I say you know—"

"Rather a means to an end," said Semi. "From now on, Mr. Dayton, we deal with material things. As to mumming, no. Call it an experiment in psychology if you will. This is hardly the time for mumming."

"That's what I thought. Good Lord, won't those chaps ever get back and tell us what they find?" Dayton moved to the rail, staring down toward the dark gash of the cañon, and the country around it.

"Has this hotel a detective?" said Semi.

"Eh? I don't know. I suppose so." Dayton turned around.

"But yes," Laredo informed. "I have met him."

"Then, Dayton, if you'll answer me a few questions?" Semi paused and waited.

The Englishman turned from the rail and came back. "Well?" He sat down in his chair.

"About the emerald and the idol; did Wingarde seem to value them highly?"

"Rather. He never left them out of his sight."

"Explain please."

"Why, he wrapped them up in some pieces of cloth and carried them in his clothes. A dozen times a day he'd get them out and look them over. He used to try and get me to praise them, too, though I couldn't get up much interest."

"But he seemed excited himself?"

"Yes."

"The Indian guides knew that he carried them on him?"

"Of course."

"So that if they had desired to rob him of them, they would have known all they had to do was to get him alone?"

"By Jove, yes."

"And a lonely walk in the night would have accomplished that." Semi nodded. "Was Wingarde a strong man?"

"No. He was too much of a student. He was wiry, but he wasn't of any great strength."

"And he was fifty-nine years old?"

"Yes. But—see here—how the deuce—"

"Oh, my calculations with his name showed me that," said Dual. "The Indians were strong outdoor men?"

"Rather—active as cats."

"Now did Wingarde ever mention the emerald's value in their hearing?"

"He told me several times that its value was immense, but its sentimental value was ten times greater."

"They could have overheard that?"

"Yes."

"Cupidity is a dreadful thing. Men have killed to gain wealth or a jewel. Men have hired others to kill for them, for the same purpose," said Dual. Abruptly he switched the subject. "Now this image—you mentioned a handle by which you thought it was held. Was the handle an actual part of the bronze casting?"

"Just how do you mean?" Dayton inquired. "It seemed to be."

"You don't know whether it was a part of the figure or joined to it— Could it have been removed as a separate part?"

"I don't know."

"I once saw an Egyptian image of Bast," Dual continued, "something like this idol you describe. That also had a handle, but it could be detached. How large was this idol?"

"About six inches long, without the handle. That was perhaps three inches long, and as big around as my middle finger."

"Wrapped up it would have made quite a parcel to conceal about one," commented Dual. "It could have been easily felt through the clothing. One desiring to steal it could have ascertained easily enough if it were upon the person of his victim before leading him away."

"*Señor,*" Laredo cut in; "you are clever. Can we doubt that if murder has been done, this is how it happened?"

Semi smiled as with pleasure. "We must see what the house detective thinks of the matter," he replied. "A light-fingered hand could surely have gained the information as I have suggested."

"Quite right," exclaimed Dayton. "I remember now that the Indian who came for the professor stood very close to him while talking, especially at the beginning. In fact Wingarde stepped back a bit right after the first."

"Hah!" said Laredo, "now we are getting at it, *señores.*"

"It's been my idea from the first that that chap was crooked," declared Dayton.

"From now on we must seek not for beliefs but for proof," said Semi Dual.

It seemed the last word. Laredo said nothing. Dayton sighed. I looked at my watch. It was three o'clock in the morning.

Dayton had risen again and gone to the edge of the porch to stand gazing off into the night. Abruptly he spoke, lifted a hand and pointed. "There! They're coming back now! I saw a light."

Laredo and I rose and stood staring. By and by a dim point of radiance flashed out of the dark. It bobbed up and down, and was followed in a moment by another. There could be no doubt that the searchers were returning. And they moved slowly, at what seemed like a measured pace.

I glanced back toward Dual. He, too, had risen and was standing. As I turned to him he also shifted slightly and looked into the lighted room at our back.

My eyes followed his glance. They fell upon Evelyn Wingarde. She had come half down the stairs from above and stood, tall and slender, a white clad figure, crowned with a mass of golden hair and a white face, from which her eyes were searching the empty lobby.

Her hand rested on the rail of the stairs, and behind her I caught a glimpse of Connie, holding her other hand, and seemingly speaking to her, for all at once, as if in answer, the girl shook her head in determined negation.

I saw in a moment how, unable to stand the suspense longer, she had left her apartments and crept out to gain some report if she could. And out there in the night the lanterns were coming closer. The best or the worst was coming fast to her now. My heart swelled.

"Shall I go in?" I whispered to Semi.

He shook his head. "Small good," he told me softly.

A sound of running came to my ears from the night. Without other warning the two bell boys panted up to the steps and began their ascent. Their mouths hung open from their running, but their faces were white and their eyes wide with the import of what they brought.

"They've found him!" the first gasped shortly.

"An' th' Indian guide, too," added the other.

"An' they're both dead!" finished the first.

A woman screamed.

The boys' panting voices, charged with excitement, had carried. In a rush Evelyn Wingarde came down the stairs, crossed the lobby and emerged on the veranda.

"Dead!" she cried out in a voice of anguish. "Who said it? Oh, it isn't true—it isn't. Tell me it isn't true."

The boys drew back abashed before her frantic appeal. Dayton leaped forward, and Dual.

"Evelyn," said the former.

"Miss Wingarde," spoke Semi.

She turned to their voices. "Have they found him? Is it true—really?"

Dual bowed his head. "My child I have feared."

I saw her shiver. I saw her breast rise and fall. "Spencer," she faltered. Dayton's arm crept about her. Connie, pale-faced and shaking, crept to my side.

"Is it?" she questioned, and I knew what she meant.

I pointed. The lanterns were almost to us. In their light we could see the slow moving legs of the men who walked and seemed to bear something among them.

They reached the steps and came up, bending to raise what they carried.

At the top they laid down their burdens, the bodies of two men, one of them red, and one of them white, both silent and wearing the strange, quiet calm of death.

With something between a sob and a moan, Evelyn Wingarde left the support of her lover and dropped down at the side of one. She lifted its shoulders up in her strong, young arms, and pressed its iron gray head to her breast.

"Father!" she cried out, her utterance grief-choked and broken. "Father—speak to me. Father, it's Eve. Oh dear God, it can't be you're dead. It can't—it can't!"

4

THE TINY PUNCTURE

THE CLERK HAD run out on Evelyn's heels, and stood staring at her. Once—twice he opened his mouth and closed it. Abruptly he spoke.

"I—I'll get a doctor and the house detective." He turned and ran back inside to begin a frantic ringing of service phones from the switchboard.

Dual turned to me. "Stay here. Keep by the bodies. See if there is any trace of the image or stone on Wingarde's. Note all that is said or happens."

Dayton had gone to Miss Wingarde's side and was stooping above her. I saw his lips move as he spoke to the girl. Once she looked up, but dropped her gaze back to the face of her father. Immediately after she bent and kissed him on the lips.

Now she laid him down gently, supporting his head as though loath to place it on the floor.

In an instant Laredo had whipped off his light flannel coat and folding it double, placed it beneath her clinging hands.

She flashed him a glance of grateful appreciation, settled her father's head back on its pillow and rose slowly. For a moment she stood looking down. Without warning her eyelids flickered, drooped, she threw out her hands as one groping blindly for succor.

Dayton caught and held her as she swayed. Dual joined him at her side. "Señor Laredo, will you ask the clerk to send brandy to Miss Wingarde's suite at once. We are going up there. Will you come, Mrs. Glace?"

Evelyn opened her eyes as he spoke. "Please, Connie Glace," she said quickly. She lifted her hands to her temples. "Oh, Spencer—I'm—I'm so dizzy. Won't you—"

Her voice trailed off. Dayton acted. He swept her up in his arms and started across the lobby.

We who watched from the veranda saw only her golden hair, and her slender limbs trailing down beyond his body as he began to mount the stairs. Dual and Connie followed. The three went on up and passed from sight.

I saw the clerk and Laredo go toward the bar, and the former called to one of the bell-boys, to come and take the brandy up to the Wingarde suite.

At that moment a man entered the lobby from one side and came rapidly toward where we were standing about the bodies. He was short, heavy set, with close-cropped reddish-brown hair, a heavy-featured face, and large hands and feet.

He walked with an assured stride and shoulders thrown back, and was clad in a tan-colored sack suit, with brown buttons. At present his eyes were not entirely free from sleep. He came out on the porch and stared at the bodies and the men who had brought them.

"Good mornin', Mr. Heffy," said one of the two guides.

"H'r'ye, Bill!" returned the newcomer. "What's the row here? These guys bumped each other off?"

"Don't reckon so," opined Bill. "Ute Charley's been hangin' round here some considerable time, an' he ain't never pulled no rough stuff."

Heffy bent closer to the two bodies. "Ute Charley?" he repeated. "Well, that's right, an' the other's that English professor feller. Say, what happened?"

"I dunno," said Bill. "They disappears together last night an' we jes' finds them like this."

"Where?" Heffy straightened and glanced around at the group.

"Up thar a ways, along the lip," Bill jerked a thumb toward the north in vague direction. "Don't know as we would have, only one of these men stumbled on Charley back of some rocks. Then we scouted around an' found a place where somebody seemed to have slid over the edge. We hung a lantern over on a rope, an' finds the other feller on a sort of ledge 'bout fifteen feet down. Had to go down an' tie him on so's we could pull him up, I did."

"Was he dead?"

"Cold. Just like Charley, when we found him."

"Funny." Heffy lifted a stubby hand and scratched his chin. "Well. I guess you better bring the bodies into one of the card rooms. Doc Osborne will want to look 'em over. An' you, Bill, you go up where you found 'em an' hang about.

"When the folks hears of this they'll wanter go up an' mill around and walk all over any clues. You stick till mornin', an' then I'll send somebody else to relieve you. Now some of you fellers pick up these two an' bring 'em in."

Several of the men bent to comply.

We formed a little procession into the lobby and across it toward the door of a card room which Heffy selected. I saw Laredo talking to the clerk as we filed past, and quite suddenly a medium-sized man, nattily dressed in blue and wearing a close Vandyke and a professional air, appeared from upstairs, running down.

At once he made his way to Heffy's side and addressed him. "What's the matter? Griggs called me."

Griggs, I fancied, must be the clerk. As it happened, I was right.

"Two dead 'uns," said Heffy shortly. "Better come in an' look 'em over."

We crowded through the door of the card room, and the bodies were laid upon tables. It seemed to me that the faces of each appeared to be puffed and swollen as I scrutinized them more closely.

So much I saw before Heffy interrupted. "Now all of you who don't know these parties beat it. Me an' the doc wants to get to work. Guess we better get Griggs in. Some of you fellers tell the clerk we want him."

"Better get the man he's talking to, also," I suggested. "He knew Wingarde in Mexico."

Heffy turned round. He puffed up. "Who—" he began and paused.

I had been waiting for the moment. From the first I had recognized him as a former patrolman from my home town. The surprise seemed to be mutual on his part.

"Go on and take another look," I said, grinning. "Who took you out of harness and slid you into plain clothes, Heffy?"

"Glace!" he shouted. "Well, good night; where did *you* come from?"

"Never mind; get Laredo—the man who was with Griggs a minute ago," I told him. "Care if I stick around?"

"Sure not," he assented, and walked to the door. From there he signed to Griggs. "Come on in an' bring your friend with you," he directed.

He came back.

"Well, say, I never looked to see you. How's the old town? They tell me you've quit the papers an' gone in for the 'private' stuff. Right?"

I nodded. "Glace and Bryce, Private Investigators," I told him.

"An' I grabbed this cinch job through a pull," he announced. "Say, if there's anything funny in this, get in an' help me. I've heard a lot about your work, but I never thought I'd get a chance to work with you. Bryce told me once you had a side-kick with a funny moniker, too. What about him?"

"He's up-stairs with the dead man's daughter," I replied.

"Well, good night," said Heffy, and turned to Griggs and Laredo, who had just entered. "Say, Mr. Laredo, did you know this Professor Wingarde?"

The Mexican answered briefly.

"Wha'd'ye know about his goin' off with Charley, Griggs?" Heffy went on.

Griggs told Dayton's story. "That's all I know," he said.

"All right. Get back on your job, then," Heffy told him.

He went over and ran a hand into each of Wingarde's pockets. He produced a handsome gold watch, a roll of bills of large denominations, and some note-books and papers. "He wasn't killed for what he had on him, at any rate," he decided, thrusting the things into a pocket of his own garments.

"Feel carefully of his body," I suggested, stepping in close to his side.

"What's that? What for?" he demanded; but he rapidly complied, patting and rubbing his hands up and down and around the outline of the corpse with a deftness which showed he had had no little practise. "I got all there was on him," he declared.

"Try the Indian now," I requested.

"Him?" Heffy threw a glance at the body on the other table. "He wouldn't have nothing but some 'smoking.' Still—"

He crossed and began a hasty searching of the Indian's trousers, which, besides his shoes and shirt, was all he wore.

I saw his eyes light with surprise and his thick lips purse as he felt to the bottom of a pocket. And then he drew out a hand, clasping a couple of ten-dollar bills. "Well, what do you know about that?" he exclaimed. "Where do you suppose he got all that money?"

I shook my head. On the other side of the body I was searching its scanty clothing for any bulky object. Quite plainly there was none to be found, and I gave over my examination.

Laredo had taken a chair and was watching our work without any particular interest. In fact, his expression was bored.

Heffy stepped back.

"All right, Osborne," he said to the physician, who had been waiting to make his examination. "Jump in and see what you can find out about it. Honest, it begins to look to me as if Charley tried to get the old boy's roll, an' got his'n, an' then the professor had been hurt so bad he'd stumbled offen the cliff, or somethin' or other like that."

Osborne was already at work, making a deft examination. Now as we watched he lifted Wingarde's head and turned it back and forth, sideways. "This man's neck is broken," he announced.

Heffy nodded. "The fall done that," he declared. "Bill said he was fifteen feet down. I reckon he toppled off an' lit on his head."

"Wait a bit," said Osborne. I noticed that he was observing the body with a frown. Now he lifted first one of the hands and then the other. After that he glanced at the stout English shoes on the feet and shook his head.

Turning his attention back to the face, he bent his own close and began to scan the skin of the neck and cheeks, while his frown of perplexity deepened.

"Looks a bit swollen and peculiar in color, doesn't he, doctor?" I threw in.

"Yes, he does," Osborne admitted. "You don't happen to know just where the bodies were found, do you, Heffy?"

"Bill didn't say, but he said Charley was lyin' back of a pile of stones, as I understood him."

Osborne grunted. He turned and gave the Indian a glance. I rose and crossed to the table. "This body looks swollen, too, though you can't mark its discoloration so well," I remarked.

Again he nodded and began an examination similar to that he had made of Wingarde, save that he drew up the trouser legs and looked at the bare limbs of the Indian beneath them. They were only a pair of overalls, and would not have offered much protection from a bite or sting, such as I fancied he was looking for.

While he was about his work I also began a close scrutiny of the upper part of the body. I lifted the Indian's chin, which had thrown his neck into shadow because of the overhead lights, and Osborne, noting my action, put down the leg he was holding and joined me.

Laredo also rose, and Heffy. They came closer to where we were working. On each side of the table the physician and I bent over the body. And then Osborne uttered a short exclamation and laid his finger on the right side of the throat.

"Look at that, will you?" he exclaimed.

We all bent forward and stared at what looked like a tiny puncture in the skin. It had not bled. It didn't look much larger than a pin prick. It was just a tiny hole in the skin, but the flesh about it was slightly more swollen than the rest of the neck.

That was all!

Laredo let out his breath in a sigh. "Something bit him, señores," he said softly. "Hah! Alone in the night something bit him so that he died. What, Señor Doctor—a serpent, a scorpion among the rocks, a tarantula—perhaps?"

Osborne appeared puzzled.

"He wouldn't die so quickly from a scorpion bite, if at all," he declared. "He'd swell from a tarantula bite, but that would take longer to kill him, too. Still—something bit or stung him in the neck, from the looks of this, and—gad, if it killed him, it killed Wingarde also—his body is swollen worse than this man's!"

"That's right," said Heffy. "Well, see if you can find out

where he was bit, then." He moved over toward the other table where Wingarde lay.

The physician followed. He began a more careful inspection of the professor's body. Abruptly he desisted.

"Hold on a minute!" he remarked. "I'm going to my room and get a glass. I want to examine that mark more closely and any others we find." He left the room with a quick, businesslike stride.

Heffy and I sat down. Laredo stood staring down at Wingarde's body, with an expression of deep consideration on his elongated face. Presently he shook his head, sighed again deeply and resumed his former seat.

Heffy turned to me with a question: "What was you lookin' to find on one of these fellers?"

"I wasn't sure we'd find anything at all," I told him. "But there was a chance that Wingarde might have had some other things on him, or that if the Indian made an attack upon him he might have taken them before he died."

I went on and told about the emerald and the image.

Heffy whistled. "But you don't know he took 'em with him last night," he said. "We'll have to question the girl about that. Perhaps he left 'em in their rooms."

A rap came on the door. Laredo, nearest it, answered. "Ah, Señor Dayton!" he greeted.

"May I come in?" Dayton questioned. "The clerk said you were all in here."

"Come on in," I called as he paused. "You'd best meet Heffy, the hotel detective."

He entered, and I presented the two men.

At once Heffy plunged into questions concerning

Wingarde, their trip, and all the rest leading up to the fatal walk of the night before.

Dayton told him much.

I rose and went back to Wingarde's body and began searching for a mark similar to that on the Indian's neck. But search as I would I could find none.

I turned my attention from the face and neck, and for the first time it seemed that I noticed his clothing closely. Besides a Norfolk jacket of tweeds, he was wearing a sheer silk shirt beneath it—and the jacket was open.

I drew it still further open, bent down and began to scan the fabric of the cream-colored silk.

After a bit I paused. It seemed to me that I had found a place where something might have passed through it—just a spot where the mesh seemed pushed aside. It might be only a flaw—still. With an eagerness I could not entirely conceal, I unfastened the shirt and drew it open. And there I found it—a tiny discolored puncture over the left breast, like the prick of a needle, and no more.

"Ah," said Laredo, "you have found it!" He had approached and once more stood beside me. Heffy and Dayton deep in question and answer had not noticed.

I nodded. The door opened and Osborne came in quickly. In a glance he noted the open shirt and my finger pointing to Laredo's observation. He crossed to the table in a stride. "What—" he began, and I took the words out of his mouth.

"I've found your pin-prick for you."

He gave it a glance, lifted a large-sized magnifying glass and bent over Wingarde's breast.

"What's that?" said Heffy, overhearing. He sprang up

and came over, and Dayton followed, taking a place at my side.

Presently Osborne straightened, went over and bent above Ute Charley's neck. Once more he scanned the tiny wound with his glass. Once or twice he frowned as before, and shook his head in silent mystification. In the end he spoke:

"This is one of the most peculiar things I have ever come across. There can be no doubt that these little wounds are the direct cause of death in both cases. But for two things I would not hesitate to express a positive opinion that they had been bitten by some extremely venomous reptile and died of the result. In fact, that seems the only plausible explanation, despite the two objections to it."

"What's them?" inquired Heffy. "They look to me like a rattlesnake had fanged them."

"They look like that to anybody," said Osborne, "but, see here—if it was a rattler he only had one fang. That's one objection."

Heffy looked puzzled. Laredo smiled. Dayton muttered his customary, "By Jove!"

"The other," Osborne continued, "is that they were struck in such odd places—the throat and breast. Now, if it had been the hands or feet or legs, I wouldn't hesitate a minute in my diagnosis."

"Couldn't the rattler hev lost one of his teeth?" Heffy suggested.

"It is possible, of course," Osborne admitted. "In some way one of its fangs may have been broken and not yet replaced by a new one, so that only the other was long enough to penetrate. They certainly look like victims of snake-bite."

"Pardon," Laredo said softly. *"Señores,* I have been thinking. If I rightly remember, the guide you call Bill told Mr. Heffy that the Indian was found behind some stones. Now, I have heard Señor Dayton say that this Indian was one who went into the mountains with the professor, an' that las' night he came an' spoke to him an' took him away.

"May there not have been something which he wished to show the Señor Wingarde? May it not have been somewhere among those rocks? May they not have knelt to examine it, and the reptile have struck, leaping upon them from among the stones? It is possible, is it not?"

"By Jove!" was Dayton's ejaculation. Heffy nodded his approval. Osborne frowned as he considered the suggestion.

"At that rate," he remarked at length, "your idea would be that the thing struck either Wingarde or the Indian, that it was torn from its hold, and in the excitement and darkness may have been thrown or swung against the other?"

Laredo nodded.

"It is possible, at least," Osborne went on. "In fact, it's the only way in which I can see it could have happened. They certainly were struck by something with a deadly venom, which killed quickly and entered through those little pinholes of pricks. As I said, I've never met a case like it."

"Which one of 'em died first, doc?" Heffy inquired on a sudden.

"Wingarde, I think," stated the physician.

"Then if it hit him in the breast, an' he grabbed it and

pulled it off, he could easy have hit Charley with it, trying to throw it away," Heffy summed up.

Osborne's eyes lighted. "You're right!" he exclaimed. "I think we can safely call it snake-bite, after all. The thing's other fang might even have caught on Wingarde's coat and been broken or doubled back so that it never scratched him. That would explain why it only had one tooth to fang Charley with."

"And how long would you say they had been dead, doctor?" I asked.

"Since perhaps ten o'clock. It is now about five. Seven hours say, roughly."

"Well—" Heffy stretched his arms with a yawn. "If it's snake-bite, that lets me out, I reckon. Let's get out."

By one accord we moved toward the door. Daylight had come as we worked, and the lights were out in the lobby, where the morning sunlight played. The night of tragedy and sorrow was past.

"But there's one thing," said Heffy. "What about that emerald Glace was speakin' to me about? Was it worth much? How big was the thing?"

"As large as a hen's egg, Dayton says," I replied at once.

"A hen's egg!" Heffy exclaimed. "Say, it's worth a fortune! Wait a mo', you chaps." He walked swiftly to the desk where Griggs still sat. "Say, Tim, any folks goin' away this mornin'?"

Griggs nodded. "Several parties, yes. Why?"

"Hold on a min'." Heffy beckoned us to him. "Say, Dayton, that stone ain't up in the professor's *sweet*, is it?"

Dayton shook his head. "No. Mr. Dual, Mr. Glace's

friend, asked Evelyn that, and she said she knew her father had it on him last evening."

"Then—" Heffy turned back to Griggs. "You tell them folks to cancel their leavin'. Nobody leaves this dump till that stone is found. Get me? As big as a hen's egg—some stone—some stone! I wanter lamp that, an' I will, too, or I pull this shack to pieces. Say, Glace, where's that friend of yourn? I wanter see him. Bryce told me onct about some of the things he done."

"Tell you what?" I suggested. "Let's all go have a bath and get freshened up a bit, and then we will all meet at breakfast and talk this thing over. You arrange for a table to ourselves, will you, Heffy?"

"Sure!" He nodded. "All right, then; see you later." Taking Osborne he walked off.

Laredo swung away up the stairs with a nod. Dayton and I went out on the veranda, where we had sat during the night. It was a brilliant July morning, with the cool of the night still in the air. We stood and drank it in. My companion's face looked tired and drawn. Suddenly he spoke:

"What became of the idol and that cursed stone?"

I shook my head.

We went back inside and up-stairs. I entered the suite and found Semi seated at the writing-table in the parlor. Its top was covered with sheets of paper on which were figures and symbols. I knew that while we had questioned each other he had questioned the stars.

He glanced up as I entered and greeted me with a smile. "Sit down and report," he directed. "Mrs. Glace is with Miss Wingarde, whom I have asked Dr. Osborne to see, as soon as she awakes. What have you learned?"

I dropped into a chair and began at the beginning. I talked straight through to the end. "What do you think?" I asked.

"That Heffy did right in forbidding any one's leaving before we lay hands on the image of Quetzal," said Semi Dual.

5

THE MYSTERIOUS TEN-DOLLAR BILLS

THE HOTEL BUZZED that July morning. Numbers of the male guests had, as I have said, joined in the search which resulted in the finding of the two bodies. As a result, the story of the night's adventure began circulating so soon as the first two got together and were joined by a third. The bell-boys, being human, talked, too.

Heffy, full of importance; stalking about the lobby and veranda, added to the general excitement in a subtle manner. Little by little it became known that the two bodies lay in the card room; that they had died the night before, and that for some reason every guest was to be held until an investigation was completed.

When I went down knots of men were scattered about the lobby talking in subdued tones—some with gesticulations. Two or three were arguing with the day-clerk. I fancied them those who had intended leaving.

I had bathed and changed my linen—a sort of vicarious substitute for the sleep I had lost; and by that time it was close to seven, as I had taken plenty of time with my shaving and toilet. Going back to the parlor I received Dual's assurance that he would join our breakfast-party later.

I slipped into the corridor and made my way below.

I found Dayton, Laredo, Heffy, and Osborne already gathered in a knot, and joined them at once. Early risers were beginning to trickle into the dining-room, and Heffy turned his eyes in that direction. "I've fixed it for a table," he announced. "Where's your friend?"

"He'll be down later," I explained. "I want to send a tray up to Mrs. Glace."

He nodded. "Shall we wait for him or go in?"

"We can wait in there as well as here," I decided.

At once he led the way, taking my arm and placing himself at my side. "I was just tellin' the others that I'd sent over and had Ute Charley's brother brought in," he remarked. "Couldn't get much out of the feller, though. He says Charley left the village 'bout eight last night an' said he was comin' here.

"I asked him if he had any money, an' he said no. Said Wingarde paid 'em for their trip, but that he took Charley's part and put it away, to keep Charley from boozing it all up. He seemed some surprised to find Charley dead. Well, we know he'd picked up twenty dollars somewheres, if we don't know where. Come on, that's our table over in the corner."

We found seats and settled ourselves in them. I looked over at Dayton. "How is Miss Wingarde now?" I asked.

"Sleeping still, thank Heaven!" he replied, his face lighting. "Really you know I shall never cease to be grateful to Mr. Dual for his kindness to her in this trouble. He has a wonderful tact."

"I believe you," Heffy cut in.

Dayton turned to face him. "You know him?" he inquired.

"I know of him," said Heffy. "I uster live in Glace's town—on the 'force.' This Dual pulled off some mighty clever bits of work back there. Cleared up some things that had us all running in circles. I never got a chance to see him work, but I heard he has some mighty funny methods."

"You know"—Dayton took him up—"I don't think I ever met a man just like him. There's something about him one can't just understand. You know—or maybe *you* don't, but Glace and Señor Laredo do—that he said right from the first that Wingarde was dead. And he was right. Now, how did he know it?"

I leaned toward him.

"See here," I interrupted. "You said a bit ago that he asked Miss Wingarde about the emerald and the idol. Did he, perhaps, ask her anything about her father's birth-date, also, or did you hear?"

Dayton lifted his eyebrows.

"By Jove, you're an odd pair!" he declared. "But you know how he works, then, I fancy. He did ask her that—got her to talking about poor Wingarde quite freely for a bit. He even wanted to know if she knew what hour he was born in."

"And did she tell him?"

"Oh, yes! I told you she seemed to feel quite at home with him from the first. Funny, too, for Evelyn isn't one to pick up with strangers, you know. But with Dual and your wife now—right from the start."

"Now," said I, "let me tell you: Dual is engaged at present in an astrological calculation, the object of which is to unravel the motive and nature of what happened last night."

The waiter slid up and sought our orders.

Dayton took tea, the rest of us coffee. "An' bring me some cognac with mine," Laredo requested. Osborne shot him a glance. "The night has been more or less exhaustive," he explained with a deprecatory manner.

Dayton pursued his subject as soon as the waiter was gone.

"Odd chap," he said. "He has a queer way of expression. You know, after he'd got Evelyn to sleep, and before I came down to the card room this morning, I asked him how he thought Wingarde had most likely been killed. Now, what do you suppose he told me?"

I shook my head, smiling. No one else volunteered a suggestion, though all eyes were turned in his direction.

"He said that, in his own opinion, both Wingarde and the Indian were the victims of a forked tongue!"

"Snake bite, by gosh!" Heffy burst forth. "They all have split tongues, you know. But—say, how did he know that, either? We wasn't sure ourselves till after you come down, an' Glace found the second bite on the professor."

"Perhaps he received Dr. Osborne's suspicions telepathically," suggested Laredo with a thin-lipped smile.

"Wait one moment," Osborne spoke quickly. "As I was coming back with the glass I went after this morning a man stopped me in the main hallway and asked me about Wingarde and Charley. He mentioned his name as Dual, and asked me to see Miss Wingarde later. I told him that we had found a suspicious mark on Charley, and expected to find one on Wingarde."

Laredo's smile became more expansive. "So much for telepathy in that case," he chuckled.

"Back up!" Heffy advised him. "Dayton was down then, and he said he'd asked before he come. How about that?"

Dayton nodded. "That's right," said he.

"So," said Heffy, "I reckon he found out about the snake-bite in way of his own. I know he's pulled stuff like that before, hasn't he, Glace?"

"Yes. I had him tell me my city editor wanted me for a murder case once—the first time I met him, in fact. And he was right. Furthermore, he helped me find the murderer, and told me what would happen to him—and it did.

"You folks can believe it or not, but he knows what he's doing, even if he doesn't use every-day methods. I can say from experience that he gets results."

I paused, realizing that my own faith and admiration for Dual were carrying me beyond the confines of a mere answer.

"An' there was that time he pinched that gang what looted the Fourth National," Heffy threw in. "Remember how he kept tabs on the main guy all day and grabbed him at night, without the feller's ever even suspectin'?"

"*Peste!*" exclaimed Laredo, frowning. "Is the man a modern magician?"

"I don't know what he is," said Heffy; "but when it comes to grabbin' a crook he's a regular whirlwind!"

Osborne had been sitting silent. Now he leaned forward. "He has a wonderful head. I noticed that this morning," he remarked. "Also, his voice has the modulation of perfect control, and he certainly has a hypnotic eye. Isn't your friend rather an adept psychologist, Mr. Glace?"

"He is," I replied; "but if you mean that he gains his results purely from psychological control of persons, you are wrong, doctor. I think he is rather a hyper-scientist, if you can make anything of that term.

"So far as I can explain his work, he has reduced all life and natural phenomena to the basis of vibration. Force to him is but vibration, in no matter what way it is exercised, whether as sound, light, or thought waves. He claims that what we call fate is but the result produced by the mean influence of the several magnetic planetary force waves affecting the earth from the stars."

Osborne's eyes lighted. "Well, well," he considered, "that is surely placing astrology on a modern scientific basis."

I nodded. "As a result he says that if he can find what influences were acting on an individual at any certain time, he can predicate what would have been that person's natural fate."

"That is how he knew Wingarde was dead, then?" said Dayton.

"Exactly."

Heffy shook a puzzled head.

"Maybe, but it was cuttin' it pretty fine to dope out he'd been bit by a snake. Darned if I can see how a bunch of stars can run a guy up against a rattler. Still—he got it, I guess."

The waiter came back and served us. I gave him an order to be taken up to Connie. Laredo poured his cognac over some sugar, set it alight, and presently sipped at his cup.

Setting it down he smiled, and shrugged his well-set shoulders in a typically Latin way. "Admitting that all this is ver' interesting indeed, an' that something may be said in favor of astrology and telepathy, like all other pseudo-sciences, in fact, or any mere belief, are we not, gentlemen, getting away from the business in hand?

"Since both the modern magi, an' the learned doctor beside us agree as to the cause of death, should we not accept it, and consider rather the only detail remaining to be settled in this unfortunate affair? Myself I should like it to be cleared up quickly, as I plan to leave here so soon as it is. I think it is Mr. Heffy's duty to act with despatch. At the presen' the innocent are suffering with the guilty from suspicion and a curtailment of their liberty."

"You talkin' about that emerald an' the idol?" Heffy demanded.

"Precisely. Since we know the cause of death, why consider it further? Your order against leaving places us all in the attitude of suspected thieves."

The room had been filling up by degrees.

For some time I had felt more than one set of eyes turned on our table. Heffy and Osborne were, of course, known to many of the guests, and they easily connected the others of our party with the events of the night.

At Laredo's words which he had not taken the trouble to modulate at all, our table became the focus of all within hearing. I saw several nod in approval of his words.

"I think it's an outrage," came a woman's sibilant speech from beyond me. "It was that stupid house detective who gave the order, of course. Give a man like that a little authority and he'll abuse it."

"Well, well, my dear," her companion rumbled. "You haven't the wonderful stone, so don't fuss yourself."

"Just the same the dark gentleman is right in his view

of the matter. The management has no right to tag us all as suspects."

Heffy's face was growing into a dusky red. I caught his eyes and knew he, too, had heard. "I'm goin' to get action as soon as I can," he declared to Laredo. "Wha'd'ye want me to do? I'll listen to any dope you got to hand out, *saynor.*"

Laredo shook his head.

"I do not wish to interfere. I merely thought we came together to discuss the situation. You will, of course, look over the scene of the unfortunate affair?"

"Sure," returned Heffy. "I'm goin' up there after breakfast, an' I want Glace to go along."

"An' then what?" Laredo's smile appeared irritating to me.

"Then if I don't find no trace of them things up there, I'll come back here and search this dump. Th' folks can like it or not. I'm within' my rights, an' I know it. I ain't sayin' who took it, but it didn't walk off by itself. An' if it didn't maybe it's up there.

"It was dark last night, an' the folks was huntin' for men, not images or sparklers. Maybe if there was a sort of fight with a snake up there, the thing fell outen the professor's clothes an' is lyin' around loose. That's another reason why I sent Bill up there to stand guard. He's a square guy, that boy."

"By Jove, I never thought of that," muttered Dayton. "Maybe there hasn't been any robbery at all."

While they talked I had been thinking. "There's more to it than that," I gave my opinion. "If your idea were the right one, Heffy, what about those two ten-dollar bills? Charley got them somewhere and he didn't get them for nothing. We ought to try to find out where he did get them, I think."

"They was new ones," Heffy said.

"Exactly, and an Indian wouldn't carry them around in his pockets very long and have them retain their freshness, would he?"

Heffy shook his head. "Nope. Charley wouldn't have carried them long anyway."

"Then probably he got them recently from some one who either had just received them or else carried them in a bill fold," I went on.

"There's something funny about the whole business," said Heffy. "D'ye know I think if we could find that green stone we'd have the key to the whole works."

"The key is contained in the image of Quetzal," said Semi Dual.

We all looked up. He had advanced down the room toward us, but so wrapped in our own conversation had we become that I, at least, had not heard his approach. Now he stood slightly smiling beside the one vacant seat at the table, his hand on its back. "Good morning, gentlemen," he went on, drawing out the chair.

Heffy was watching him, all eyes, as he sank into his seat. Since Osborne had met him in the hall the detective was the only one who did not know him by name. "Dual," I began, "this is Heffy, the hotel detective."

"Mighty glad to know you, sir." Heffy ducked his head, and half raised a hand from habit, in salute. "You mean the whole business hangs on this here idol I've been hearing about?"

"Exactly."

Dual unfolded his napkin and spread it across a knee, as the waiter slid up. "Bring me some fruit, a cup of cocoa, and a pitcher of milk, with some bread, cut thin," he directed and came back to his theme.

"From all accounts it was a most peculiar and interesting object. One is led to believe that we of to-day do not give anything like due credit to the skill possessed by the ancients, though as explorations go on we find more and more proof that they were in reality engineers and artificers of no small degree of achievement.

"Egypt and Babylon have yielded up a mass of very interesting data. In America the ruins of Palenque show it to have been an immense city, the equal of ancient Thebes in area, with temples and public structures of a magnificence undreamed of among us of to-day. It was accurately laid out four square, with a mathematical precision which excites one's wonder and admiration.

"The Spanish *conquistadores* found among the Aztecs so many beliefs of religion similar to their own that they alleged the devil had given them a parody of the Christian doctrines, in order to confound the priests of the Mother Church. Their rites of marriage were sacred and holy; they baptized their new born, and said masses for their dead; they had a sisterhood of nuns, who gave their lives to the service of mankind and the gods; their judiciary was in some respects more fair than ours of the day, and was divided into district courts and supreme courts, with the right of appeal from the lower decision to the higher.

"The rudimentary forms of our own present alphabet are carved on the Maya temples now in ruins, and this image of which I have spoken was made by some artisan of that ancient race which was overthrown by the invading whites. From the description given by Mr. Dayton it was very similar to images recently found in Egyptian tombs.

"And we must not forget that a great many of the inhabitants of that section of this continent where it was created are literal descendants of the nation which worshiped it once, despite the years of slavery and subjection to the whites they have undergone. In a way there is a pathos in it all. They were so grand a people in the Western eyes.

"Then came the white, and disaster. In a short time they were vanquished, their temples desecrated and robbed, their gods o'erthrown, their lands, their cities wrested from them; yet clinging fanatically to a belief in a restoration by some miraculous means. It must have been a faith truly fanatic which urged some body of priesthood to transport this little image and the emerald temple jewel through all the miles from there to here and set up its altar in the ruins of a cliff house in the mountains to the north. Such a faith is sublime. Could it be rekindled in the descendants of those people, it might work the miracle they have about forgotten to even dream of."

It struck me as a rather odd sort of speech at such a time, and I could see by the faces of my companions that they shared my feelings in the matter.

Just at first when I had heard his soft, assured tones my heart had leaped with the thought that now at last the master hand had arrived and things would begin to move. Even his words had foreshadowed a certain knowledge, which seemed to me to say that his calculations alone in our rooms had borne fruit.

Yet starting from the assertion he had first made he

had run off into a dissertation on the ancient nations of the earth, both Eastern and Western, which, while proving the image of Quetzal to be an object of interest to the antiquarian, did not, so far as I could see, serve to throw any light upon its present probable whereabouts or that of its accompanying gem.

Yet Heffy seemed called upon to make some comment.

"I reckon, that's so," he remarked, as though not quite certain of what he was saying. "I always did feel a sort of pity for the under dog myself, but jes' what does it lead to?"

Dual smiled.

"Merely to the fact that there is really nothing new under the sun, Mr. Heffy. That has been said before, but it was true even then. Human nature changes but little after all; and it is very much the same in its basal impulses and motives now as it was at the time of Moses or of the Aztecs. Like us they had their loves and hatreds, their desires for wealth, self aggrandizement, power.

"Like us they planned and plotted, and struggled to win what they wished, sometimes by fair means and sometimes by foul. The things men do live after them, so the things men make may live after them also, and affect other men hundreds or thousands of years after the hands which formed them in the first place have crumbled back into dust. And now, if you will kindly let me see the currency which you discovered on the Indian's body, Mr. Heffy, perhaps we can determine how recently it was made."

Heffy's face was a puzzle as he passed over the bills.

Dual spread them out on the cloth of the table, glanced at them briefly and gave them back. "They were made quite recently," he remarked.

"Of course," said Heffy, "but honest, I think we ought to get busy. It's going to be some job to find that green stone, an' if I don't dig it up pretty soon, the folks in this joint are going to raise merry hob with the management."

Dual took a sip of his cocoa. "On the contrary," he returned, "I do not expect any great difficulty in recovering the stone."

Laredo started, appeared about to speak and desisted. Dayton looked his amazement. In pure elation I grinned.

"What we have to do," Dual continued, biting into a peach, "is to discover such proof as will enable us first to accuse and later convict the one who took it."

"You mean you know him?" Heffy leaned forward and shot out his jaw with the question.

"I have no proof of his identity as yet," said Semi; "at least very slight evidence at best."

"Then—how—" Heffy stopped. A boy was coming among the tables. "Mr. Dual! Mr. Dual!" his treble rose over the buzz of the conversation, which whispered through the room.

Semi signed him to him, took from his tray a single flimsy envelope of yellow, slit it deftly open and gave its contents a glance. Thereafter he placed the message in its cover and the latter in his pocket and pushed back his plate and cup.

"On the whole," said he, "I think you may as well remove your embargo on the departure of the guests, Mr. Heffy. I spoke to the manager of the hotel as I came in to breakfast, and told him I thought it would be possible to do so before long. I think you may safely do it now. It will not be necessary to inconvenience them further, in order to clear this matter up."

6

THE EXAMINATION

"TURN 'EM LOOSE? All of 'em?" stammered Heffy.

"Exactly. Several meant to leave this morning, I believe."

Heffy grinned, and nodded. "I getchu," he said in a tone almost sprightly. "I don't know how you done it, but you've located that danged stone and the image."

Dual shook his head, smiling. "Not yet," he confessed.

"Then, wha'd'ye mean turn 'em loose—openin' th' gate—tellin' the guy what's got it to beat it?" demanded Heffy, growing more and more hopelessly involved in the situation.

"Mr. Heffy," said Dual quite calmly, "it is my belief that the one who obtained possession of that stone would be a person of too great strategic perception to leave at this time."

Heffy considered. Little by little his grin came back. "Well, maybe," he admitted. "I'll go tell th' boss to tell th' folks they can beat it when they're ready."

"That will not be necessary," said Semi. "He was to do so unless we sent him word to the contrary by this time. I took the liberty of assuring him that you would notify him unless you were in accord with me on this point, as I felt you would be."

"Sure," assented Heffy. "Your idea about the thief not tippin' himself by leavin' is a better one than mine, I reckon. That bein' settled, what next?"

Dual nodded.

"I am glad you agree. Next we should, I think, take steps to close the incident as speedily as may be." He turned to Dayton, who had been maintaining a nonplused silence.

"You, Mr. Dayton, permit me to suggest may as well go up to the Wingarde suite. Miss Evelyn was awake when I came down and asking for you. I assured her I would send you up.

"I am sure you will be very glad to know, gentlemen"— he swept us all into the scope of his remarks—"that the young lady has shown her admirable balance by rallying bravely from the first shock of her bereavement and is now in a much more resigned frame of mind. Her control is in fact praiseworthy indeed, robbed of her father in a strange country as she is.

"Mr. Dayton, as her *fiancé*, is, I think, the logical supporting influence which she should now be given. I am therefore going to ask him to devote the rest of the day, until such time as we may want him, to giving her his society and moral support, and diverting her mind thereby so far as he may from the trying position in which she finds herself just now.

"It is in times of trouble that those we love can help us most, and the man to whom a woman intends to commit herself and her life, is more fitted to shield her than any other should be. It is at such times that the man should be a firm support for the more impulsive and emotional female.

"One of the most beautiful things in life is a man and

woman standing in mutual strength against the buffetings of environment. In such we have man's nearest approach to real happiness on this plane of existence. Heaven itself smiles on the true mates, who find their true aim and object in each other."

"By Jove," said Dayton softly. "You—er—that is you think Evelyn wants me?"

Dual nodded. "She asked me to send you up."

"Then I'll go, you know." Dayton rose. "I'll be there if you want me. I—er—good morning." He walked off very erect and square shouldered.

"Bravo!" applauded Laredo. "An' while Señor Dayton consoles his *fiancée,* shall we not discover the missing image, and the emerald, perhaps?"

"An' the proof of who took it," Heffy added.

"And of who gave Charley the bills," I threw in.

Dual shot me a glance of what I felt was approval. "Exactly," he said. "First, if Dr. Osborne will permit it, I should like to inspect the bodies of the Indian and Professor Wingarde?"

"Certainly," Osborne assented, "I would be glad to have you do so. While there seems small doubt about my diagnosis, I confess there is an unusual atmosphere about the affair—the locality of the wounds, and—well, I'd rather like to hear your opinion."

Semi Dual nodded. "Mr. Glace told me. Shall we go to the card room at once?"

Osborne rose and the rest of us followed. In a group we passed toward the door, finding our way among the tables. In the rear with Heffy I noted many eyes turn and follow Dual. It was always so when he appeared with his quiet, commanding bearing, so in keeping with his splendid figure and poise.

We passed out of the dining-room and into the lobby where groups of the hotel's guests were still lingering in conversation, and on across it to the closed door of the room in which the night's victims lay stretched on the green tables where so many games of chance had been waged, none more bizarre or unexpected in outcome, however, than the one they had played with fate, and lost.

Osborne set the door open and motioned Dual inside. Laredo, Heffy and I came after, and then the physician closed the door, and we five were alone with the dead.

They lay as we had left them, save that Wingarde's face was rapidly becoming mottled with purple patches, which shone from the puffed waxen skin in a gruesome manner, and spoke more plainly than ever of the deadly virus which had been injected into his veins.

Under the clear light which now shone into the room from the outer day, he looked frail, weak, pitiful, with his high-bred features framed in iron gray hair.

Heffy at once bustled forward beside Osborne and Dual. Laredo went over and dropped into a seat by a window, after the barest scrutiny of the bodies on the tables. I noticed his dark eyes turn now and then to where we were gathered about Wingarde; but he made no movement to join us, maintaining the attitude of an onlooker rather than an active participant in the scene.

Osborne threw back Wingarde's coat and drew open the shirt. "Here is the wound," he said, pointing to the puncture in the breast.

Dual bent slightly forward to inspect it closely.

"Yep, that's it," declared Heffy. "Glace found it, but it was my idea that the snake fanged the professor first and that he pulled it loose and flung it away an' it hit Charley and bit him in th' neck. Gosh, can't you see the danged thing settin' its teeth through that thin shirt the professor's got on, an' hangin' there wriggling?"

"An ingenious theory surely," said Semi, still viewing the little blue puncture which had not bled even enough to stain, by so much as a speck, the silken fabric of the shirt.

Heffy nodded.

"It was that made Osborne finally conclude it could be a snake bite," he averred. "Before that he was puzzled. Seynor Laredo thought that might be the way of it, too."

Dual nodded slightly. His eyes turned from the wound to Laredo.

The Mexican met his glance squarely. "I thought, *señor*, that there might have been something venomous among the rocks, where the Indian was found," he remarked.

"There was doubtless some deadly thing in that region," said Semi. "This is a typically envenomed wound, made by an exceedingly sharp and pointed object, which doubtless conveyed its poison without cutting any vessels, exactly as a hypodermic needle may convey a solution beneath the skin without drawing blood. Absorption of the fatal substance would be very rapid."

"An' the nature of that substance? You imagine what the thing could have been?" Laredo continued to stare directly toward us as he spoke.

"I imagine it to have been probably of an animal toxin in nature," said Semi. "Its effects on the blood organization of these two men would rather indicate something of the protein strain of poisons. They, you know, are the natural poisons really.

"Humanity first drew its knowledge of toxicology from Nature itself. The earliest application, and the most primitive, is the poisoning of arrows and spears and darts, by substances made from animal sources. The Aztecs and American Indians used a special material obtained from rattlesnake venom, and the South American Indians still use a venom made from the saliva of a variety of large toad, the *Bufus horridus.*"

"You mean the peculiar appearance of the bodies leads you to believe that their blood cells were disorganized to some extent?" Osborne queried quickly. He was observing Semi with what I judged was deep interest and a growing respect for his scientific qualifications.

Dual nodded. "Yes. As a physician you evidently agree, judging from your diagnosis."

"Most surely," Osborne appeared pleased at this support.

"In my estimation your diagnosis is absolutely correct, doctor," said Dual. He walked over to the Indian's body and began an inspection of the wound in its neck.

Laredo rose and joined him. He even began to whistle softly the measures of a Spanish waltz, while Dual made his examination.

Abruptly Semi turned to Heffy. "In which pocket did you find the money?" he inquired.

Heffy grinned. "In neither one," he replied. "All I found in a pocket was a hole. I put my fingers through it and found the bills inside the feller's pants. He'd a lost it if he hadn't been killed, I reckon. It'd worked through an' there was just one end stickin' fast enough in the hole to still keep 'em from droppin'."

Dual made no comment. Instead he lifted one of the dead man's arms and let it fall stiffly back into position. "Still rather rigid," he remarked. "I was wondering if it would be possible to place him in a sitting position." He paused and appeared to consider. "He could be forced into it I imagine, however."

Amazement appeared in Osborne's face.

Doubtless it showed also in my own. As for Laredo, he frowned, as seemed to be his habit when he did not exactly comprehend what was forward. Only Heffy, however, made some verbal expression of what we all felt in regard to the matter.

"What for?" he demanded as Semi paused.

Dual turned his eyes upon him and answered at once. "Because I desire to complete my examination with his body in that position, Mr. Heffy." Swinging back he next addressed the physician: "Doctor, do you happen to have a laryngoscopic mirror in your equipment?"

"Yes," said Osborne. "You wish to use it?"

"If you will be so kind. Bring the reflecting mirror when you return also, unless the throat-glass is equipped with an electric light. Also, if you have an exceedingly fine probe—"

"Very well." I caught sight of Osborne's face again as he spoke. Its expression of deep mystification had increased. Still, he asked no reasons as he turned and walked from the room to obtain the instruments Semi desired.

At once Semi beckoned to me and to Heffy. "If you will lend me your assistance," he suggested. "Take the body by each shoulder while I lift its feet. Señor Laredo, place a chair with its back to the window, where we will obtain a good light, if you please."

Laredo complied without words. Heffy and I took the positions assigned us. Dual lifted the Indian's feet. Together we swung the body from the table and carried it across to the seat prepared for its reception.

Dual lowered the feet to the floor.

Heffy and I drew the shoulders up onto the back of the chair. Semi placed his sinewy hands on the dead man's hips, and while we held him steady, forced them backward, as one might bend a rusty hinge, so that they bent slowly and slipped into the seat of the chair.

Holding them there with one hand, he took each partly flexed knee and bent it down and backward until Ute Charley appeared to be sitting with his back to the window, waiting for the return of Osborne with the little mirrors and probe.

In fact, we all waited.

Semi and Laredo and Heffy dropped into chairs. Myself, I walked over to the window, the lower sash of which was of semiopaque glass, and stood gazing up through the clear pane of the upper frame to the blue of the outer sky.

I wondered what Connie was doing—how she felt!

I hadn't seen her since the night before, because I hadn't wished to intrude into that suite of sorrow where she had remained while Miss Wingarde slept after Dual had lulled her first wild grief of bereavement. I wondered if, perhaps, she were not lying down and resting, and I hoped she was.

Then the door opened and Osborne came in with the laryngoscope, its reflector, the probe, and a tongue depressor and mouth-gag, which he laid out on the table from which we had just lifted Charley.

Dual rose and joined him. He nodded. "Good," he approved. "You brought all we shall need, I think."

He took up the gag and came over to the dead man in the chair, drawing up a seat for himself directly facing. Separating the Indian's lips he inserted the blades of the little instrument between the strong teeth and forced them apart with a little clicking of the ratchet-catch. The Indian's mouth gaped open and exposed his tongue—bluish in color and swollen, like that of a parrot.

Osborne, watching him, lifted the reflector and extended it toward him.

Semi took it, manipulated its strap, adjusting it to his head, and slipped it into position so that its reflecting surface stood like a Cyclopean eye above his own; reached up and drew it about on its ball-joint, until its central hole exactly covered his right eye, and hitched his chair closer still to the body in the chair.

Sunlight was coming through the window. Dual caught a ray on the reflector and threw it back into the mouth, held wide by the gag. It swayed and flickered, searching out the reddish blue cavity, steadied and played on the back of the throat in a tiny circle which brought out the swollen veins under the membranes.

Dual put out a hand backward toward the physician.

Like a trained surgical assistant, Osborne was ready, and handed him the tiny throat mirror on its long, slender handle. Semi took it, and the tongue-depressor which he had laid on his lap at first.

Slipping the latter over the tongue he forced it down,

thrust the tiny glass into the mouth and back into the ray of the mirror on his forehead, turning and twisting it this way and that, to at last hold it steady and peer intently at the diminutive reversed picture it revealed.

For a long minute, he continued to gaze into the lifeless cavity of the throat; then without words, beckoned Osborne to him. The physician came, bent and peered along the luminous ray to the surface of the mirror. It seemed to me that he started slightly.

His face swung from what he had seen and he looked squarely at Dual. His eyes had come open, his lips were slightly parted. His entire expression was that of one deeply affected by some totally unexpected sight or occurrence. As their eyes met, Semi Dual shook his head shortly.

Osborne's eyes narrowed again and he turned them back into the Indian's throat without a word. I could see Heffy and Laredo watching the two closely, and myself I wondered what in all reason they could have lighted upon to excite their evident interest.

However, Semi Dual offered no explanation.

He drew out the mirror, removed the tongue depressor, rose, and took the gag from between the jaws, which he pressed back into place. Followed by Osborne, he went back to the table and laid the instruments down, picked up the slender probe which lay there, and then went over to Wingarde's remains.

He bent down and seemed to be seeking to insert the tip of the probe into the tiny wound in the old archeologist's breast.

Whether by purpose or otherwise, both Osborne and he stood so that their actions were completely screened by their bodies. It was Osborne who spoke abruptly in a voice of exclamation: "Good God!"

Dual straightened, went back, and gathered up all the shining articles of craft, and passed them back to their owner. Osborne's intelligent face was paler than its wont, and I could see that he labored under an illy controlled excitement as he took them and thrust them into a pocket of his coat.

Abruptly Semi turned and, picking the body of the Indian out of the chair, lifted it up and swung it back on the table, where he released it and straightened it out.

Heffy broke the silence which seemed to have clogged our tongues during that wordless period of action.

"Well, wha'd'ye find?" he interrogated. "What's struck you two, anyway, I'd like to know? A feller'd think there was something mighty mysterious about all this from the way you're actin'. Why don't we get after that green stone? We've taken time enough on a couple of snake-bites, it seems to me."

Dual swung to him.

"Things are not always what they seem, Mr. Heffy," he said.

"Meanin' what?" the hotel official demanded.

"Meaning that while Dr. Osborne is perfectly right in his diagnosis, he has been essentially wrong in his deductions therefrom," said Dual.

"I don't get you. Put it to me straight," Heffy insisted.

"Briefly, then," said Semi, "Professor Wingarde and the Indian were murdered."

Heffy's jaw dropped. His eyes popped.

"Murdered!" he gasped. "Then—then—how'd they git them snakebites?"

"That is the thing we must endeavor to prove," said Semi Dual.

7

MORE VALUABLE CLUES

I CONFESS THAT for a moment I felt a personal sympathy for Heffy. So completely had he accepted Osborne's declaration that Wingarde and Ute Charley had met death from the bite of a reptile, that Dual's pronouncement of murder, robbed him of all power of consecutive thought. He gulped once or twice before he managed to get out his next question: "Prove it—prove it how?"

"To begin with I would suggest that we now visit the scene of last night's tragedy," said Semi. "We intended that anyway, I believe, and it is time we set out. Señor Laredo, you will accompany us, will you not? You have been so closely associated with the entire course of this regrettable affair."

For the first time since the somewhat startling statement regarding the manner of death, I gave the Mexican a glance.

I found his dark eyes narrowed to something like slits and fixed on Semi's person. He had not moved from the chair he had taken before the examination of the Indian's throat had been made. He sat with feet apart and long fingers interlaced, hanging down between his thighs, his shoulders bent slightly, his head thrust a little forward.

As Dual spoke he straightened.

"But yes, Señor Dual, if you wish, I shall be happy to go along. It is a beautiful morning for a stroll, if nothing more. I am rather tired of being shut up with the dead men. Let us go by all means, and at once."

"Come on," said Heffy. He turned toward the door. "If there's any proof up there how two men could be murdered by a snake bite, let's go git it. Was the murderer carryin' a killer around with him for a pet?" Something akin to petulance was growing in his tone.

Dual nodded. He favored Heffy with a glance of slow regarding. "In a sense you are not far from correct," he responded.

"And he lifted the emerald an' the image after he had croaked 'em?" exclaimed Heffy in a growing excitement.

"He killed to obtain them," said Semi Dual.

"*Dios!*" muttered Laredo. "Then why did he not make his escape before anything was discovered?"

"It is my opinion that he never dreamed of being suspected," said Semi. "He fancied himself safe, and that to remain would be as safe as to depart. Come, let us go up and see what evidence the three actors in last night's murder have left for us to read."

"Three?" said Laredo.

"Three. The two who remained and the one who came back to the hotel."

"*Dios!* You seem sure, *señor,*" the Mexican made comment.

"One should be in a matter like this," Dual answered. "Come."

Heffy pulled the door open. We passed out and he

locked it behind him. We went out to the veranda and down it to the sun-lighted grounds. The porches were full of women in the light, fluffy things of summer.

Dual led the way with Osborne, the two walking along, their voices now and then speaking in low-toned conversation. Heffy and Laredo and I came next. We went out of the grounds and turned up along the course of the cañon. We went up along its edge toward the spot where death had stalked the night before.

Abruptly we came on two men walking back toward the hotel. One of them nodded to Osborne as they came up.

"This place is getting worse than a private park," he observed. "They've got a man up there to warn every one away from the spot where those two men were found last night. Maybe they'll let you look around, but nix on the rank and file."

"A precaution to avoid the obliteration of any possible clues," the physician explained.

"Oh," said the fellow. "Well, you know, I never thought about that." He walked on with his companion.

Heffy grinned. "I reckon Bill's still on the job," he remarked. "Yep, there he is, standin' right on the edge."

I looked forward to see a dark figure outlined against the sky. Plainly the guard had been faithful to Heffy's instructions. At least any signs which had escaped the trampling of the rescue party the night before would be visible still.

And now Dual abandoned all seeming mystery in the matter, and became on the sudden the every-day detective in search of clues. Turning to Heffy he requested him to have Bill point out the exact spot at which the Indian's body had been discovered the night before.

Without a question the fellow turned and led us all to a jumbled piece of tumbled stones a little way further along and back perhaps some fifty yards from the edge of the cañon. In a few words he described how one of the searchers had noted its shadow in the darkness, and walked in that direction to stumble over the body and give a halloo which had brought them all to him.

"Charley was lyin' all doubled up, like as if he'd had a fit or somethin' before he died and hadn't straightened out," he explained. "It was right here we picked him up."

As if to confirm his words, we could see the blurred outlines of some object which had lain there on the ground, and about it the imprint of several pairs of feet.

Dual went down and began an inspection of the ground and the footprints. Heffy and I stood by and watched him. Laredo went over and sat down on a pile of stones; lighted a cigarette, and sat smoking, with one leg crossed over the other, apparently at ease.

Dual, crouched low, was moving slowly about the outline where the body had lain.

Suddenly he paused, bent lower, and knelt down. He beckoned Osborne, Heffy, and me to him. He was pointing toward the outline of a footprint—a long, narrow footprint. "Distinctive from the others if you will notice," he remarked. "Observe it closely. There may be others hereabouts."

"Other what, *señor?*" came the voice of Laredo.

"Footprints," Dual told him with a sidewise glance.

"Doubtless," he responded. "The searchers tramped around much, it appears. But this particular footprint?"

"Is distinctive." Dual rose and dusted the knees of his trousers.

"It is that of a man of say five feet nine or ten who walks more on the outer edge of his foot, so that his weight comes on the outer edge of his sole and heel, making an easily recognizable impression. Furthermore, he wears a French make of shoes—Villet et Cie's if I am not mistaken, which I do not think likely."

Laredo removed his cigarette and inspected its tip for a moment. "You profess to recognize the make of shoe from its imprint?" he inquired at length.

Dual merely nodded. He turned to Heffy, who was waiting wide-eyed at this turn in affairs, and addressed him once more. "And now, Mr. Heffy, if your guide will show us just where he discovered the body of Wingarde, I should like to examine that spot also."

The hotel detective nodded to his man.

Bill moved off at once, leading us still farther up and nearer the brink of the cañon. Heffy and I followed, and Laredo left his seat and came along. I noticed Dual closely.

He was walking close behind Bill, and scanning the ground as he went. Heffy, too, never took his eyes from the stooping figure, yet he managed to speak:

"Say, now, do you think he can do it?"

"Do what?" I gave back.

"Tell what company made a shoe from the mark it leaves, like he said."

Almost I felt sorry for the fellow. But my pity did not prevent my adding to his growing bewilderment in the least. "Of course he can if he says so," I replied. "I saw him recognize the handwriting of a forger several years after he'd seen it written on an envelope once, even though the first time it was used in writing a different name. But he was right, and the man was the same."

"Yes, I know," said Heffy; "but—but shoes—"

"Hah!" Laredo cut in. "Is it not true that there is a Bertillon record of the various brands of shoes? It was a matter I had overlooked."

"If there is Dual has a copy of it, you may be assured," I responded. "Señor Laredo, my friend never makes a statement he does not feel able to support."

Osborne nodded. "He is analytic to a degree."

"One moment," Semi addressed the guide. He paused and waited until we came up. "Another one of the prints," he observed. "If you will notice it was going toward the pile of rocks, not from it, and—yes, here to one side is another track—no, two—pointed in the same direction, but made by a different sort of shoe—one with a cracked sole, worn by a person who walked flat-footed, as shown by a slight dragging in the outline. The wearer had an almost shuffling gait."

"Charley for a thousand then!" exclaimed Heffy on the instant. "The feller hated shoes, went barefoot or in moccasins mostly; but he always wore shoes if he came up to the hotel."

"As he did last night," said Dual.

"Well, then," Heffy concluded, "he was able to walk when he went *to* them rocks, all right. This other wouldn't belong to the professor, would it, Mr. Dual?"

"No," Semi responded. "The professor was English and wore an English shoe, as I noticed this morning in the card room. You are right, however, in thinking the other made

by Charley. If you'll look at his shoes on our return you'll
see that the right has a broken sole. The print which shows
it here is that of a right shoe also."

He motioned Bill to go on.

"Then," declared Heffy, "either he walked by here alone
or with the party makin' this other track. Say—you don't
think he could have been walkin' *with* the guy what croaked
him?"

Dual turned his head quickly. "Why not?" he said.

"*Before* he was croaked?" Heffy was growing incoherent.

"Naturally," said Semi, and followed Bill.

He led us quite to the edge of the lip, where he stopped
and pointed to a blurred, dragging mark in the soil—a
sickening thing, which showed where some object had
slipped over and gone hurtling downward into that dreadful abyss where the mist of distance swung between us and
the writhing river so far below.

"He just happened to light on the ledge down there," he
remarked, pointing over. "I reckon whoever shoved him off
thought he would go all the way. It was *meant,* all right."

Semi went quite to the edge a short way beyond the telltale drag on the brink, got down, and peered over. In fact,
we all looked down to where a narrow ledge had caught
the body and so stayed its plunge into the terrible depths.

Bill began dilating on the recovery as we looked. "I had
'em tie me to a rope, an' I slid down an' tied the body fast.
Then they hauled him up an' let th' rope down again for
me. Tell you that there ledge is a shivery place to stand on
at night, all right."

Dual came back to the dragging mark, which showed
where Wingarde had been thrust off.

He moved slowly about it, searching, as I fancied, for more of the slender footprints. And he found them. We all crowded close as he pointed them out, partly smudged by the later walking over the spot, but yet discernible to a trained eye which knew in advance for what it was searching. One pair of them pointed directly toward the brim of the cañon, and were printed deeper at the toe, as though the full weight of the maker had been thrown on the forward part of his feet—and they were directly back of that point where the suggestive sliding mark showed on the edge.

I looked at Semi. "He laid the body down and shoved it off by pushing against it," I suggested. "That would explain the pressure on the toes of his shoes, I should think."

He nodded.

"Exactly, Gordon. We may picture the murderer bending and forcing his victim over the edge. He expected the body to drop to the river, and either sink to the bottom or be carried far down and so removed as an accusing object. The chance ledge and the concealing darkness betrayed his plan without his knowing it had happened."

I glanced at Laredo. He was standing not far from the edge, and drawing his feet slowly backward and forward in a nervous manner while he watched our investigations. His dark face was intent, tense, full of the keenest interest in our actions.

"You would have thought, if he had thrown the body off, he would have tried to see if it really went all the way down," I said to Semi.

"Let us see," he remarked softly, half rose and moved in a crouching attitude to the very edge of the gash in the earth, skirting the mark of the body as he went, and sinking to his

knees again as he reached the brink. On the other side of
the sliding impression Osborne and I followed suit until
we, too, knelt just back of the rim, yet so close that I could
look over and down to the shadows, which the morning's
sun had not yet been able to dispel.

Dual was speaking.

"The natural impulse of one having thrown the body of
another over such an edge would be to approach the edge
himself and look over. And because it was dark he would
exercise caution. That he did so we can see by the fact that
he pushed the body over rather than having held it up and
thrown it out and down. He would in all probability creep
forward and seek to look over. Look for the marks of hands
rather than feet here, Gordon."

He was right.

I saw it even while he was speaking. Heffy heard, too,
and joined in the search a little way beyond Dual, on the
other side of the spot where I was working. We all began
to scan the sandy soil along the edge, seeking if possible to
determine if some one had knelt there, rested his weight
on his hands, and peered down into the night-filled chasm,
into which he had cast his fellow.

I bent and scanned the reddish-brown sand closely,
hunting for the print of a hand if, perchance, it should be
there.

And it was! I found it. Close to the edge, pressed well
into the surface, the mark of a thumb and four fingers,
spread out to support the weight of the body which had
rested upon it, until it resembled almost the impression of
the claw of a huge bird.

I caught my breath as I found it, and Semi Dual heard.

He lifted his eyes, and they met mine. I nodded. At once he came over and sank down beside me. Together we studied the thing I had found.

"You were right—you always are right," I said in a voice which trembled. "He knelt here and rested on his hand and looked over, and the darkness kept him from seeing the ledge—and the body caught on it. See, Semi, it is the mark of a hand with long, slender fingers and a narrow palm!"

My friend nodded. "One of the fingers is partly missing," he pointed out.

You mean in the print or on the hand?" I questioned quickly. I, too, had noticed that the mark of the little finger was short out of all proportion to the others.

"From the hand itself. A valuable clue," said Semi. "Observe, Gordon, that the soil at the end of the short finger has not been disturbed any more than that about the others. The man who made this has lost a part of one finger—the last on his left hand."

"Sufficient for identification in itself," I suggested.

"Conclusive with the footprints," said Dual.

"No doubt about it," agreed Osborne with emphatic assent.

"That settles it," declared Heffy, who had drawn up beside us and listened with poorly controlled impatience. "Come on. We'll go back and hunt up a guy with a part of one fin missing. If he's got toothpick feet to boot, then we've got the goods on him for fair. I gotter hand it to your friend, Glace. He's the pure quill."

"But, *señor*," questioned Laredo, "is it not possible that one of the searchers may have leaned so and looked down, last night? I distinctly heard it said that they lowered a light on a rope and, later, this guide here. Might not such a mark have been made at that time?"

"It might," snapped Heffy shortly; "but we can soon find out. If any of them searchers is shy a finger-tip or two, all right; if not, then the thing holds, an' I bet you it does. The feller who made this here print had a long hand, like he had feet—that is, if it was the same man, which is likely."

"Precisely," said Semi Dual. "Both hands and feet were long and slender. Your point is well taken, Mr. Heffy. Now, one moment more. Let us find the place where Professor Wingarde was killed."

"Killed!" Heffy erupted. "Why—say! What's wrong with this place?"

"Much," said Semi. "We all agree that the murderer laid the body down and pushed it over, and later looked over to mark its fall. The mere fact that he could lay it down and slide it over the edge shows that the actual death occurred at a different point, and the assassin then carried his victim to this spot in order to dispose of the remains."

"Good glory! You're right again," howled Heffy. "What do we do? Look for more of them slim slippers?"

Semi nodded. "Start here at the lip and walk in a half-circle back to the lip above. Return at a wider distance and repeat. In that way we should cross the trail to this spot if there is one."

Heffy started. I turned to assist. Osborne, too. Dual had stooped again, and was carefully measuring the length and breadth of the handprint. Laredo still stood, coldly observant, taking no part in the hunt which was forward. He stood quietly smoking, his hands thrust into his pockets, his eyes peering off across the distance of the landscape.

But Heffy found it.

His jubilant cry took us to him. He was pointing to another of the slender footmarks, turned toward the lip of the cañon, from a direction still farther along its brink than we had come. "It's pressed pretty deep, this here one," he declared with no little pride. "I reckon he was carryin' double weight, all right, when he made it. Come on, Glace. Let's find some more."

And we did.

Now and then we found a telltale mark to guide us, until at last we came to a spot where the soil was trampled, and other marks mixed and crossed and blended with the slender ones we followed.

"This is the spot," said Dual. "Here they struggled, and the weaker was overcome and slain. These other marks are those of English shoes of a make and size corresponding to those Wingarde wore and—" Suddenly he strode a little to one side and pointed. "Here are more of the first. Some one stood here and shifted his position from time to time. He was waiting—for Wingarde."

I lifted my eyes from observing the fresh signs and met those of my friend. "Wingarde was lured here and ambushed," I remarked to him. "The Indian was the agent who lured him."

Semi Dual nodded slowly. "Wingarde thought he knew him," he said quietly.

"An' th' money was guv to Charley for bringin' him up here!" cried Heffy. "Gosh, th' whole thing's gettin' clear! Wingarde come, an' th' other feller jumped him. They fought, an' Wingarde got his. Then th' other guy frisked him of th' stone an' th' image an' dumped him off th' bank. But where is he now?"

"Caught in the net of eternal justice," said Semi Dual. "Come; it is time to go back. We have learned the story of the crime. Let us now, as agents of eternal justice, devote our efforts to bringing it to pass. Señor Laredo, we are going back."

Laredo turned.

Still standing, inspecting the tumbled panorama of the cañon, he seemed to have given no attention to our later actions whatever. Now, however, he tossed away his cigarette and bowed.

"By all means, if you have finished, *señor*, let us go back."

We set off. I managed to place myself beside Osborne. Heffy was forging ahead, and Dual had dropped back beside Laredo. Bill was talking steadily to the detective in uninterrupted flow. I turned to the physician and asked a question, which had been crying for expression for an hour.

"They weren't snake-bites at all, then, doctor, were they?"

He gave me a straight glance out of a pair of very steady eyes. "Your friend is a very remarkable man, Mr. Glace. I have given him my word to answer no questions until this affair is ended. I do not know that he meant to include you in the restriction, but he said 'all' were to be refused an answer."

I grinned at him. "Just the same, you *have* answered," I told him. "But never mind. I know Semi Dual, and if he said that, he had a mighty good reason for it. If I can judge from my former knowledge, you won't have to keep still very long, however. He's getting ready to act!"

8

THE ALL-IMPORTANT QUESTION

"NOW WHAT?" SAID Heffy, checking his progress as we neared the hotel.

Dual answered: "I think that now we should proceed to recover the emerald and the idol and apprehend the one who slew to take them."

At the time I do not think any of us noticed the sequence of his remark, and it was only later that I saw how his wonderful penetration had predicated the order of events thus far in advance.

Then he gave us no time for consideration, but continued, addressing Laredo: "It would be well to talk matters over in quiet before going further into the affair, however, in order that there may be no misapprehension, no confusion, when the final solution occurs. Mrs. Glace is in our suite at present, and Miss Wingarde and Dayton in hers. *Señor*, may we go to your apartment for the discussion?"

Laredo assented; "But yes, *señor*, if you wish it."

"Then," said Dual, "let us go there at once."

Heffy shrugged. "More talkin'," he growled to Osborne and me. "I never seen so much chinnin' in all my born days. Why don't we *do* somethin'; I want to lamp that stone an' that image. Why don't we scout for a three-fingered guy?"

Osborne smiled slightly.

"Why don't you get wise to the fact that we're babes on the bottle at this game, Heffy?" he suggested. "Do you know, my friend, that our tall acquaintance yonder could put out his hand and hand you that stone inside ten minutes, if he wished."

"Eh? What's that, doc? *Yes,* he could? Why, we ain't even found the guy what—"

Osborne dug him in the ribs. "Oh, can some of your own talk, old man," he said.

"All right," complained the house sleuth. "But it gets my goat."

"I know it," said Osborne. "Mine, too. Come on up-stairs and watch the wheels go round. I've read about it, but I thought it was fiction. I didn't know they made men like the gentleman in gray."

We entered the hotel. "Keep your eyes peeled for some narrow shoes, Glace," whispered Heffy, at my elbow, "and lamp every guinea's hands."

I nodded, and we crossed the lobby, mounted the stairs, and turned along the passage toward our own suite and Wingarde's. Heffy was the last in our party. He had put his own instructions into effect. At the top he gave me a glance and shook his head in fruitless negation. "We come through too quick," he said.

Dual stopped at the Wingardes' door and rapped.

Dayton himself answered. Through it I had one glimpse of Evelyn sitting in a great padded chair, big enough for two. She was hastily patting her skirt into shape and adjusting a lock of hair. For a moment I felt a whimsical wonder if the chair had been doing capacity; then Dual spoke: "If you will come with us, Mr. Dayton."

"In a jiff," replied the Briton.

He closed the door. We could hear his voice briefly, and then he came out and joined us. We went on down the hall, and Laredo unlocked the door to his room. We entered, and he followed. "Find yourselves seats, *señores*," he invited, himself crossing and taking a place on the bed.

Osborne sat down at his side. Dual took seat in a chair. Heffy and Dayton and I found others.

And then, as by common consent, we all turned to Semi. In that moment we all made silent admission to his leadership. He swept us briefly with his eyes and opened his lips:

"Let us, at the beginning of this final chapter, sum up the entire causal element of this affair and arrange the incidents in their proper sequence before proceeding to the last step, which must ever be a painful one in a matter of this nature. Theft in itself is a reprehensible action, but it concerns merely material substance.

"When one accuses another of the taking of life, he must be careful lest, by imperiling the life of the one he accuses, he do an incalculable wrong, little less great than that of the one who has killed. But should he know, then he should speak that justice may be done and the guilty compelled to pay for the irreparable theft of life, than which no crime is greater—since he who takes life sins not only against man, but against God himself.

"Therefore, I shall run over the incidents as we know them; and if any of you find a flaw in my words do not hesitate to name it. In the beginning, Professor Mathias Wingarde, an archaeologist, went to Mexico, and there he met

Señor Laredo. In some way not known to us, the professor learned of a temple jewel and an idol—an image of Quetzal which had been brought from there to this region and left in a cliff dwelling, and he determined to find that if he could. That he succeeded we know. He came here and, with Mr. Dayton and two guides, went north and recovered the objects he sought. What happened then?

"Gentlemen, you are aware that I believe in the science of astrology, and that I believe in telepathy as well. When I first heard of the professor's disappearance from the hotel, I made some calculations which showed his probable death.

"Later, from data furnished me by his daughter, I set up a figure for this year of his life, which confirmed that suspicion and showed other things, too. I do not ask you to accept this statement, save as events with which you are familiar or will be shall prove it. But I assure you of its truth.

"If one can intercept the thought waves generated in the murderer's brain, one can learn much more of the actual nature of the crime. One way to accomplish that purpose is to produce a continual, at least a partial concentration of the murderer's brain on his deed, so that it constantly would give off waves dealing with that subject.

"By so centering his mind one could gradually gather more and more information, not only from his thoughts, but from the words and acts which they inspired. This is a psychological fact known to all physicians and criminologists. Dr. Osborne will tell you that I am right."

Osborne nodded.

"The association of thought reflexes is well known to medicine to-day," he declared.

Semi Dual smiled. "And the effects of expression suppression, doctor."

Again Osborne nodded in satisfaction.

"Sometimes an associated idea will produce the expression of a suppressed thought, I believe?"

"Indeed, yes."

"So that, by remark seemingly innocent in itself, another may be made to reply in a way which will strengthen or weaken suspicion," said Dual. "Now to continue. The bodies of Professor Wingarde and the Indian were found dead as I might have predicted, but almost immediately after there occurred a conflict between the results of my calculations and the surface seeming in their death.

"My calculations had shown that Wingarde would die from a wound inflicted at the hands of another man, armed with a pointed weapon—in other words, that he would die by murder. Yet, Dr. Osborne's diagnosis was that both the Indian and he died from snake-bite. It became necessary to harmonize the two variant opinions."

"But you yourself said they died from snake-bite," Heffy interrupted. "If forked tongue wouldn't mean snake—"

Dual smiled slightly. "You placed a literal interpretation on my remark to Dayton," he replied. "Treachery has been called by the words 'a forked tongue.'"

Heffy's hand crashed on his knee. "By granny, that's right. The Indians say a liar has one—a forked tongue, I mean."

"Exactly," Dual went on. "I therefore decided that I must myself examine the bodies. You saw what I did, but only Osborne knows what I found. It was a small clot of blood in the throat of the man Ute Charley. It was not larger than a pin-head, but it was adherent to the membrane on the right side of his throat at a point slightly below the level of the wound in the outer surface of his neck.

"Yet it was sufficient to indicate that the puncture ran entirely through the muscles of his neck and entered the cavity of the throat. It was therefore clear at once that it had not been made by the fang of any snake, because of its length alone. No rattlesnake ever recorded has a fang which could reach such a depth.

"At once Dr. Osborne and I probed the wound in Wingarde's breast. We followed it to a depth of some three inches—far enough to prove that it had reached the heart."

Dayton had been showing signs of excitement as Semi continued.

"Good God!" he burst out at last. "Then they were murdered? Mr. Dual, I want you to find out who did it. Find him and give him to justice. Make him pay for the life of that mild-mannered old man. Make him—"

"Patience," said Semi Dual. "Believe me, Mr. Dayton, he shall be unveiled and justice shall be done. The mills of the gods, Mr. Dayton, are in operation as much to-day as at any time in the past, and—they grind 'exceeding' fine."

"Quite right. I beg your pardon. I was shocked. You see I have not followed your later work in the matter." Dayton subsided.

"Thus," Semi resumed, "I found my calculations once more supported by material fact. It became evident that Wingarde and the Indian had died from the effect of wounds administered by a stab with some poisoned weapon.

"Poisoned because of the condition of their bodies,

which showed the effects of the toxic substance, in the swelling and discoloration—the very thing which caused Dr. Osborne to seek an explanation in a possible fight with a serpent in the dark. The next question presenting was the natural one as to what the weapon might have been. I found an answer ready.

"Gentlemen, I once saw a small image of the cat-headed goddess of Bast. It, too, had a handle something like that described as being attached to this image of Quetzal which Professor Wingarde found. But the handle to the Egyptian idol was really the handle of a slender dagger of which the image was but the masking sheath.

"That dagger was steeped in a poisonous substance, so that a prick from it meant death. As you will recall, Mr. Dayton, I last night spoke of the similarity between the basal natures of mankind, past and present, and of the skilfulness of the artisans of other days. At once I drew an analogy between the image of Bast and that of Quetzal, and I felt that I knew the weapon which had been used in this case, and that, as in the Egyptian instance, it had been a poisoned blade, dipped in some venom which had maintained its active nature throughout all the years since it was made."

"Have you any idea of the nature of the poison?" Osborne inquired, with acute interest. "Its physical effects resembled snake poison so closely."

"There is even a possibility that its source was snake venom," said Dual. "We know that that substance contains various alkaloidal principles which give it its toxic effect. The Aztec priesthood may have known how to use them in preparing their poisoned weapons, even as the Egyptian priesthood did."

Osborne considered. "They had a fiendish ingenuity," he said.

"Having determined the actual cause of death," Semi once more took up the interrupted thread of his exposition, "I next determined to visit the scene of the crime, to see if perhaps it were possible to read the story of the murder at that spot.

"We were aware already that Wingarde had been led away from the hotel by one of his Indian guides. That, of course, presupposed a purpose on the Indian's part and a supposed object on the professor's side for going.

"But as the Indian had been killed also, and as he was in possession of some new currency notes, it appeared that he had been merely the agent of a third party who had paid him to act as a decoy. You will remember that I asked to see the bills found on the Indian's body.

"The serial numbers upon them were P 9174, 66374, and E 857752A. They were of an issue made by the Anglo and London-Paris Bank of San Francisco."

Heffy dug into his pocket and produced the bills.

"You're right!" he exclaimed after a brief inspection.

Dual nodded.

"And three days ago this hotel received a shipment of small denomination bills from that bank, as the clerk himself and also the manager told me, before I joined you at breakfast. Furthermore, the bills found on Ute Charley are of the same series, and were evidently given out by this hotel to some one from whom the Indian had them."

"By Jove! Did you find out who got a bunch of those bills? "Dayton asked.

Dual shook his head.

"Patience. One step at a time, Mr. Dayton. That was the obvious course. I inquired, certainly, and received a list, so far as the clerk could remember, of such guests as had received any of the bills. There were several names. Now, you all saw what happened at the scene of the crime itself. Suppose that we draw a mental picture of what occurred there some hours before.

"The Indian, acting as a decoy, had induced the professor, carrying the image of Quetzal and the jewel, to accompany him there. In all likelihood he told him he had found some object of interest or discovered some one who knew something in which Wingarde would find material of interest.

"It is easy to deceive one who is wrapped up in a subject. Such a one will ofttimes overlook inconsistencies which a less biased mind would sense. They had come through the night, therefore, to that spot where the one who bought the Indian's service was waiting for his victim, his mind centered on obtaining the great jewel he knew he carried upon him, and which Charley was to know was present before he brought him, as owing to its bulk he could easily ascertain while talking to Wingarde at the start.

"Wingarde was not of a suspicious nature. His going as he did shows that. Not until he arrived at the appointed spot and found one he did not expect did he conceive of treachery in the affair.

"The one who waited demanded what he carried on his body. What he proposed may never be known, but Wingarde refused. The other sought to take them by force. The footprints at that spot show that they struggled. But the thief was the stronger.

"He wrested the image from Wingarde's body and, knowing his man would never rest quiet under the theft, he saw that his death alone would serve to render his own possession secure. He wrenched out the handle of the image and plunged it into Wingarde's breast, wounding his heart. The poison on the blade acted quickly. Wingarde sank dying. It was easy enough then for the one who had slain to complete his purpose and possess himself of the gem.

"But he knew that the discovery of the body would excite comment and suspicion. It must be concealed. The cañon was at hand. A fall to its bottom would either conceal his work by allowing the body to be washed away or, failing that, by making it appear that Wingarde had stumbled over the edge in the dark.

"Lifting him up, he carried him to the edge and pushed him off. Thereafter he followed the natural impulse and looked over, and so left the convicting mark of his hand as well as the prints of his feet. And the fact that he laid the body down and pushed it off showed him to have been a man of no exceeding strength or stature. A man far larger than Wingarde would have hurled his man from the cliff.

"A man of the same size, or nearly, would have done as this man did. Therefore, we know that our man is of ordinary stature, from the three details—the record of his action, the size of his shoe, and the print of his hand. To this we add the detail that he walks slightly on the outer side of his foot, and that the last two joints of the little finger on his left hand are missing. That gives us a fairly good description, I think."

"Gosh, yes," said Heffy. "When you get done I'll grab him, if he's anywheres around this dump. That's as good as a photograph of the guinea. You think he's got the image an' th' stone anywheres near him?"

"I think so—at present," said Semi Dual.

"Having disposed of the professor," he went on, "he was now confronted by the Indian as a witness. I scarcely think he meant to destroy his agent at first, but now circumstances compelled the deed. He conceived a crafty scheme.

"Returning to the Indian's side, he walked with him toward the pile of stones. As he walked he lifted the dagger from the image and plunged it noiselessly into his companion's throat. But he did not seek to conceal the body.

"He reasoned that Wingarde and the Indian had been seen. Therefore he left the latter lying by the stones to be found and to show by his body's condition that he had died of apparent snake-bite. It might even be supposed that the two men, Wingarde and his guide, had stumbled across a venomous serpent, and the Indian being bitten and Wingarde excited, the scientist had started for help, become turned around in the darkness through the shock of the occurrence, and so ran directly off the lip of the cliff.

"And his belief was plausible, I think, for he had no reason to believe that any one would have reason to suspect him. In fact, he had planned to make it appear that he could not possibly have had any connection with the affair. In pursuance of that plan he took from the Indian's body the price of his betrayal of the professor and left him where he lay.

"But here again the fortuitous fate, which at times seems to pursue the guilty, played him false. He took not all of the price of Judas, but a part. The hole in the dead man's pocket betrayed him.

"Two of the bills slipped partly through it, and he missed them in his hurry and the darkness, and perhaps in part because of the reaction from his deed. So he took part and left the others to point to the fact of a third party's presence, and so induce a search for himself.

"He came back to the hotel and was seen about it. Doubtless he concealed his booty in some spot he believed perfectly safe. It lies there now, shut away from searching eyes. Himself, he went down and was seen and spoken to by others, so that when the discovery was made it would appear that he had been about the hotel at the time. Perhaps he even told some of them that he had been in his rooms during the earlier evening. Thus he hoped to build up a fictitious alibi to account for his time.

"And he might have succeeded had it not been for the watchful stars.

"But the stars, gentlemen, said so plainly that foul murder had been committed that they inspired me to search for the one who had killed, and his motive. Save for the stars, Dr. Osborne's diagnosis of snake-bite would have been accepted, and the mystery of the idol and the jewel might never have been cleared up.

"Surely there was nothing to point to the true solution in the surface seeming. But my calculations showed the murder clearly. They, I may add, even showed an astral picture of the one who killed; and long years of study have taught me, my friends, that the stars do not lie; that if error creeps in, it lies in their reading, and must be charged, not to them, but to human failure to see and understand."

He paused, and we all sat silent. I think we were each picturing for himself the scene as Dual had described it. As he spoke it had seemed not any theoretical structure, but an actual account of the thing as it had occurred.

Dayton sat brooding over its logical phases. Osborne, scientific, trained in deductive diagnosis, wore a slight frown as he weighed its parts and sought to find some vital error. Quite slowly he shook his head.

Heffy simply sat staring at Semi as though he had met something he found totally beyond his comprehension. Laredo's face seemed to wear something like a swarthy pallor to me, as he perched on the edge of his bed, his feet drawn back beneath it, his hands thrust down into his pockets, his shoulders drooped from their square breadth, his head slightly bowed.

At length he shrugged slightly, rose and walked over to a window which gave on the grounds of the hotel. He stood there with his back to the room, looking out at the sunshine, and the cañon off beyond, and after a bit he spoke:

"There is no saying that, your picture of the thing may not be what actually occurred, *señor.* But you have asked that we who listen should point out a flaw in the case you built up, if we saw one, perhaps. All which you say might ver' well have occur'.

"If—an' mark me well now, *señores*—if that one who is supposed to have waited—an' to have bribed the Indian to act the decoy—an' who slew—an' took the jewel an' the image—had known of these things in advance. But I know that Wingarde had but come two days ago to this hotel from his trip. I knew him in Mexico, *señores,* yet even to me he spoke not of what he had found. The Señor Dual's ingenious description would presuppose a previous knowledge on the part of the one whom he would accuse, in my estimation. An' we have not seen this image.

"We do not know that it contains a dagger. Let us not be blind to that. Yet Señor Dual says plainly that the one guilty knew the image sheathed a weapon. Then that one must have known of this image before. Señor Dayton, did the professor know of any dagger in this image?"

"Not that I know of," Dayton replied.

"You never saw him take it out?"

"Good Lord, no!"

"Did the Indians, perhaps, see him do so?"

"I don't know, Laredo. All I know is I never saw it or heard Wingarde say a word about it."

Laredo turned directly toward Semi. "This I claim, *señor,* is a flaw in your deduction. None but one who knew fully of this image could have known of the dagger, if it existed. Are you justified in presupposing such knowledge?"

Dual raised his head and met his challenge fully.

"I think so," he made answer slowly. "I shall know in a moment. Señor Laredo, it is not, perhaps, an unfitting time to ask you for exactly what motive you killed Professor Wingarde last night?"

9

WHERE IS THE IMAGE?

SILENCE AFTER THAT.

Yet I saw it all in a flash, and whatever conceit in my own powers of detection I may ever have held seemed to fade swiftly away. Why is it the obvious so often escapes observation? Is it that we blind ourselves to the near at hand in seeking to look further?

The one who advised us to hide a thing in plain sight knew the truth of that, doubtless.

All the long night and to-day Dayton and Heffy and Osborne and I had gone looking into what seemed a baffling complexity of facts, seeking to see through them to the guilty beyond, and never regarding the one who walked beside us as a possible suspect at all. Only Dual had seen with his unerring vision, and so actually *kept* that one at his side until he had gathered up all that material proof needed to support his strange occult knowledge, and make his charge binding to the minds of every-day men.

Now I saw it all clearly; that Laredo was of the physique he had mentioned; that his feet were long and narrow; that one heel was slightly worn off on its outer side, showing that he walked partly on that edge of his foot—and I recalled that the night before, as I watched his skilful manipulation of his cue in the game I had played him, I had noticed the partial absence of the last finger of his left hand.

And I think of all in that room, save, perhaps, Dual, the Mexican himself was the most utterly controlled.

Perhaps he had even sensed the thing coming, and had nerved himself to it, for now he played what must have been a premeditated part. He started back a pace. Surprised incredulity rather than fear looked out from his eyes—that and, perhaps, resentment. "I, *señor?*" he cried. *"Dios!* A sorry jest to make such an accusation."

"Sorry, indeed, if a jest," said Dual.

"Then"—Laredo drew himself up to the full measure of his inches—"then, *señor,* I must tell you that you are mistaken. I was Wingarde's friend. I helped him in his Mexican work. I, too, was interest' in his same pursuits. I, Rodriguez Laredo, am well known in my country. You have but to inquire."

"I have," said Dual. *"Señor,* pray sit down."

"But I am accuse'. I demand proof," Laredo insisted, seating himself and keeping his eyes upon Semi.

"You shall have it," said Dual. "As often happens, throughout this entire matter, you have, from time to time, made remarks which drew my attention to yourself—and I told you I read minds, if you will remember. *Señor,* I read you from the first. My whole endeavor was to prove what I read that others might believe."

Laredo shrugged. "It would be needful—I should think."

"Exactly. A few moments ago, however, you once more brought up the one point of weakness in my story as an argument, as you hoped, in favor of yourself. In reality it acted against you. For you were right. The man who planned the theft of the emerald and the image would have needed prior knowledge.

"By your own confession, you had it, so far as Wingarde's trip here was concerned. He obtained his knowledge of the objects in question in your Mexican city. May you not also have obtained a similar knowledge? This morning when I inquired about the bills your name appeared in the list the clerk gave me concerning those who had received some of the smaller bills.

"And, *señor,* your physical description tallied with the man shown by the stars as being the one who killed.

"With the double suggestion to go on, I cabled to Mexico City to a man well known to myself. He is a man in touch with sources of information, and one to be relied on. I asked for information concerning one Rodriguez Laredo. You yourself saw his message of reply delivered to me this morning at table. It reads—"

Thrusting his hand into a pocket he drew out the telegraph form and gave us its contents:

"Rodriguez Laredo, resident this city—travels widely, however, seldom long resident here. Suspected by government agents of endeavoring to incite uprising of various Indian tribes against federal government for past two years. Under surveillance much of time by secret service. Left lately, assigned destination United States—exact locality, unknown. Sometimes calls himself Prince of Montezuma.

"You see, *señor,*" he continued, putting the message away, "you are well known indeed; and it is mentioned that you have sought to produce an uprising among the Indian tribes, which should doubtless elevate you, the self-styled Prince of Montezuma, to a temporal power, if successful.

"Señor Laredo, you have dreamed a dream, and in dreaming—in working for the object of your dream among those Indian tribes descended from the old Aztec stock—you have heard of the Image of Quetzal in the mountains of the north, and of the Eye of Quetzal, that great intaglio emerald from the temple, which had been taken away and must be restored, according to their legend, before the children of Quetzal could be free.

"And in your dream, *señor*, you imagined that could you procure this talismanic stone—could come back among them and say: 'See, I, Prince of Montezuma, whose forebears were of the great king's blood, have brought back the stone to assure your final triumph.' Then they would rally to your standard, and you should once more ascend the throne from which the Spaniards thrust the final Montezuma ere they enslaved his people and looted the splendors of his realm.

"Shall we not see now how closely my theoretical story matches the facts? You came here a few days ago. You learned that Wingarde had gone north, taking the most available guides, but would return shortly. You waited. No doubt, you had learned before you started that he had heard of the gem.

"We may assume so much to account for your presence at this time. You waited then until he came back, and you questioned his guides. One told you all that you wished to know. Him you took into your plan and bribed to lead Wingarde to you.

"That you met him we know, for the print of your foot is up there, a record against you. I knew when I saw the print at the first, for I had noticed your feet, and the imprint was of a similar nature and made by a similar brand of shoes.

"Back in my present residence I have a record of every civilized brand of shoes—their imprints, the number and arrangement of their pegs and nails, the shape of their heels. And so I knew that you wore shoes imported from France, the factory of Villet et Cie.

"And the imprint showed that form of shoe. You yourself knew I was correct, for after that, as I knelt and you stood on the brink of the cañon, you shuffled your feet from time to time in order to blur their marks.

"And the imprint of your hand is there, too, *señor*—the hand with the missing portion of the little finger—pressed into the soil of the cañon's lip to make the identification sure.

"So you took the image and used its dagger, and you took the emerald, and you brought them back to the hotel and hid them, and went down to the billiard-room, and there you were joined by Professor Wingarde's daughter and Mr. Dayton. What did you say to them?"

"I suggest a game of pool, *señor*," said Laredo.

"Dayton?" Dual demanded sharply.

"Why—er—he told us he'd been up-stairs, writing letters all evening, you know, and said he'd take us on for a game or two if it suited our fancy."

Osborne shook his head. "There's your attempted alibi," he remarked. "God, it's all checking out!"

Heffy reached into a pocket in a manner entirely suggestive. I could imagine what he was after. "Well, I reckon it's my cue, ain't it?" he questioned.

Dual glanced briefly in his direction. "First search this room," he said.

"*Señor,*" Laredo protested, "this is an outrage! You accuse. You allow no refutation. You order a search of my room. You transcend all bounds of endurance. I shall appeal to my national representatives in this matter."

"Go on an' appeal," snarled Heffy. "I kin get done wid dis coop before you git an answer." He rose heavily from his seat and glanced slowly about the apartment, as though seeking a point to begin. It was an ordinary bedroom with bath. After a moment Heffy walked over and disappeared into the latter.

"But I say," broke out Dayton, "you wouldn't think a chap would hide the things in his bedroom. You'd think—"

"What you were expected to think, Mr. Dayton—of every other place. Therefore, the bedroom. Señor Laredo is a man of no mean intelligence in material matters. He would have been successful in this, save for unforeseen and unforeseeable conditions which arose to confront him. You must admit his remarkable finesse and control, in that throughout our entire association he aroused no suspicion in the minds of any of you. Yet his position was one of the most trying," said Dual.

Quite unexpectedly Laredo rose. He bowed. "*Señor,* I value the compliment of your words." He laid a hand on his heart. "It is too bad we should oppose one another."

"Indeed, yes," said Semi. "I am grieved always to see a good mind devoted to objects unworthy. It is such needless waste of God-given power, and leads to only ruin in the end."

"Mine, of course, in this matter?" the Mexican suggested.

"Yours, Señor Laredo."

"But, no, *señor*. Admit that your deductions are clever—that they appear true. How prove them true, *señor*, without the emerald and the image, which none of us have seen? I, as I told you—I have heard stories of this stone. Are stories proof that it exists?"

"Dayton has seen it," said Semi, calmly.

"Ah, yes—I forgot! Then it does exist. But unless found, could you prove me guilty of what you accuse in a court of law?"

"No."

"Then—" Laredo paused and smiled thinly.

"Heffy is seeking it now," said Dual.

"Ah, yes! Heffy—" Again Laredo smiled.

I felt a sudden desire to chuckle. Gripping as the situation was, I could not help it. The Mexican's *sangfroid* was splendid, and he had said so much in the one word "Heffy." It was an expression of absolute contempt.

I threw my eyes toward the bathroom, from which various sounds advertised the hotel detective's search. There was a scraping of feet, a grunting, as he doubtless stooped to peer here and there; the sound of water running, as he possibly tested the pipes. And then he appeared, shaking his head to show us clearly that his search had been vain.

But he was on the trail, and had no notion of desisting.

As by a common accord, we all fell silent and watched his effort. Without pause he attacked a dresser and drew out its drawers. He took them clear out and poked into the space behind them. Without ceremony he dumped their contents on the floor, and replaced it bit by bit in order to overlook nothing.

In the end he got down and looked under the dresser itself.

Next he attacked the pictures on the wall, looking behind them; and from them he climbed up and poked over the top of the window and back of its shade; got down and inspected the drawer of a small night-stand by the bed, straightened, and scratched his head.

In a moment he made up his mind and attacked the bed itself.

"Say, doc, if you'll move—" He addressed Osborne, laid hold of the bedding, and swept it on to the floor. On the exposed mattress he got up and began a careful prodding and feeling, and a careful search for any evidence of rips or tears.

He lifted the mattress itself and inspected the springs; put the mattress back and shook out each sheet and comfort and blanket as he laid them back one by one. After that he uncased each pillow and went over them closely. One by one he threw them from him, darted into a closet, and kept up his examination.

And all the time his heavy face was growing redder and redder. He was so in earnest that once more I felt that insane desire to chuckle and to cry, "Hotter, colder!" to him as we used to do when playing a childish game.

Now and then as he worked I saw him throw a half-pleading, half-resentful glance toward Semi, as though he suspected some sort of a game at his expense. But Semi did not seem to notice.

Since Laredo's last words he had been sitting partly relaxed, leaning back in his chair, his eyes fixed straight before him, seeming to stare at the bed in a total oblivion as regarded Heffy's frenzied search.

Sounds of that search still came from the closet.

I glanced up to find the eyes of Osborne and Dayton upon me in a mute sort of question. I shook my head. I was as much mystified by it all as they were. Save the closet it seemed to me every possible spot of concealment had been exhausted, and surely no man in his senses would have put such objects in his trunk. Where then was the gigantic emerald and the Image of Quetzal, with its poisoned dagger, which Dual felt so sure it contained?

Without it, as Laredo had said, I could see no chance of conviction. The mere fact that his footprints and the mark of his hand had been found at the scene of the tragedy of the night would never serve to fasten the crime upon him.

What, then?

The strain was telling. Dayton rose and walked to the window back of Laredo. Osborne went over and stood looking down at Laredo's trunk, as though half-minded to have it open. The Mexican followed his movements, and once more I saw the thin-lipped smile writhe across his face.

He had been sitting half turned, apparently listening to Heffy in the closet. Now his eyes came on around from the physician and fell on Semi Dual. Of a sudden I saw them widen, then narrow as quickly to slits. Without a sound his lips moved slightly. He cleared his throat as if to attract attention.

Heffy came out of the closet.

"I'm beat," he complained in a growl of disappointment. "Unless he's planted 'em in his trunk, which ain't likely, they ain't here. Still—"

"Never mind the trunk, Mr. Heffy," said Semi Dual without moving.

"Huh!" Heffy paused in his advance.

"That which you seek is not in it," Dual spoke again softly.

Laredo rose quickly. "Then, *señor*, your wonderful structure of suspicion comes tumbling to the ground."

Dual shook his head without shifting its position or changing his eyes' direction. Though addressing Laredo, he never so much as glanced toward where he was standing. "Not yet," he said.

"But the emerald and the image—the things on the finding of which the entire matter rested—"

"Are here."

"In this room you mean, *señor?*"

"Yes."

"They have not been found—here, *señor.*" Laredo threw out his hands.

"No. Not yet." Still Dual leaned, lolling in the great chair which held him. Still his eyes stared straight before him.

And the rest of us stared at the two men who pitted their wits in well-nigh mortal combat. We were all on our feet, save Dual. We all stood and waited, while the tension grew and grew.

Dual alone seemed calm, inscrutable, unmoved, as he fenced with his mental opponent. Laredo, on the other hand, I could see was breathing quickly, leaning slightly forward. He seemed seeking some point in Dual's subtle attack through which he could break.

"Perhaps, *señor*," he said slowly, at last, "you imagine you know where they are?"

"Yes."

Laredo's hands clenched at the answer. I saw his eyes blink in involuntary contraction. Yet, the next instant he shrugged, and the faint smile came back to his thin lips, pressed close together.

"Where, *señor?*" It was a question, a challenge.

"In the least likely to be suspected, and therefore the most probable place," said Dual. "*The place of which you are thinking.*"

He rose from his chair. "The place at which you are *looking*, Laredo."

In a stride he had reached the bed.

It was of brass; one of those molded affairs, with head and foot posts fully five inches in diameter, massive in appearance, yet hollow. Without a glance in our direction Dual laid hold of the top cap on the foot post beside which he stood and began to unscrew it.

Laredo's control vanished. He gasped. The look of a cornered fox leaped into his face.

"You cursed devil!" he cried hoarsely. His hand darted swiftly inside the left breast of his coat and came back with something short and sinister and as venomous in its way as the fang of a snake. He swept it out and around and—

Dayton acted.

Standing nearest the Mexican, he saw and hurled himself upon him. His powerful hand closed in a numbing grip on the slender brown wrist of the other! He forced it downward and inward till the fingers of its hand loosed their hold on the weapon and it clattered to the floor.

I leaped to his aid, but Heffy was before me.

With an agility surprising in one of his build, he saw the moment he had waited for and rushed to meet it. As he came his hand dragged something which glittered from his coat.

He reached Laredo's side; there was a struggle, a flash, a sharp click, and the detective straightened, gloating. Circlets of steel bound Laredo's wrists together.

"An' that will be about all from you, I reckon," said Heffy. "Maybe I ain't such a much at detectin', but you bet I've had practise with the irons."

Our eyes came back from Laredo to Dual.

Throughout the brief moment of peril he had gone calmly on with his work. As we turned he had quite removed the cap, and stood holding something in his hands. He lifted it up and held it for all to see—a slender bit of wire to which were attached a peculiar image of bronze and a monstrous-sized green stone.

He seized the image in his hand.

With his other he laid hold of its handle. In a wrench and a pull he tore it out of the idol, and drew with it a slender bit of tempered copper some sixteenth of an inch wide at its broadest point and perhaps four inches long.

Tossing the rest on the tumbled bed, he turned directly to Heffy, the dagger in his hand. "You have done well, Mr. Heffy," he observed. "Here"—he lifted the fatal weapon—"is your single fang. And there"—he waved it toward Laredo—"is your snake."

"Scotched!" chuckled the hotel official. "Hold him a

minute, will you, Dayton? I wanter go lamp that stone." He crossed to the bed, lifted the Eye of Quetzal, and turned it in his hands.

Abruptly he cast it from him on to the bed and came back to lay hold on Laredo. "Come on," he growled. "I reckon you ain't to be trusted in sight of them things. I'll put you where you're safe."

He led the Mexican toward the door.

Heffy was a far better policeman than detective, when all was said.

LAREDO HAD BEEN turned over to the local authorities to be held. His dream of an Indian empire with himself at its head completely shattered, he had lapsed silent and refused to affirm or deny any or all details of his actions of the night before.

The great green stone of ill omen lay somewhere beneath the boiling water of the Colorado. Dual had advised it, and Dayton had given his sanction. We had gone down, Dual and Dayton and I, and cast it from us and watched it sink out of man's ken.

Ute Charley's brother had taken his body, and Dayton had arranged for Wingarde's remains to be sealed and shipped. Dual had kept the Image of Quetzal, and he has it yet.

As the green stone had vanished Dual had turned to Dayton. "So," he remarked, "we free mankind from its menace, as you, Mr. Dayton, freed me from the menace of Laredo's automatic, for which I thank you. The episode is ended. Let us go back."

And that night Evelyn Wingarde and Dayton sat with

Connie and Semi and me at a little supper served in the parlor of our suite, where privacy reigned.

The girl, her blue eyes wet with quiet tears, had thanked Semi gravely for his actions in her behalf, and he had replied, as was his wonted custom, in a way to place her at her ease. Still later she addressed him again:

"You have been so more than kind, Mr. Dual, that I want to impose still further upon both your kindness and wisdom. Spencer and I have a question which we wish you to decide."

Our eyes turned to Dayton. He grew red in the face. "Why—er—that is, you know," he made embarrassed response. "You see, Evelyn here is so awfully much alone. I fancy I told you we were engaged. So, you know, I imagined there was really no reason for waiting. If we were married I could take care of her rather better than if we were not. So I suggested—that is, I proposed—"

Dual smiled. The expression lighted his whole strong face benignly. "That you marry at once, Mr. Dayton? Is that it? If so, I think I approve. Why not?"

THE WEB OF DESTINY

1

A FLY IN A WEB

I WONDER: DID you ever, out of the collected experiences of life, notice how some incident, seemingly trivial in itself, may take position as the basal note of a train of subsequent happenings? And from that initial circumstance other things follow in a gradually ascending scale like notes on a musical stave until the grand, crashing climax is reached and leaves us thrilling with the vibration of its meaning.

In my work as a newspaperman and later as a detective, I have. Yet who could have suspected that a fly caught in the meshes of a spider's web was the initial occurrence of a drama of human life—would strike the key-note of the things which followed in unbroken sequence for days to come?

The train had stopped at Salida, where the road over Marshall Pass and the line to Leadville separate to meet again at Grand Junction. The mighty grandeur of the Royal Gorge of the Arkansas had been left behind us, though its influence still lingered as a lesson of man's smallness when opposed to the forces of nature.

At Salida they hook on a helper engine, and there is usually some delay before the train again takes up its western climb. Connie and Semi Dual and I had descended from the observation platform from which we had viewed the wondrous cañon the river has cut through the mountain barrier, and were spending the time of the wait in walking up and down the platform beside the string of Pullmans.

That was how Connie came to notice the spider's web in the first place. The depot building and platform are of wooden construction, and the sun was hot on the June day which found us there.

Dual had gone on up the train toward the front, and Connie drew into the shade cast by the overhanging of the depot's eaves. I followed, and we paused close beside a window, where, on the upper corner of the frame, a spider had spun its web.

"Look," said my wife, pointing. "Every time I see anything like that I want a broom."

I nodded. "The housewifely instinct," I responded. "The spider, however, is merely trying to make a living in the only way he knows. He—"

"Oh," cried Connie, "he's caught a fly!"

He had. While we were talking one of several of the insects which had been buzzing about the platform had circled and darted squarely into the outer segment of the web, where it now buzzed and whirred with a great flutter of wings and ineffectual efforts at escape. Under its struggles the web vibrated violently, and presently a small dark body appeared from the funnel-like opening close up by the frame of the casing.

"Spider knows he's got a bite," I remarked.

The fly ceased to struggle and lay still. It might have been dead already save for a faint quiver of the wings. One could imagine that it lay in its bonds and panted with its efforts and a sort of fright.

Connie touched my arm. "The poor little thing. Gordon, set it loose," she urged.

Dual spoke. While we had been absorbed in the minor tragedy being played out before us he had approached from his stroll up the platform and now stood directly at our back.

"Pity not the unwitting fly, Mrs. Glace," said he, having manifestly heard her outcry. He smiled: "On the face of the thing it is but a matter of food-catching by the spider. Looking below the surface it is an illustration of the working out of the laws of the universe, which says that ignorance is no defense or excuse from the paying of the penalty of our acts.

"The act must bring its effect with immutable surety, be it greater or less. The fly which unwittingly flings itself into the meshes of the web is as certainly lost as though it had deliberately cast itself therein. In either instance the penalty is death for the fly—food for the spider. The advice, 'Christian, walk carefully,' is exceedingly worthy of consideration by all of us. Its application would save much pain."

Connie turned her eyes upon him as he spoke.

"Just the same, it seems like a cruel law," she rejoined as he finished. "The poor little fly was so happy, and now—I was asking Gordon to help it escape."

A smile lighted the warm olive of Dual's face and shone in his gray eyes.

"It's the law of immutable justice to which there are no exceptions," he replied slowly. "It operates for each plane of existence in its own particular application. Hence it follows that its application on a higher plane may transcend its working on a lower—thus."

He put up a finger and thumb and deftly extracted the prisoned insect, held it a moment, and tossed it lightly into the air.

"The quality which we call mercy is but the transcending of the lower by the higher application," said he.

"Splendid!" exclaimed Connie "I'm so glad to hear you say that, Mr. Dual. Not, of course, that I doubted your innate mercy, but when you begin to speak of the law in that manner, I always feel as if I didn't understand."

"So few of us do understand," said Semi. "And because of that so many of us suffer. As for mercy—yes, I believe in it. But, Mrs. Glace, one must be careful in its exercise lest he allow mere sympathy to pervert his understanding, and so cause him to transgress his true position. He who seeks to become an instrument of destiny may often precipitate more harm than good. It is a choice to be made with care."

"Apropos of that," I joined in, "in view of the present swat-the-fly crusade, isn't your recent act in freeing the fly open to question on the grounds of the greatest good to the greatest number?"

Dual's eyes twinkled.

"Well sped, my verbal archer," he made answer.

"Besides," I went on, "you robbed the spider of his dinner. How justify that?"

"By the conjunction of time and place," said Dual. "You who know my belief that nothing happens from chance in this world of ours scarcely need ask, friend Glace. Still—" He paused and grew utterly serious in his manner. "Had the destiny of that little insect which I freed just now demanded its ultimate dissolution, I personally hold that neither you nor your wife nor myself would have been at this place at this time. And because we were here at this time, I hold that the fly was to be saved, and that in liberating it from its peril, I acted as an instrument of fate, regardless of any considerations of sociological hygiene."

Again he paused and appeared almost to listen, stood so for a moment, and shook his head. "It may be," he resumed, "that there is a hidden meaning in all this, wholly apart from the seemingly trivial incident under discussion. It has come to me in the last moment that there are etheric vibrations about us which I may read if I so elect. Would you object if I retired to your stateroom—until you wish to use it?"

"Of course," Connie assented. "Oh, dear, this interests me immensely. What is it, do you think, Mr. Dual?"

Semi shook his head.

"Not now—later," he made answer and walked across to our car, mounted the steps, and disappeared within.

Connie turned her eyes from watching his retreating figure, and rushed a question at me.

"What did he mean? What's he going to do? Isn't he the queerest and finest man that—"

A rattling bump ran along the line of Pullmans. I glanced forward and saw that the two engines were coupled up. I shook my head.

"All aboard now, Hon," I suggested. "We'd better get on now ourselves. Where do you want to go—inside or back on the platform?"

"Back," decided Connie. "I want you to tell me a lot more about Mr. Dual. I want to ask you some questions."

We went back, and because it was a hot day there between the hills in the little valley, and because people are like sheep in a way and followed each other in or down from the platform when the train stopped, we found it deserted, and settled ourselves in a couple of chairs well back under the overhang.

"And now," said I when we were seated and the depot buildings were beginning to slip past us, "what do you want to know about Dual?"

"Everything," my wife made most comprehensive reply.

I smiled. "I've told you pretty much all of that for the last few years, if I remember," I remarked.

"But I didn't know him then," Connie countered. "Now that I do, I want to hear it again—how you met him, and about his theories of life, and all of it. Go on." She turned half toward me and prepared to listen.

And so as the panorama of the mountains unrolled on either side and the train crawled up toward the west, I told her again of how I had first gone to see the strange person whom we now called friend: how I had gone to interview him for the *Record* long before Bryce and I organized our detective bureau, and found him dwelling in the magnificent quarters which he had made for himself twenty stories up in the air on top of the Urania building, where his garden of flowers and vines and shrubs bloomed the year around under its sheltering roof of green-yellow glass, and where Semi Dual pursued his strange studies in the application of universal laws. At the end Connie's eyes were glowing.

"He's a sort of modern magician, isn't he, boy?" she remarked in an awed little voice. "And yet there must be something in these studies of his. Look how he found the rubies."

I nodded. I knew to what she referred. It was too recent to have faded in the least in my mind. In fact, it was an episode of our present trip.

This, in reality, was our honeymoon, upon which we had come as the guests of Semi Dual. He had suggested it quite as a surprise to us at our wedding, and taken us first down the coast to New Orleans, then up the Mississippi by steamer, and now on west toward the ultimate destination of Goldfield, where dwelt his friend and partner, John Curzon, manager of their jointly owned mines.

On the steamer a theft of some beautiful gems had occurred, and Dual had recovered them in his own peculiar way. This was in the week before.

"I prefer to call him a modern metaphysician, however, Connie," I said. "Magician is hardly the word, because, after all, Semi uses only natural forces in gaining his results. In fact, he says there is no such thing as a supernatural force, but that what we so regard are but higher manifestations of natural law. I honestly believe that Dual knows more about the subliminal self, subconscious analysis, chirography, astrology, telepathy, suggestion, and pure psychism than any other living man."

Connie moved slightly.

"What a fearful power a man like that could wield if he wished," she murmured.

"Either for good or evil," I followed the suggested thought. "But Dual only uses it for good. Connie, I tell you, he is the most wonderful person I ever knew. With the ability to do anything he wishes, he uses his mighty power only to help others. There are times when I have actually felt a sense of veneration for him. I have sat in his presence when I seemed to sense something beyond the mere man-life, as though he were almost godlike in his calm defense of right and justice."

My wife's hand fell on my own.

"Don't," she whispered. "You make me feel strange. Little as I know him, I have felt that same thing in his presence. He has done some wonderful things of which you have told me. He sent you to Goldfield once to find a man nobody knew was alive, do you remember?"

I smiled. "Rather. It was there I met a girl Dual and I afterwards went half around the world to save from danger."

"Alice Parton," said Connie.

"Née Sheldon," I amended. "She was single at that time, the daughter of old Colonel McDonahue Sheldon, who had succeeded in getting his brother mixed up in a bad mess through trying to put over a stock-deal. I want you to meet them when we get to Goldfield. The colonel is a character, believe me."

"What you'd call 'crooked,' isn't he?" said Connie.

I chuckled. "I don't know," I told her. "The fact of the matter is, I like him. He's a very nervy old goat, and when Dual pinned him down, he stood the gaff like a soldier—never whimpered, and offered to pay or stand the shot in any way. Said he'd had enough of the devious path, and was going to stick to the straight and narrow. I don't know if you can call a man like that crooked or not. I know he's run straight ever since, and he certainly loves his girl and her baby!

"Has Alice a baby?" Connie sat up and took immediate interest.

"Girl," I responded. "Dual is its godfather as it happens."

Connie smiled softly.

"I shall like to meet them," she decided. "It won't seem like meeting strangers, but more like old friends, because I know their stories and they know you and Mr. Dual. I think it will be awfully jolly."

She glanced into the car behind her and back to me.

"What do you suppose he is doing? What was it that happened back there on the platform?" she asked.

"Dual sensed something subconsciously," I ventured. "I have known him to do it again and again. The first time I ever met him, you know, he sensed a murder and Smithson's desire for my presence. At another time he sent me on another similar case. He can sense etheric waves which are imperceptible to us of lesser evolution, though at times we unconsciously do the same thing. The difference is that Dual does it consciously and at will."

"Just as at times when you were thinking of me or coming to me I have felt it," said Connie.

"Exactly, Hon. You and I felt it in a vague way. Dual feels it in a perfectly conscious manner, just as he senses the meaning of any occurrence. That is telepathy, so called. It is nothing but the ability to allow the subtle vibrations of thought-waves to influence our subconscious minds and then translate their meaning into the objective plane of thought."

"That, then, is what he meant by saying he could read them if he elected?" said Connie. "And then he said he wanted to occupy our stateroom instead of his section.

Gordon—what do you suppose he is finding? It makes me shivery clear down to my toes. You remember he said he read that man's thoughts on the boat. What do you suppose this will be?"

"Heaven knows," I answered. "If Dual wishes he will tell us. Probably he will because he told you 'later,' and Semi never says a thing unless he means it. He says a person has to account for every thought and word as well as every action."

"Goodness!" said Connie. "Do you suppose that's so?"

"I hope not," I told her. "I'd hate to answer for some of the things I've thought every once in a while. If they were known they might hang me."

"Br-r-r!" laughed Connie. "Of course every one knows you're a desperate man."

I joined in her laughter. "Before I got into the business with Bryce and made good, I used to think about robbing a bank every now and then," I declared. And that reminded me. "I wonder how Bryce is getting along? Things must be quiet; he hasn't let a word out of him in days."

"Now, no business," chided Connie. "You're a very lucky boy. You got me without robbing the bank, and you've got a partner who used to be a police detective and knows how to run the business while you're gone, and you've got a friend unlike any friend of whom I have ever heard. Take a real rest and don't worry about the affairs of 'Glace & Bryce, Confidential Agents.' I myself told Mr. Bryce not to bother you unless he had to."

"The deuce you did?" I exclaimed. "What did Bryce say?"

Connie giggled. "He said he didn't think you'd be of

much use for at least six weeks, anyway, and that he'd try to struggle along."

"Under which circumstances I suppose I may as well enjoy the beauties of nature," I remarked, and stared full into Connie's face.

Connie flushed and promptly pointed out some cattle grazing in a mountain meadow, knee-deep in lush grass.

The afternoon wore on in a peaceful drowsiness, while the train climbed up and on around the shoulders of hills, across gullies, past hills clad in the dark greenery of the pines, across upland valleys where little cabins sat amid the trees.

Others came out and occupied chairs on the platform. Connie and I ceased to talk, save for perhaps an occasional word. Rather we sat and watched the receding landscape and thought our own thoughts while the wheels pounded out the lengthening miles.

Part of the time I watched the mountains, and part the girl beside me. Even yet at times it seemed hard to realize that the hope of years, when I struggled to save enough from the salary of a reporter to make our life together a thing of reality instead of dreams, had at length been realized, and that as man and wife we now faced the future together.

And yet, thanks to the work of those other years, and to the help of my friend Semi Dual when Inspector Bryce and I had formed our private bureau of detection, we drew a steadily increasing patronage through our doors—for the credit of clearing up more than one puzzling tangle was mine.

Dual would never appear as the real solver of the mysteries which had more than once baffled the police, though I must confess that it was his work which brought them to an end. And it was on his advice that I opened my offices in the first place.

Always Dual led and I followed, and I would have followed no matter where he led. Some men can make others feel like that—Dual more than any other, I believe.

"What time is it, Gordon?" Connie asked at last.

"Six." I looked at my watch.

"Goodness," said she: "and Mr. Dual hasn't come out! I wonder if it would be all right to go back? I want to freshen up a bit for dinner."

I rose and gave her a hand. We went on to the second coach, which was ours. The door of our stateroom stood open Semi sat in his own section, poring over a railroad folder.

He glanced up and smiled his pleasant smile as we passed and turned to his task again. Yet in that fleeting moment I caught something from him which told me, who knew him, that he had found the thing which he had sought. I passed on after Connie, mentally questioning what it might be he had learned.

But it was not until the first call for dinner had gone and we were seated at a table in the diner and our order had been given, that he elected to speak.

"Mrs. Glace, it has been my pleasure to find you of a sincerely sympathetic nature, as witnessed by your attitude on several occasions and lastly in the affair of the spider this afternoon."

"I hate to see anything suffer," said Connie.

"I too hate to see anything suffer," replied Semi and

lapsed into a momentary silence. "Life is life," he went on after that pause in which he seemed to have decided upon the course he would follow, "and it makes small difference whether it be that of a fly or a man, though most of us would judge the life of a woman, for instance, as worth that of several million flies, and rightly, for the woman has evolved to a superior plane and is just much farther along the road of attainment. Mrs. Glace, would you mind if I changed the itinerary of our trip?"

"Why—certainly not," said Connie, while I sat up and opened my ears. It was coming now; I felt certain, though I had no idea what it was to be. That it was important I knew if Semi was changing his plans in order to meet it.

"I think then," he was saying, "that instead of stopping at Salt Lake we will go directly on to Goldfield. I have looked up the schedules, and I think we may be able to catch a train out of there, provided the Western Limited is late, as it generally is at this time of year."

"What's wrong in Goldfield, that somebody was wishing you out there?" I inquired.

Dual smiled and nodded.

"Correct, Gordon," he admitted. "It was a telepathic flash I caught this afternoon. They want us there very badly right now."

"Who does?" I leaned forward with an odd little feeling of rousing interest such as I had known many a time before in the presence of some such remark of my friend.

"Colonel Sheldon," replied Dual.

Honestly I started. It was so blamed sudden, and Connie and I had been talking about Colonel Mac, as you know.

"Colonel Sheldon!" gasped my wife and paused at the

sound of her own voice. "Er—the man who forged the check?"

Dual turned his eyes toward her.

"The man who had the check forged and thereby learned a much needed lesson, Mrs. Glace. There is much in him to admire."

"What's happened to the colonel?" I asked.

"Nothing directly, I think," said Semi, "but at the same time he wants us both very badly."

"Alice and her baby?" suggested Connie in a rather indefinite question.

Dual shook his head in perfect understanding.

"Gordon has evidently told you all about them," he returned, smiling. "They are safe. However, I have reason to think the matter concerns a woman in trouble. Now you see my reason for hurrying on."

Connie's eyes were wide with interest, her lips were slightly parted.

"Hurry; yes, hurry," she whispered. "Do you think we will be in time?"

"That lies in the future," said Semi. "Ah, here we are at Leadville. A lot of Western history as well as many a fortune was made here, Mrs. Glace."

He plunged into a series of stories of the town at which we were stopped, and said nothing more of the need of his presence at Goldfield then or later in the evening.

Immediately after our dinner, however, he went to his section and began covering sheets of paper with series of numbers and figures. I realized that he was already at work on his answer to the voiceless cry for assistance, which had come to him from the invisible void of space.

Time and again I had seen him mark down those symbols of his and from them gain information which led him to strike with unerring precision at the root of violence and crime.

I have heard many sneer at the astrological science; I had even done so once myself, but now I know that in the hands of a sincere seeker after knowledge it can unlock both the future and the past.

And so I left Dual at his work and led Connie out on the back once more, where we watched the moon flood over the mountains and spoke softly together in whispers until it was time to retire for the night.

Dual's section was already curtained and dark when we went in, so that we did not see him. Once in the night I woke and looked out, attracted by the blue white glare of an electric arc. I caught one of those half-retained glimpses of the wakened sleeper on a train.

It was of an area of light flooded platform and building, of a trundling baggage truck and a man passing in uniform, with a lantern caught over his bended arm, its light making a blur on his coat. Then came a woman's voice raised in question, and a man, evidently our porter, replied:

"Gran' Junction, ma'am."

Up forward I could dimly hear the hiss of steam and a man bawling some words of question or direction. Footsteps ran past outside. The man with the lantern slipped it off his arm and raised it. The train trembled and the arc-lamp slipped slowly away. I turned and slept again.

Yet while I slept others waked, and immutable Fate wove its web and material agencies worked to prove correct the statements of Dual, and demonstrate once more the verity of the things he said.

When daylight broke we were running across the arid stretches of eastern Utah, where the great ragged buttes rear their torn and gashed masses as far as the eye can reach from the train.

I have never slept soundly on a train and I rose early, but early as I was I found Semi Dual laving his face in the dressing-room when I went in.

"Hello!" I greeted. "Have a good night?"

"I was awake at Grand Junction," he replied.

"Did you find out anything from your astrological figures last night?" I questioned.

Dual wiped the water out of his eyes and faced me. "Enough to predict that I shall probably interrupt your honeymoon," he said.

"Then the matter is serious?" I lighted a cigarette and took a deep puff.

"Yes."

"What is it?"

Dual smiled slightly.

"A fly in a web," he made cryptic answer. "If we don't catch the Western Limited at Salt Lake I shall engage a special. Finish your toilet for the present." He slipped into his coat and left the room.

It was at breakfast that he next spoke of the matter. After we were seated he drew a yellow envelope from his pocket and extracted a telegraph blank. This he extended to Connie and me, with an explanatory remark: "This came aboard at Grand Junction."

I glanced at the words of the message, and read the

confirmation of Dual's words of the previous evening. It was from my partner Bryce, addressed to Dual:

> Communicate Sheldon, Goldfield, at once. Important. Have wired him your probable address—Salt Lake.

2

THE NATURE OF THE WEB

CONNIE'S EYES LIFTED from the paper. "You were right," she said softly. "It seems even more wonderful now that you show us this. I think I feel a little bit like I used to do when I heard a ghost story."

Semi Dual nodded.

"And yet it is only an example of the operation of the natural law of vibration," he answered. "Because your husband and I were wanted and Colonel Sheldon was thinking about us, and had telegraphed to Gordon's firm and so caused Mr. Bryce to begin thinking about us also, their thoughts set up a strong current in our direction, which I finally sensed. It is simple, after all, and not strange, or a cause for any thought or emotion of awe.

"If you strike a musical note in a room with a harp or piano, its strings vibrate in sympathy with the note you strike. So thought-waves may affect a sympathetic mind. At the time I first sensed this message we were speaking of a thing which I now know was in a way related to our need in Goldfield. That sensitized me to the thought-waves of Sheldon. Do you see?"

"You mean the fly in the spider's web," said Connie; "but what else do you mean?"

"That I have an idea we will find some person caught in the web of circumstance at the end of our journey, Mrs. Glace."

"You wired Sheldon?" I questioned.

"Yes—of course—at Grand Junction. Now suppose we return to our muttons—or, to be exact, to our melons— which I see the waiter is bringing. There is something decidedly refreshing in a nicely iced melon for breakfast. There is no need of anticipating trouble, so enjoy the day. We make Salt Lake this afternoon and take the first train for Las Vegas."

Our waiter served us, and Dual at once attacked the cantaloup before him. He ate with a relish which neither Connie nor I could imitate, inured to strange situations as I had become; and after breakfast he sat with us for a while, explaining to Connie all about his relations with Curzon and their Goldfield mine, and telling her of Colonel Sheldon's mines as well.

To have heard him one would never have imagined that he had a care in the world, or have suspected that even then he was rushing to the front to engage in one more of those battles he had so often waged in defense of right.

And there is little to tell of the rest of the trip. We made Salt Lake on time; Dual called a taxi and had us rushed from one depot to another. Luck attended us there, and we caught the belated Western Limited some five minutes before it left for the South.

From Salt Lake to Las Vegas was made in the rest of that day, and the night and the next day saw us running up from the latter station to Goldfield, where we arrived in due time.

Colonel McDonahue Sheldon met us as we stepped off the train. He was the same old Colonel Mac, little changed so far as I could see. Perhaps the hair under the light Stetson was a trifle grayer than the first time I had met him; but the steady gray eyes were the same, and his mustache bristled as stiffly as ever. Under it his thin lips were now wreathing into a smile as he came forward to greet us, dragging off his hat in deference to my wife.

"My Lord!" he burst out, gripping Dual's hand, "but I'm sure glad to see you. Got your message yesterday mornin'. I reckon that feller Bryce muster headed you off, all right. I got my first long breath after I got your wire. Howdy, Glace—an' I reckon this is Missis Glace, ain't it? Dual tipped off the marriage in his message. I hope I see you well, ma'am. Say—you folks come over to the car, an' I'll get you home, *pronto*. Then we can talk. Hot, ain't it? Hey, Moto, grab these here bags!"

An intelligent-looking Japanese in the uniform of a chauffeur came forward, picked up our cases from where we had placed them on the platform, and carried them toward a handsome motor at one end of the station.

The four of us followed his lead, and, while Colonel Mac held the door, Dual, Connie, and I climbed into the tonneau. Then the colonel slapped his hat on his head, lifted his five feet ten of bone and muscle aboard, and spoke to Moto.

"Let her out, son." He sat down.

The car leaped away with a dash of gears. Sheldon turned back to us with an audible sigh.

"It was sure mighty good of you to git action so quick," he ran on. "When it happened I said to Alice an' Archie, 'I ain't goin' to fool with none of these here police or private detectives. No, sir. There's jest one man on this little old ball of dirt as can put the Indian sign on whoever done it, an' that man is the feller who put it all over Colonel Mac himself.'

"Homer thought it was kinder foolish, but I says, 'I'm runnin' this thing, my boy,' an' I got busy with the wires. Then somebody signin' hisself Bryce wires me you're headin' this way already, an' I could catch you at Salt Lake if not sooner, an' then I gets your wire from Grand Junction. I reckon Bryce wised you up, eh?"

"He wired me to communicate with you," said Semi.

"Eh? Didn't he tell you what had happened?" Colonel Mac seemed a good deal surprised.

Dual shook his head.

"Well, my—Lord! How'd'je know then? You wired me not to take any steps till you got here. How—" He paused, as though struck by a thought, and a grim smile twitched the lips above his fighting chin.

"I reckon you don't need to answer," he said slowly. "I've seen some of your work before this, Mr. Dual, an' I mighter known. I'm mighty glad you're here. Now I reckon we'll find that girl."

I felt Connie's fingers close on mine at the words, and knew she had not missed their meaning. I saw her eyes resting on the gray-clad figure of the colonel, with its heavy gold watch-chain looped across its brocaded vest.

"What do you think of him now?" I whispered in question.

She turned her eyes, and I saw they were dancing. More than that, her lips were smiling.

"I like him," she said.

Colonel Mac had lapsed strangely silent. Presently he drew a caseful of his favorite black panetelas from his pocket and extended it to me.

"Smoke, Gordon," he invited, "or kin he smoke, Mrs. Glace?"

"He does whenever he wants to," laughed Connie. But I shook my head. "A little too strong for me, colonel; I'll stick to cigarettes."

Sheldon chuckled, selected and lighted one of the slim brown rolls, and put away the case. "I been smokin' like a chimney for four days, an' I cribbed this caseful when Allie wasn't lookin'. She's kickin' about my smokin' too much, but there wasn't nothin' else to do; only send telegrams, an' I had to smoke to dope up what I wanted to say in them."

The car swung in from the street and stopped at the side of the house where once I had called upon Alice Sheldon in the days before her marriage to Parton. The colonel helped us out and led us up to the wide porch, where Alice herself waited to greet us.

So far as I could see she was still the same brilliant brunette I had not seen for two years, save that there was an added matronliness about her which was rather becoming. She gave both her hands to Dual, and then turned to me while I presented Connie.

"I have known your husband for years," she said, smiling, "but we didn't know of his marriage until we had Mr. Dual's message. I am so glad to meet you. Mr. Glace spoke of you many a time in the past. This is my husband," she added as Archie Parton came forward, and he bowed over Connie's hand.

The introductions completed, Connie and Alice went off to see the Parton baby and Sheldon took us men into the library, to "get action," as he said. As we entered the room a young man rose from a chair of Spanish leather and stood while the colonel presented him as Homer Reich.

He was a dapper appearing individual, clad in blue serge and tan oxfords, a soft shirt with French collar and belt. He was what one would denominate a handsome man on first impression, of an almost tawny complexion, brown eyed, and wearing a great mass of wavy light hair, brushed straight back from where it grew low on his forehead.

His brows like his hair were tawny, his nose high of bridge and slightly long, and his rather large mouth was thin lipped, blending into the general, long, slender lines of his face as a whole. His figure, too, was slender and his hands long. So much I noted before he was introduced to me.

"Homer was Lilly's *fiancé*," explained Sheldon, "an' I thought you ought to meet him. I had him come up an' wait here, when we knew you was comin'. Now thet you know him, I guess we'd better dope this thing out jest as fast as we kin. Sit down an' let's get to work. First off though I want to show Glace a Goldfield highball." He struck a bell on his desk.

A white jacketed Chinaman answered the ring and to him Colonel Mac gave his order, by holding up four fingers, and then separating his two hands about six inches.

"Long ones, Lee," he directed and glanced at Semi who shook his head. "An' a lemonade," said Colonel Mac.

The servant grinned and shuffled from the room.

"An' now," resumed our host, "just how much of this here are you wise to, Mr. Dual?"

And Semi Dual answered promptly. Even to me his words were a surprise, for remember there had been no way for him to learn the things he said save by his own peculiar methods. Yet he smiled slightly as the colonel asked the question, leaned back in his chair and spoke.

"Merely the main points, Colonel Sheldon. As I understand it, a young lady is missing. She is a woman, in whom you feel an interest, though she is in no way related to you. She may be described as of some five feet four inches in height, medium complexion, brown haired, and with brown eyes and a well rounded figure. She has been in peril for some time, but it was not until five days ago that the climax of her danger arrived."

"Well, my lord," ejaculated Sheldon. He took his cigar from his mouth and turned his eyes about our circle of faces. "Can you beat it? An' he never saw Lilly, I'll gamble. What do you think of that Homer, my boy?"

"Quite a coincidence," said Reich.

"Coincidence your grandmother," began Sheldon. "He kin do that any time he wants—"

"I might add," Dual interrupted, "that Mr. Reich was one of the factors in causing her disappearance."

"What do you mean by that?" Reich sat forward and half rose from his seat. "We may as well understand one another first as last," he went on with a good deal of heat. "I was engaged to marry Miss Lawton. Do you think I'd be apt to—"

"Steady, Homer," Colonel Mac cautioned. "Don't you go to goin' off half cocked. Mr. Dual says you was a factor, an' you was. That telegram said you was about ready to kick in, an' that's why Lilly left in the first place. You want to keep cool an' not leave your feelin's lyin' around like a cat's tail. Nobody's aimin' to step on you."

"Perhaps you had better tell the story, Colonel Sheldon," suggested Dual.

The China boy came back with the drinks and served them on the desk. When he was gone the colonel picked up his and took a long draft, set it down, and stuck his cigar back in a corner of his mouth.

"Well, then," he began. "I reckon I will. Lilly's last name was Lawton. Her dad was a foreman in my mine, an a mighty fine straight man as they go. We had a cave-in a year ago an' he got killed. That left Lilly stranded as you might say, an' I says to her, 'little girl, I knowed your pa and I liked him, an old Colonel Mac ain't goin' to see his gal want for nothin'. You come over to my house an' help Allie take care of the kid, an' wave a feather brush once in a while, an' we'll take keer of you till some likely feller sees what a nice gal you are.'

"Well, she come, an' barrin' missin' her dad she had a good home, an' we tried to make her fergit her pa every way we could. Then Homer here gets into the game. He blows into town about two months ago, an' he meets Lilly at a dance.

"Then, after a bit he begins to call on her. First thing I know Lilly comes to me an' says he's asked her to keep house for him steady. 'Do you love him, gal?' I asks her, an' she says 'yes.' Well, bein' as her pa was dead, I tells her I'll have a look at Homer's pedigree, an' if its clear, I won't put up no holler.

"I sends for Homer an' asks him a few leadin' questions, an' he answers 'em all right. He said he was thinkin' of buyin' into a movin'-picture show here in town, an' settlin' down. I goes to see the feller who was runnin' the show at present, an' he tells me Homer an' he's a hen on, an' expect to make a deal. So I say, all right to Lilly, an' the next thing I know they've set the date for the last of this month. That was up to ten days ago about.

"Then Homer has to go to Salt Lake to see about gettin' some new stuff for the picture-house, him an' the feller havin' agreed that that was the way Homer would buy in— by gettin' the new stuff for his interest, and then five days ago there comes a telegram from Salt Lake for Lilly. Wait a minute, I got it here."

He opened a drawer in the desk and took out a yellow telegraph form.

"Here it is."

Miss Lilly Lawton,

    Goldfield.

    Care of Colonel McDonahue Sheldon.

    Homer Reich injured in automobile collision. In Holy Cross Hospital. Injury fatal. Wants to see you. Will meet you at train and take you to him.

                  Dr. Morehouse.

He tossed the message down on the desk.

"Lilly was pretty near crazy an' she come to me with the message. 'Little gal,' says I, 'don't you take on that-away nohow. Maybe it ain't as bad as it sounds Doctors don't always kill everybody they aim to. 'Course you kin go to Salt Lake, an I'll telephone the station to fix your ticket right now, an' Allie will help you pack your bag and git ready.' Then I takes her down to the station and she catches the first train out, an' we ain't heard a blamed word from her sence."

"A fake message," said I.

The colonel nodded.

"Sure, cuss the yeller dogs what sent it. The second night after Homer comes to the house. 'Where's Lilly?' says I, 'cause I was so surprised at seein' him, when he was supposed to be all hashed up.

" 'Ain't she here?' he says, as surprised as I, an' then we hed it out. It seems he hadn't had no sort of trouble an' he didn't know a thing about the message, but he was acquainted in Salt Lake, an' he was dead sure there wasn't no such man as Dr. Morehouse in the place. Gad, you kin imagine how we felt."

The colonel threw the cigar which he had chewed to rags into a basket beside his desk, lifted his glass and finished his drink.

"That's about all," he resumed in a moment. "Homer and I spent a day telegraphin' to every one he thought likely to know anything about it in Salt Lake, an' then I started to round you up."

"Did you notify the Salt Lake police?" I asked.

"Nope," said Sheldon. "Homer wanted to, but I told him that if I could get Mr. Dual, he was better'n all the bulls in the country. I made him wait, an' I had a fine time holdin' him level."

Reich, who had sat with face resting on his knuckles, arms on knees, raised his head.

"You can imagine how I felt," he burst out. "We were to have been married in a few days. She went to me—because she thought I needed her—to say good-by to me, as she thought—and it was a trick—they used her love to betray her. Ah!" He rose and began to pace the floor. Suddenly he paused in front of Semi.

"Mr. Dual, you were right—I was a factor in her betrayal," he said.

"There remains then the opportunity to assist in her rescue," said Dual.

"But couldn't you have stopped her by a telegram on the train?" I questioned.

"No, Homer didn't show up here till it was too late for that," Colonel Mac responded. "I reckon he passed her train when he was coming down the other day."

Reich nodded.

"I was near enough to almost reach out and touch her."

He pressed his lips closely together and walked over to a window, snapping his long fingers in a nervous way as he went. I followed him with my eyes.

Dual said nothing. Of a sudden he had lapsed from all apparent interest, sinking down in his chair, with drooping lids and hands lying idly folded in his lap. I gave him one glance and knew that behind his seeming lack of attention, his mighty brain was alive and at work in its own way upon the problem of this human soul in danger.

Sheldon glanced at him, opened his mouth to speak, caught my eye and filled his parted lips with a fresh cigar rather than words.

Parton smiled in a satisfied manner. He surely had reason to trust Semi Dual who had saved him his wife from a deadly peril. Reich turned away from his staring into the outer sunshine, came back and mutely questioned us others with his eyes.

We sat on. The silence seemed to get on Reich's nerves. He licked his lips and eyed Dual with impatience.

"What is he—a trance medium?" he whispered to Colonel Mac.

"Shut up," hissed Sheldon.

Dual opened his eyes and turned them on Reich. I knew then that he had caught the words.

"Mr. Reich," he began, "I must make you a slight explanation. My methods of gaining my results are, viewed from the usual police procedures, somewhat unusual—peculiar, if you prefer. I do not in the least expect you either to understand or sympathize with them. At the same time I have present three witnesses as to their capacity for gaining results, and so I fear you will need accept their word and for the rest await the end."

His manner and words were almost apologetic, and I marveled. Never before had I seen a person question Dual and not be forced then and there to acknowledge the subtle something about the man, which spoke of superior knowledge and force. I saw Colonel Mac frown as Dual finished. But it was Reich who spoke.

"It's results I want, Dual."

"You shall have them, I promise," said Semi and turned to Sheldon. "I think that after some preliminary steps here, Glace and I had better go to Salt Lake."

"Me and Homer'll go too," declared Sheldon, nodding. "I'm standin' in on this to the end, Mr. Dual. I'm takin' the place of that little gal's pa, an' all I want is to git within range of the bunch of dirty rustlers what pulled this thing off. I'm on my own range now, an you bet nobody can run anything like that over me, an' keep a water-tight skin if I sight him. You can count us in when you begin to deal."

Dual smiled.

"I rather anticipated your attitude, colonel," he responded. "And all I ask is that you allow me to handle the matter in my own manner. Aside from that I shall be very glad to have both you and Mr. Reich as companions."

"You bet you'll handle it," chuckled Sheldon. "I ain't goin' to make any fool plays, an' tip over the beans. But when we meet up with the bunch of jaspers who put this across, Gawd help 'em. Lawton's gal was the finest thing Gawd Almighty ever made—a clean woman, but she wasn't wise to th' sort of white-livered pups we have nowadays who don't respect nothin' at all. Any man what tries to double cross that sort of a girl oughter be got, and got good and plenty, an' I'm willin' to help with the gettin'. Well what do we do now?"

"Call your car," said Semi. "Have you searched Miss Lawton's room?"

"Searched her room—what for?" queried Sheldon.

"For anything which might bear on the matter in any way," Dual answered. "However I see you have not, and I will ask Gordon to request Mrs. Parton and his wife to examine the room, while we men are gone. A complete search, Gordon."

I nodded and rose to hunt up Connie and Alice Parton. Archie came with me, and when we returned we found Sheldon, Reich, and Dual waiting to go down to the car. I joined them and we were soon under way.

"Have your man drive to a point a little way from this moving-picture house Mr. Reich intended to buy into," Semi directed, as we started. "I want Glace to talk to the present owner."

"What for?" Reich took him up as Sheldon spoke to Moto.

"I want to see if Miss Lawton could have met any one at the picture house who might have in any way been responsible for what has happened."

"But how do you know she went there?" Reich appeared puzzled.

"I supposed that as your prospective wife, you might have taken her there," said Dual.

Sheldon chuckled. He seemed to be feeling much relieved now that Semi had taken hold.

"There ain't no use in your bein' surprised at what he knows, or what he does, Homer," he made comment. "As a matter of fact, Lilly was singin' in that house for about three weeks, Mr. Dual. She had a good voice an' she wanted to earn some money for her trousseau. I told her she didn't need to, but she wanted to do it, an' as Homer was bringin' her home every night, I let her."

"It was generally known that you were to be married?" Dual turned to Reich.

"Yes," said Homer. "But I'm sure she didn't meet any one at the movie who could have tried anything like this."

"Still, I'll have Gordon see the man. What is his name, Mr. Reich?"

"Green."

"And in the meantime, I'll go to the telegraph office and look over the messages you sent to Salt Lake," said Semi.

"While Colonel Mac and I are at that, Moto can take you to your rooms, and wait while you pack a bag for our trip to Salt Lake."

"Do you think they'll let you see the messages?" asked Reich.

"I think they'll let me see them," Dual smiled. "Don't worry, I usually get what I want, Mr. Reich."

The car rolled to a stand. "Ah, Gordon, here is where you get out. Go up and talk to Green and meet us at the colonel's when you get through."

I climbed down and saw them roll away. Then I turned toward the gaudily postered entrance of a motion picture-house a little way down the street. I admit that I grinned. It felt good to once more be in the game with Dual directing the moves.

Time and again I had gone where he sent me and found what I sought, and brought it back to see him weave it into the complete fabric of his scheme of things. I could easily understand how his cool directions should amaze and half pique Reich, smarting and confused by his loss and the danger which he must feel threatened the girl he had been about to wed.

Mr. Reich impressed me as a very much demoralized young man. I turned into the entrance to the movie, and asked for Mr. Green.

He proved to be a quite likeable young fellow, with a round face and a rotund body, an ingenious smile and baby-blue eyes. I made myself known and promptly got down to business.

"Just how much do you know about Reich?" I asked.

"Not much. He seemed to have coin, and he wanted to

buy in here," he responded frankly. "He seemed rather a live wire to me, and as though he might be able to help build up the business. Had a lot of original ideas for advertising and that sort of thing. I needed more money, and he said he'd buy the new machines. He went up to Salt Lake to see about that."

"You knew his *fiancée?*"

"Miss Lawton? Sure. She was a fine little girl. I gave her a job here singin'. She had a swell voice."

"How did she behave around the theater? That is, did she pick up any acquaintances or carry on any flirtations, or—"

"Nit!" said Green with emphasis. "She was as straight as a string. She'd hardly talk to me 'cept on business. Reich always took her home."

"Did he seem fond of her?"

"Who, Reich? Why, they never made love around here, but I rekon he was, if they were goin' to get married. Reich never talked about her to me, though."

I didn't seem to be getting much beside second-hand information. I paused and considered, but I couldn't really see what more I would be likely to gain. I rose.

"I guess that's all then, Mr. Green, and thank you," I remarked. "I'll get on up to Colonel Sheldon's and meet Reich and the rest. We are going to Salt Lake to-night."

"You goin' to see Reich?" he asked quickly.

"Why, yes."

"He ain't been around since day before yesterday," said Green. "I suppose this business puts our deal out for the present, though he did tell me he'd bought some machines. Ask him to leave word for me what he wants me to do, and here's a letter. It come this mornin'. I was goin' to send it to his room if he didn't show up. Don't know if it's important or not, but it's marked 'missent,' and seems to have been a long time getting here from Denver. Maybe you'd take it to him?"

I assented and he gave me a somewhat soiled and mussed envelope bearing the Denver postmark and a return address to a post-office box. I pocketed it and walked out. When I got up to Sheldon's, none of the others had returned, so I laid it on the hall-tree when I hung my hat, and hunted up Connie and Alice.

I found them playing with the baby, and they reported that their search of the girl's room had revealed nothing, save a picture of Homer in a leather folder. Across the back of the card on which the picture was mounted Reich had apparently written: "Your loving Homer." I put it in my pocket and chatted with Connie and Alice until I heard the motor run in and stop.

I went out and met the returning men. They came up the steps—Semi Dual, Sheldon, and lastly, Homer—carrying a couple of cases. Dual entered first and hung his hat on the rack, glanced down and spied the letter, picked it up, gave it a glance, and handed it to Reich.

"For you," he remarked.

"For me?" Reich took it, scanned its address, and thrust it into his pocket.

"Green asked me to bring it up and ask you what you wanted him to do while you were gone," I explained.

He nodded.

"Thanks. I've been too worried to care about Green or business. Still—I suppose I ought to see him. I'll go down there now, I guess."

"You got two hours. Moto can take you," said Sheldon, and went out to see him off.

I gave Dual the folder from the girl's room. He took it with a nod, and walked into the library, where Sheldon joined us a moment later.

Colonel Mac threw himself down at his desk and banged his bell for Lee.

"I gotter have a drink," he explained. "Glace, will you join me? Gad, I ain't felt so bad since Allie was kidnaped. Here it's over three days, an' nobody knows what's happened to Lawton's girl. Did you find out anything at the picture-show?"

I shook my head.

"Dual an' I seen the messages, but there waren't nothin' in 'em. A drink, Lee—two long ones," he broke off to order. "What did the girls find here?"

"Nothing but Homer's photograph."

Colonel Mac made no comment until Lee came back.

"There you are—just a lot of nuthin'," he resumed, raising his glass and taking a thirsty gulp. "Gad, I wish it was time to start for Salt Lake. I want action. I can stand a lot of that, but what gets my goat is this runnin' around an' gettin' nowhere. Right now we don't know nuthin'—"

"That is hardly correct, colonel," Said Semi Dual. "In fact we know quite a good deal. I hardly expected to learn much to-day, save perhaps to collect material for future needs, which, I think, I now have. At the same time I believe that we now have sufficient information to warrant us in saying that Miss Lawton has fallen a victim to the white-slave organization."

The hand lifting the glass again to the colonel's lips

paused midway, then was slowly lowered. The thin lips of the old fighter closed with something like a snap, making his mustache fairly bristle.

"That bunch?" he faltered. "My Gawd!"

3

AFTER THE SPIDER

DINNER AT SHELDON'S that evening was not a pleasant function. Dual's words as to the probable fate of the girl had thrown out an atmosphere of depression.

Dual and I had not unpacked our bags and Sheldon made short work of his preparations. Connie at my side ate little.

"Be careful," she whispered and I pressed her hand to reassure her.

Semi alone seemed utterly calm and undisturbed by the fact that he was soon to measure forces with the organization which to-day preys upon the youth and beauty of the nation and hesitates at no crime to gain its ends.

Reich telephoned asking us to pick him up at the theater and as soon as dinner was eaten, Sheldon ordered up the car. Good-byes were said and we three set out for the station.

We got Homer who was waiting outside the movie, and went on.

"Get it fixed up?" I asked in low tones after he had settled into a seat.

He nodded.

"We canceled the order for the machines by wire," he

said shortly. "I don't want to be bothered by business until this thing is settled. And the Lord only knows how long that will take, because I'm going to find that little woman if I have to hunt the whole world over."

"Nonsense!" I told him. "You don't want to take it that way. The trouble is you don't know Dual. Unless I'm greatly mistaken we'll find her all right and that before long."

He shook his head in unconvinced fashion.

"I don't know your friend," he admitted. "Neither do I see how he can do anything quickly. Why, we haven't a thing to go on. All we know is that she was last seen when she started for Salt Lake. We don't even have a single idea as to who may have sent that phoney message, or why, or what they did when she got there. We don't know a thing. Not a single thing. What is there to go on?"

"But," I cut short his confession of impotence, "already Dual has gone a lot farther than that. He told Sheldon and me just a little while ago after you left that he had reason to believe she was a victim of the white-slave people."

"My God!" Reich drew away from me and turned a wild visaged face upon me. "What makes him think that?" he faltered, when he had regained a fraction of his shattered control.

"He didn't say beyond the mere statement," I responded. "But if he says it, he means it, Reich. So you see he is already at work on a probable theory of the case. You know Salt Lake is one of the centers of operation for that bunch of people. The thing looks plausible to me."

"Then," he said dully, "we might as well give it up. What's the use if those devils have got her. How can Dual or any other one man expect to win out against them? Why, the government has fought them for years, and done little or nothing. What can Dual or I do? It's no use. If he's right she's gone."

"Don't you believe it," I encouraged. "I've seen him do things equally as hard. He'll get this girl."

"If he does," said Reich. "If he does." He glanced at Semi's back, clenched his hands and bowed his head.

He seemed pretty well worked up to me and I sought to encourage him as best I could until we reached the station, but my success was not marked enough to notice. He followed us aboard the train and sank dejectedly into a seat to sit staring out of the window.

I confess I felt sorry for the chap, and wished I knew some way to lighten his gloom. He seemed like a person distraught, uncertain of each step he was taking, yet fighting by sheer will to maintain control.

Yet I had said all I could and I sat silent while we made the run to Las Vegas, as did Dual. Sheldon fidgeted in and out of the car, to and from the smoker like a restless soul. Taken all in all it was not a cheerful trip.

We caught the limited east bound, and were off on the next lap of the chase. Every one seemed to be in bed save the porter, and a tip induced him to seek a different place to lounge in other than the dressing-room.

We settled ourselves in its narrow quarters by Dual's suggestion. For the first time since the trip began he now seemed to take an active interest in affairs.

"Well, we're here," said the colonel, after the porter had taken his *pourboire* and gone to arrange our berths. He drew a flask from his pocket. "Anybody want a drink?"

"I do," declared Reich, reaching for the liquor. He tilted

its neck to his lips and drank several swallows before taking it down.

"This is a terrible business!" he broke out in nervous excitement. "What are we going to do? She's gone—gone, I tell you! Glace says Dual thinks the slave gang have got her. If that's so, what's the use? There isn't any good trying to buck that bunch of people. Even if we should get her, her life would be ruined. Oh, God!" He lifted the flask again.

Colonel Mac took it away.

"Here—that's enough, sonny," he cautioned. "I thought you looked like you needed a pick-up, but you don't need to get all lit up, for all that." He put the flask away.

"That is the terrible thing," said Semi Dual slowly; "that through no wrong of her own she should find her life in ruins. It is a fearful business—this dealing in human flesh and blood. In fact, it is a hell of a business; and surely if there be a hell—the men and women who control the trade should go to its lowest depths!

"Yet it is an established trade, with its agents in nearly every large city in the country. They lurk about the cheaper theaters, the cheaper hotels—along the streets. They go from town to town inducing girls to leave home by offers of legitimate employment, which proves in the end to be but the lure to deliver them into the trap of the hunter.

"They prowl like beasts of prey—ready to pounce on the unsuspecting victim. They respect neither youth, innocence, beauty, virtue, hope, faith, love, nor any other emotion save the greed of the dollars they get as the price of their morsel of human blood and bone. They—"

"My God!" said Reich hoarsely. "Stop it! He compressed

his lips and clenched his hands. "What good does it do you to say this to me?" he went on in a moment.

"It does me no good, of course," Dual made answer, "but the subject makes my blood boil. Take this case, for instance—what of the girl? They have used the holiest of human passions in order to betray her—her love for the man she was to marry. She responded to the call of love, as they knew she must, and they met her. Then she was in the web.

"Where did they take her? To some foul room, where she was probably shut in like a caged beast, whose cries and entreaties would fall on deaf ears. What must she have suffered when she realized her fate—that she was trapped in a net by those who were lost to all human feeling.

"What did she feel? What did she say and do? Did she beat on the doors and cry to her God for help because only He could longer avail to help her? Did she struggle vainly, and then worn out with terror and grief, throw herself on a poor bed and look into a future more cruel than death?

"And remember—death would be denied her. They would take good care that their new captive should live until she reached a market. Was she a woman to them, a potential mother, a thing to be respected, a human being with an immortal soul?

"No! She was only a marketable something, capable of putting dollars into their pockets. She excited no more compassion in their breasts than the trapped creature in the fur hunter's snare. And this was for what? To supply food for the most material of human cravings—the perverted appetite of degenerate men—a sacrifice to the Moloch of passion, offered on the bloody altars of lust—the vicarious expression of a false civilization, an improper manner of living.

"We shudder at the living sacrifice of the ancients and call it inhuman. As God lives, it was gentle! They only destroyed the body. Modern man destroys body and soul. Mr. Reich, I shall find your sweetheart, and when I have found her, I shall free her, and then some one—the one who is guilty, I promise—*is going to pay!*"

"My Lord, I hope so!" boomed the colonel. "I'd like to see the jasper stuck in a cage for about one natural lifetime. Killin' would be a little too good, I reckon. Let him try a taste of the slavery end himself."

Dual shook his head. "Female life and happiness are too cheap for that in the opinion of our lawmakers," he said in a tone almost bitter. "At least, however, we can see that he gets a few years."

"But how?" Reich burst out. "So far, all we've done is talk. Talkin' never amounts to much. What are you going to *do?* You seem to know a lot of theory, Mr. Dual, but while we are talkin' those people are working. You don't think they'll keep Lilly where we can reach out and take her, do you?"

"Not intentionally," said Dual. But I have always noticed, Mr. Reich, that when good and evil cross swords—good generally has just a bit of what Sheldon would call 'edge' on the evil. As for acting, I shall act when I deem action is demanded."

"An' you can gamble on that, too, Homer," averred Colonel Mac. "I told you about how he helped me one time. I couldn't see where he was goin', no more than you can, but you can bet he arrived."

He turned to Semi.

"He's pretty well hipped, Mr. Dual. First off, he wanted to chase off to Salt Lake an' try to run things down on his lonesome. I said no, an' I had to most hog-tie him to hold him. You can't blame him, I reckon, either. Gad! do you remember me an' Archie when Alice was in trouble?"

"If he loved her he would naturally feel that way about it," Dual responded. "I do not wish Mr. Reich to act in any way not natural, believe me! I sympathize fully with any man who finds a loved one in such a danger, and I shall spare no effort to free her as soon as I practically can do so. I think of the woman herself as well as the man."

"I don't mean to seem antagonistic," Reich stammered. "But I like to see where I'm going. I want to get the thing settled. Sheldon's kept me idle for days, and my nerves are ragged. If I could *do* something—"

"I would suggest that you go to bed," said Dual.

"Bed?" Reich laughed shortly. "I couldn't sleep."

"Let me have your flask a moment, colonel," Semi requested.

He took the metal cap from the top and filled it with liquor, set down the flask, and surrounded the filled cap with both his hands. Raising them in this position he held them before his face for perhaps thirty seconds—and suddenly extended the cap to Reich.

"Drink it and sleep," he directed.

"What the devil!" Reich rather drew back from the proffered draft.

"Sleep for you," said Semi Dual.

"What did you put in it?" the youth demanded.

"Sleep," said Semi Dual.

"No thanks," objected Reich.

Dual smiled. "Did I put anything in it, colonel?" he asked.

Colonel Mac shook his head.

"Drink it, son. It ain't doped," he advised. "This ain't no come-on bunch."

Reich put out a hesitant hand, lifted the cap, and took a tentative sip, rolled it on his tongue, and quite suddenly drank the liquor off. "That won't make me sleep," he remarked.

"If you think not, suppose you try fighting it off," said Semi. "Now suppose we all get what rest we can."

Reich nodded and walked out of the room. Colonel Mac turned his eyes from his disappearing figure to Dual.

"What did you do to the stuff?" he inquired.

"Nothing," declared Semi. "I merely fastened his mind on the sleep thought by a material suggestion. He'll try to fight off sleep and keep his eyes open till they tire from the strain, after which he *will* sleep. It's an old trick."

Sheldon picked up his flask with a grin.

"A lot of your old tricks are new ones to me," he remarked dryly. "That's the first time I ever heard of putting a *hombre* to sleep—by makin' him stay awake. Good night!"

The rest of the trip passed without any moment. Dual sat around and scribbled on bits of paper now and then. Sheldon smoked panetelas until I wondered at his endurance.

Reich slept until the last call for breakfast, and after that patronized the buffet a little too well. I spent my time between the men. We reached Salt Lake in due course, and Dual took a taxi to the Hotel Utah. We registered there and were shown to a suite of rooms.

It was 2:30 p.m. and at once Dual assumed direction.

Hardly had the page closed the door of our suite behind him than he turned to me.

"Gordon, take a taxi and go to police central. Interview the chief or his representative in his absence. Request him to send a dependable operative to this suite at his earliest convenience, then return to us here."

There was a snap in his words which spurred me to action. I swung on my heel and started for the door. I caught a picture of Reich staring at Semi in a surprised sort of way, and then I was outside striding down the green carpeted hall toward the bank of elevator cages. I had a mission to perform. Vaguely I realized that at last Dual had played a card in the game.

I caught a cab outside the hotel entrance and directed the driver to get me to police headquarters quickly. It wasn't far, and two minutes saw us drawing up before a squat two-story stucco structure, within whose hall I caught a glimpse of khaki clad forms.

I climbed out, told the chauffeur to wait, and went in, preferring my request for the chief of the sergeant behind the desk. I had no difficulty at all. The sergeant called a patrolman and directed him to take me to the chief's office. He in turn led me down the hall to a lettered door and rapped, swung the door open, and left me standing in the presence of the man I sought.

Chief Brant sat in a large room, furnished with a desk, a leather couch, several chairs, a rug, and a cuspidor. He raised his face crowned with heavy hair and trimmed with an iron-gray mustache, and silently gazed in my direction as I advanced, then waved me to a chair, and continued to stare.

I lost no time in making myself known and explaining my mission.

Brant listened until I was done and then nodded. "I shall be glad to help you, if I can," he said. "As it happens, there has been a good deal of this sort of thing going on here of late, and I think I can get you the sort of assistance you're needing. I'll send you up a detective as soon as I can get the person I want. Was there anything else?"

"No, that was all," I answered, rising. I shook hands and left with a feeling of satisfaction. Outside I found my cab and returned to the hotel. At last it seemed that we were about to get to work.

Dual and Sheldon were each reading papers. Reich was standing at a window staring out into the street and drumming on the pane above his head. He whirled around at my entrance. "Well, did you get your bull?" he inquired.

I nodded, more at Dual's eyes above his paper than to Reich.

The latter snorted, "I could have done that much three days ago, if Sheldon had let me come up here," he sneered with impatience. "That's just three days wasted, and God knows what's happened to the kid in three days. Where's the tec you were to get?"

"Coming up," said I.

"Still in the future," he growled. "Oh, this business makes me sick! Wait—wait—wait! We haven't all the time there is, have we? I'm tired of waiting." He turned to Semi. "Can't we do something, Dual?"

"Wait for the detective," said Semi.

Reich threw himself into a chair and thrust fingers into his tawny thatch of hair.

"Good Lord," he groaned, "when you get tired of waiting, I suppose you can wait some more."

"See the chief?" inquired Dual.

I nodded. "Yes. He'll send us his best man on the case as soon as he can locate him, he says."

"That's the stuff!" exclaimed Sheldon. "Then we'll get action. I'm goin' to ring for a drink. My nerves is gettin' kinder jumpy, like Homer's, Glace?"

I shook my head. I wanted to think. To tell the truth there was something funny about the thing. I couldn't exactly blame Reich or the colonel, even considering the former's peevishness of demeanor.

In all the years I had known him, Dual had never puzzled me more. Not that I doubted him for a moment. I knew him too well. Neither, I am sure, did Colonel Mac. It was only Reich who was wholly unacquainted who did that. At the same time his utter apparent lack of endeavor, his unbroken calm of manner, his what I once heard a physician describe as masterly inactivity, gave me an odd feeling of uncertainty in things.

Here we were confronted with a matter whose every detail was gripping, warranted to excite to the most rapid of action—which would justify almost any means to bring about its successful issue, and Dual's one word seemed to be summed up in the counsel to wait. Like Reich, I asked myself what we were waiting for? It seemed almost as though the answer came in a knock on the door.

Before I could more than turn Dual had dropped his paper, crossed the room, and swung the portal open. Framed in its rectangle appeared the figure of a woman.

She was young, brown-haired, brown-eyed, of medium

height, and a strong assured figure and carriage, clad in a tan khaki skirt, a pongee shirt-waist, with soft collar and tie to match, and wearing tan walking shoes A soft hat of tan felt was caught on her head by a strong silver pin, and she carried a pair of gloves in her hand, with which she tapped her skirt.

"Mr. Dual?" she inquired.

Semi Dual bowed.

The woman stepped into the room in a perfectly contained manner and swept it with her warm, brown eyes.

"Shut the door. I am Lucile Foote. Chief Brant sent me up at your request," said she.

Reich lifted his head and stared. Colonel Mac's jaw dropped and remained so for possibly half a minute before he remembered to shut it.

A smile wreathed the face of Semi Dual.

"My dear young woman, this is indeed good fortune," he returned quickly as he closed the door. "Your chief was wise in his selection. Please take a chair. You understand the case?"

Miss Foote took a seat, crossed one leg over the other and nodded.

"The girl left Goldfield six days ago. That would be five since she reached here," she said. "As the phony message came from here they probably grabbed her when she arrived and rushed her to some joint where they could keep her till they could slip her out again. There's been a lot of that going on of late, and I've rather been helping out with the Federal men. I've been working on the lodging-houses and that end of the game. That was why Brant picked me for this."

There was a straightforward directness about her which made me like her. Save for her sex she might have been a man speaking to men. As she finished her lips parted and gave us a glimpse of strong, white teeth in a rather wide mouth.

Dual seized the opportunity for introductions.

"This is my friend, Mr. Gordon Glace, a detective."

Lucile gave me her hand frankly.

"We ought to get on together, at that rate," she remarked.

"And this is Colonel Sheldon, who was acting as Miss Lawton's guardian."

"Pleased to meet you, colonel," Miss Foote smiled.

"And this is Homer Reich, Miss Lawton's *fiancé*."

The girl swept the boy with a level glance and nodded.

"How'je do?" she said "Have any of you folks a picture of this girl?" she asked.

"Homer has in his watch," replied the colonel.

Miss Foote put out her hand. "I'll slant that if you like," she suggested, took the watch Reich produced and stared for some moments at the portrait in the case. At the end she nodded.

"The sort they'd be apt to grab," she sighed and returned the watch. "Pretty and not too wise. Poor kid!"

"How long had you known her?" she turned to Reich.

"Two months. I met her just after I went to Goldfield," said Homer.

"Where'd you jump there from?"

"Salt Lake."

Lucile shook her head.

"Before, I mean. You're not a regular here."

"Denver," said Homer.

"What's your line?"

"Movies."

"You were engaged to Miss Lawton?"

"Yes. Say, I lost the girl, I didn't steal her."

"Nobody said you did," replied Miss Foote. "Know anybody in Salt Lake?"

"A few."

"Tell any of them about your coming wedding?"

"No."

It was my first experience of the policewoman, but I confess I was favorably impressed by Miss Foote. She was all business from the first to the last of my knowledge of her and contrary to the usual opinion she wasted no words. She dropped Homer as quickly as she had taken him up and turned to Dual.

"Mr. Dual, just what prospect of running this down exists I can't, of course, say. Just at present we are watching one part of this city pretty closely. I haven't had any report from there for several days, however, and this thing may have been pulled off without attracting attention—probably was. The slave people have recently been making use of the foreign colony here help in their work.

"There is a part of town known as Greektown, where very few natives live. On several cases girls have been found secreted in the lodging-houses in that part. We have rescued some, but we have reason to believe that we have missed others. At the same time I believe that if this girl was kept here at all, it was down there in some room in one of those places. They've even tried to capture school-girls here in the last year. Well—I'm a woman, and there's nothing I'd like better than to find this other woman and get her out of their clutches, and there's nothing I wouldn't do to do it."

"Good for you, ma'am!" Colonel Mac's voice boomed out in sincere admiration. "A girl like you, who is wise to the tricks of these fellers, kin do an awful lot of good, I reckon. I've heard a lot about policewomen of late, an' I'm mighty proud to hev met one, an' that goes as it lays. Put it there!" He rose and held out his hand.

Lucile Foote took it and met his clasp in all frankness.

"I, too, am glad to have met you, colonel," she told him. "One meets so few of the old school nowadays."

Sheldon chuckled. "I wouldn't have never picked the force as a place for a girl," he said, grinning. "But I ain't like a dead man. I can change my mind. If this keeps on—that stuff about the 'finest' won't be no joke. It'll jest be plain facts."

Reich interrupted. "Just why do you think this Greektown would be the gang's hangout?" he questioned.

"Because," said Miss Foote, "to use a Western expression, we are keeping them rather close herded elsewhere in town. The nature of the population in Greektown makes our difficulties greater.

"That sounds like sense to me," averred Colonel Mac.

Dual picked up the girl's eyes.

"Then I may understand that you will give this matter your attention?"

She bowed in affirmation.

"Yes—at once. Not only as a detective but as a woman."

Their eyes met and held for a single long moment, and Semi Dual smiled.

"Once more, I am glad of your chief's choice," he said

softly. "You are the person we needed, and you have been sent to us. You will find what you seek, and contribute your part in freeing one from bondage. It is now four o'clock. Will you begin your work at once and dine here with us at six? I expect you to win, because I perceive that you are competent to sympathize."

Lucile Foote dropped her eyes as he spoke.

"You— I—" she began and flushed slowly. "I will meet you at six," she accepted and rose.

Dual crossed and opened the door. As she came toward him he bowed above her hand and spoke in a whisper. She smiled slightly and nodded as one quite in accord— and was gone. Dual was still smiling as he closed the door behind her, came back and sat down.

"And now what do we do," queried Reich— "investigate the bill of fare and dope out a menu while we wait for the dinner-party?"

"What else?" said Dual as he picked up his paper. "Everything is running along nicely."

"Running along nicely? Well, for—" Reich paused for an apparent inability to find words to express his feelings. But he rallied.

"Well, say—you said your methods were peculiar, and they sure are. They're about as effective as a pink tea in a war office. I thought you were running this, and now you say, 'What else?' How should I know? But I do know one thing, and that is—that I'm tired of waiting. I want to do something, and if you can't think of anything better than turning the job over to a woman, I'm going to start something on my own. How about that?"

"Quite interesting," said Semi Dual.

"It may be," flared Reich. "I don't know how much there is in the notion of this squab cop that the deal was put over in Greektown, but I'm going down there. I know a fellow—a Greek by the name of George Stakos—who's runnin' a movie down there. He used to be in Denver, an' I met him last week when I was up here. Maybe he can steer me up against some sort of information. Anyway, I can try, and I'm going to do it."

Dual's answer was almost facetious. "All right, run along and see George," he assented as he turned a page.

Reich fairly snorted. His muttered comment contained something about four-flushing as he passed me on his way to the door. He wrenched it open, slammed it shut, and was gone.

"He's been tryin' to break loose ever since it happened," said Colonel Mac.

I saw that Dual still smiled.

"Is there anything you want us to do?" I suggested.

He shook his head.

"I think I'll send a telegram. Do what you like till six," he replied.

I cupped my hand and lifted it at the colonel. He nodded, and we went down-stairs. After some liquid consolation I suggested a game of billiards, and the colonel took off his coat, stuck a long cigar in his face, and proceeded to lick me as easily as a father does his six-year-old son.

Thereafter we took a walk about the streets and came back a little before six—to find that Miss Foote had already arrived. She looked up and nodded and went on talking in low tones to Dual.

A waiter brought in a table and spread it for dinner and

left. After a bit he came back with a companion and served the dinner himself. We sat down.

"I reckon Homer must 'a' seen George," opined Sheldon when Reich failed to appear.

"George?" said Miss Foote.

"Yep-a friend of his'n. After you left, ma'am, Homer an' Mr. Dual had a run in 'cause Homer can't noways understand Mr. Dual's way of runnin' this thing, an' Homer reckoned he'd go down to Greektown an' see a feller what's runnin' a moving-picture show—what he met here last week. He thought he might be able to dig up a nigger or two outer the wood-pile and learn something."

"Oh, I see," Lucile smiled. "The fact of the matter is, I don't believe that the little girl is in Salt Lake at all. The mere fact that they dated their message from Salt Lake would indicate that they moved her on quickly. They would naturally expect the first search to be made here.

"At the same time, as I explained to Mr. Dual before you came in, I have laid the lines for the investigation. Just between ourselves, we have at times to adopt some peculiar stratagems to get our information. What would you think if I were to tell you that the cashier in a Greek café is really a secret service agent, and that a waiter in another is the same? Yet I assure you it is so. I have given them both their information in this matter, and I fancy they will learn as much as poor Mr. Reich. By the way, you said he was in town last week and met this Mr.—"

"Stakos," supplied Semi Dual. "Yes, Reich was up here, according to his statements, which I see no reason to doubt. Mr. Reich is impatient of my reticence regarding my plans. He desires the matter settled."

"And has small confidence in the policewoman," laughed Lucile.

"The sentiment does not extend to us, however," Dual told her. "As I remarked this afternoon. I expect you to gain us information of value."

"Heaven knows, I hope so!" Miss Foote responded. "I ought to, if any one can. Something inspires me to speak in confidence to you three men, and I'll tell you that one page of my life makes me a fitting person to trail such things as these. As you, Mr. Dual, said this afternoon, I am competent to sympathize—and to know how they act and think."

I looked into her eyes and was dumb with amazement. They met me squarely and did not shrink, and it seemed hard to accept what her words implied. Yet, if true, here then was one doubly fitted for her employment.

It was Sheldon who broke the somewhat uneasy tension.

"Thank Heaven, then, ma'am, that you decided to git into this game! You kin do an almighty lot of good with your knowledge, an', God knows, what a lot of poor girls you may save! If you help us save Lilly, I'll never forget it, an' when Colonel Mac says that, it's a lot. I talk a whole lot, but sometimes I mean what I say, an' this is one time. I was tryin' to be a sort of foster dad to that little gal, 'cause her pa was killed in my mine, an' if we kin jest git her back, there's a good home for her to go to, an' damn the man what says a word about her!"

He paused and vociferously blew his nose.

Lucile's face was beaming as she put out a hand across the table.

"Colonel—" she began, and the shrill clamor of the phone on the wall broke into her words.

Dual nodded to me, and I went to answer the ring. "Hello!" I called, and glued the receiver to my ear.

After a bit I put my hand over the mouthpiece and turned back to the room.

"It's Reich," I announced. "He's somewhere down in Greektown, and he says he's picked up a clue. He wants us to come down."

Semi Dual nodded without hesitation.

"Tell him we will come," he directed, "and ask him where we shall meet."

4

THE TRAIL LEADS ON

I PUT THE question to Reich, hung up the receiver and came back to the table.

"Is there such a place as Second South West Fourth in this town?" I inquired of Miss Foote.

She laughed.

"You mean Second South and Fourth West. Our street enumeration always does bother the newcomer. Still it is simple. If you take the temple square as the center and count numerically, adding the point of the compass, you have the street name. Easy when you catch it. As it happens Greektown lies west of Fourth West along Second South. Mr Reich evidently intends to meet you at the intersection."

"He said he'd be on the southwest corner in about an hour," I explained.

"Why the delay?" said Miss Foote.

I shook my head. "That was all he said, Miss Lucile. His voice sounded as though he were excited."

"Maybe *he's* dug up a nigger," opined Colonel Mac. "Well, my Lord, I hope so."

Lucile frowned slightly, knitting her brows as though seeking to grasp some point of thought. At the end of a moment she rolled her napkin into a ball and pushed back her chair.

"I think," she began, "that I'll get back on the job. Of course Mr. Reich may really have picked up something, but I have learned to be rather doubtful of information gained in those sources.

"Veracity in dealing with others is not a shining merit of our foreign population. They are as apt to get more than they give, than anything else. I think I'll go down and endeavor to check up what Mr Reich learns."

"You mean you're goin' into that place alone at night?" demanded Sheldon. "Ain't that rather risky for a girl, ma'am? Now looka here, I'm just sort of a useless dub in this matter. Glace an' Dual are the real show.

"Me an' Homer are just sorter trailin' along in case somebody needs a strong arm play or to burn some powder. So you see they kin git along without me all right on this little *pasear* they're takin' with Homer. You let me go along with you. I don't reckon a girl oughter be prowlin' around among a lot of wops an' dagoes at night. You take Colonel Mac along."

"Colonel!"

Lucile's eyes turned upon him and I thought they glistened. She went swiftly around and stood beside him and she laughed with just the least catch in her voice.

"You're a dear," she went on. "But don't you see I can't do that. This is business, and I have to act on the quiet. I'm used to the work—it's my regular employment.

"But don't think I don't appreciate your offer. I do, and I wish—I wish— Oh, I wish I'd had a dad like you. There—

"Mr. Dual," she turned to Semi, "I'm going to try and

verify or disprove what you may hear down in that quarter to-night. Of course Reich's information, if he finds any, may be straight, but I doubt it. I'll report whatever I learn to you later. Better go armed, but not let any one know it. Good-by now."

She walked to the door which Colonel Sheldon opened, and was gone.

"Whew!" ejaculated Sheldon. "My hat's off to that little woman. She's sure one live wire. Maybe she's made her mistakes, but a lot of us have I reckon. I can respect a person who gets up after fallin' down. That's what takes the real nerve."

"You hold with Browning, then, that, 'we fall to rise again, are beaten to fight better, sleep to wake'?" said Semi.

"Never heard of him, but if he said that he was handin' out straight talk," declared Sheldon. "Ain't I right?"

"Decidedly right," Dual assented. "The real man or woman profits by his reversals and misfortunes, and learns therefrom a lesson for his farther walk in life. Whom the Lord loveth, He chasteneth, in order that the well-learned soul may bear divine fruit of knowledge. In the pursuit of knowledge, I think it is now time we set out for our rendezvous."

We left the hotel, took a taxi and stopped some moments later somewhere on a thoroughfare traversed by a railroad crossing. As our chauffeur's orders carried him no farther he climbed down and opened the door.

We left the cab on the east side of the intersection and walked slowly across, keeping an eye out for Reich.

He appeared suddenly from the door of a corner saloon and came to meet us. For the first time since I had known him he seemed free from restraint and his manner was one of poorly suppressed excitement.

"That's what comes of getting out and stirring things up," he began as soon as he was beside us. "I came down here and found Stakos, and it didn't take him a minute to get wise. He said he knew a couple of fellows who would be likely to know about this business if any one would and he left his show and came along with me to find them.

"And here's something we've got to keep under our hats. It isn't generally known but the two chaps he steered me to, while full-blooded Greeks, are naturalized citizens of this country and are government men—sleuths. D'ye see?

"Well I put the matter to them, and they came through at once with the tip that they knew about Lilly, but said they thought we'd better talk it over all together.

"They make a business of hanging out in a café down here and they said I'd better get you folks and George and I could come in like you was a party doin' the town, an' out for a time, an' then George could pretend to spot them, and we'd all get at a table and talk so nobody would suspicion. Oh, Lord, but it's a sweet mess, from what they tell me, but come along. Let's go get George and keep the date."

"You say they know Lilly was here?" rumbled Sheldon.

Reich nodded. "Yes. Oh, it's a mess. But come along."

He turned beside us and led us down the street toward an illuminated sign above the mouth of an alley, turned into this and stopped before some steps leading up to the door of a building which bore a Greek lettered sign.

The sound of a piano and violin floated out as two men emerged, and I caught a fleeting glimpse of a picture flickering on a screen, before the door swung shut.

"This is George's place," Reich explained. "I'll get him if you'll wait." He ran up the steps and disappeared within.

He was back in a very few moments with a squat, heavy-set individual, with auburn hair and a wax-tipped mustache, whom he introduced as Stakos. The Greek shook hands around and spoke in fair English:

"I am glad to meet my frien's frien's. I am entirely at your sarvice."

"Then let's get along," said Colonel Mac.

Stakos bowed, linked arms with Reich and turned out to the street. They then swung back along the way we had come and presently paused before the entrance to a narrow hallway, directly below a transparent sign which announced the "Kaffenion Poseidon" that he who ran might read.

Reich pushed in and we followed into the hall which ran straight back from the street for some hundred feet.

Its walls were painted green with yellow panels, stenciled in arabesque designs in black, interspersed on one side by windows, which showed that the passage flanked, first a bar, and secondly a small room like a cheap restaurant, furnished with tables, napery, and glass.

Streamers of red, white, and blue tissue papers festooned the top of the passage and waved above our heads.

At the far end the hall opened into a room some seventy-five feet square, its walls like those of the entrance, painted and stenciled in glaring colors.

In the center a metal fountain squirted a tiny stream of water, which fell back into a basin containing goldfish. Ranged around the room were tables and chairs, and a cigar-case, and the cashier's desk occupied the far corner.

The ceiling like that of the passage was practically hidden by the paper festoons.

Early as was the evening, at least half the tables were held by men of swarthy complexion, interspersed with an occasional blond type. At a table back in a corner a man was playing on what sounded like a zither, and a phonograph beside him gave promise of a different sort of music.

A young woman, of not unpleasant features, sat back of the cashier's desk reading a book, as we came in, glanced up at our entrance and gave no further heed.

I noticed, however, that as Stakos led us to seats at a vacant table, and bade us sit down, more than one head of the other denizens of the place turned in our direction. Colonel Mac attracted still more attention our way.

Hardly had he taken his chair, when without warning his voice boomed out above the other noises of the room: "Well, my Lord, look at the goat!"

I had noticed it already, but it was evident that Sheldon had not. Now, however, we all turned and looked at the little animal which ran about the tables.

It was white, with pinkish eyes and the merest suggestion of a tail, and seemed very much at home. It was roaming from group to group of patrons, accepting a bite of bread, or cheese, or bologna, or a mouthful of salad, very much like a pet dog might have taken a scrap of meat.

More than one dark face greeted the colonel's outburst with a flashing smile at his recognition of what was evidently an established custom of the place. The colonel, as usual, was sincere in his enjoyment, and in no way sought to detract from the prominence he had gained.

Instead, he leaned over and snapped his fingers in a desire to be friendly.

"Here. Billy—C'm'ere," he wheedled. C'm'ere, you funny little devil. Well what d'ye know about that?"

In the midst of diversion Stakos rose and excusing himself approached another table well back beside the cigar-case, where he spoke to a couple of men. After a moment he came back and in quite audible tones requested that we come over and meet his friends.

It was well played and I'm sure one not informed of its true purpose would have been completely deceived. We rose after a bit of urging and accompanied him half across the room to the place where the other two sat.

Introductions followed.

We learned that the larger of the two men who were both dark was called Paulos, and the smaller Hermostyple. At their invitation we sat down. A waiter slid up and after a friendly byplay Stakos ordered the drinks, and we were alone. Not until then did Reich speak.

"These are my friends of whom I told you," he explained in a low voice. "They want to know about the girl."

"Mr. Dual an' Mr. Glace, the detective, an' Mr. Sheldon, quite so," said Paulos. "Those were the names you gave us. Very well. There is not such a very large quantity to tell. Perhaps Mr. Reich have tell you what we air?"

"We're wise," muttered Sheldon.

Dual and I nodded. For no apparent reason Hermostyple saw fit to duck his head also.

"Well then," continued Paulos, "the ozzer day it was teeped off to my very good fren' Hermostyple an' me, zat zere was a girl in a room in a house down in thees parts. Zat have happen before, have it not Hermostyple?"

Again the little man nodded.

"Ze one who was inform us of thees, say zat they think perhaps thees girl was wat you call detain' agains' her will, an' was not zere of her own accord. Zen it was to us to investigate in w'at you call offeecial capacity, was it not?"

"It was," rumbled Sheldon. "Did you?"

Paulos opened his brown eyes in surprise, then shrugged his shoulders in deprecation.

"But—" he began and paused once more as our waiter returned with our order. "But of course," he resumed, lifted his glass of beer and sunk his mustache in the foam, "Hermostyple and I acted at once. What did we do? What should we do? We go to thees place, an' we deman' to see thees girl, an we ask her the question 'Have you experience?' to which she say, 'Oh, yes.'

"Then what could we do? Wis her nozzing. She say she is of the age, she haf no people. Is she doin' anything wrong? We may know but can we prove it? Eh, Hermostyple, my fren'?"

Hermostyple answered by a nod, and went on consuming beer.

"You asked her if she'd had experience. Whad'je mean?" said Colonel Mac.

"Eet is contradisinction from persons who have been persuaded or led away from home by false representations," explained Paulos. "As one would say, 'do you come of your own free will?'"

"An' she told you yes? She wouldn't do it. I don't believe you."

Sheldon's voice threatened to rise to an unwise pitch.

"*Sssh!*" hissed Reich laying a hand on the colonel's arm. "Maybe she had to. Maybe they scared her into saying what they told her. Colonel, they're devils. They've killed girls who wouldn't do what they told them, haven't they, Mr Paulos?"

"Indeed, yes," declared the Greek. Hermostyple nodded.

Colonel Sheldon's gray eyes hardened. "All right," he muttered. "I ain't very wise to this game I reckon, but I got a hunch that that leetle gal wouldn't 'a' been afraid to cash in if that was th' only way to slip this bunch. Go ahead. I won't butt in any more. I reckon I kin think to myself. What did you do then?"

"We investigate, sair," replied Paulos, coldly. "We try to fin' out where she come from, an' we fin' she came from the south. Then we decide to see her again, because there has been too much trouble here of lately an' when we go to see her yesterday we find she is gone."

"Gone where?" I asked.

"We do not know. We ask the man who runs the house. He say, she say, she goes to Seattle. That is all."

"They moved her, that's all," said Reich dully. "They knew we'd follow and they wouldn't take chances. We were just too late. If only you'd let me come up when I wanted to, Sheldon. I'd have met these men and identified the girl, and we'd have grabbed them before they got action. Oh, God what a mess! I'm sick—sick, I tell you, I—" he paused abruptly and turned his face away.

"How are you sure this girl was Lilly, anyhow?" Colonel Mac's tones were strangely throaty.

"I showed them her picture—the one in my watch,"

choked Homer. "Oh, it was her all right. This is what happens from waiting. And I won't wait any longer. I'm going to Seattle."

He half rose.

Behind us a girl laughed shrilly. Aside from the cashier she was the only woman in the room. She had come in while we were talking together, with a young fellow of a handsome though dissipated appearance, and taken a seat at a table to the side and back of ours.

She was young and pretty in a way. Now she lay half across the table laughing into the face of the man. As Homer pushed back his chair she glanced at us and laughed again loudly.

Colonel Mac reached out and pulled the boy back to his chair.

"Steady, boy," he cautioned. "Maybe I was at fault in the first place. It begins to look like I was, but this ain't no time to cry about that. I told you I'd see you through an' I will. I reckon I think a little of Lilly myself. We'll go back to the hotel an' talk this over in a minute. You sit down."

Throughout his words I had noticed Semi Dual. He had not spoken once since he acknowledged the introduction to Paulos and Hermostyple, but now I saw that he was listening intently to the talk at the table next to ours.

The half maudlin girl had followed her laughter with a stream of rapid speech directed to her companion, and though it was all an unintelligible jargon to me, I became imbued with the belief that Semi understood.

Reich sank back into his chair and gloomed straight before him. I glanced at Stakos, who lifted his eyebrows in mute interrogation. I nodded and he arose.

We made our adieus and after thanking the two Greeks for their information, led Homer from the place. The boy seemed completely beyond self-control and staggered as he walked beside Colonel Mac. His actions had attracted considerable attention again toward our party, and I was glad to get him outside.

Even there, however, he refused to listen to anything either Sheldon or I could say, and at our rooms he slumped into a chair and burst into bitter speech.

"There isn't any use of you fellows talkin'. I suppose *Mister* Dual will say everything is running along nicely, but I say the thing's been hashed from the start. I won't listen to anything except takin' the first train to Seattle to-morrow. There's one in the morning, and now I'm going to bed."

"I reckon you'd better, son," agreed Sheldon. "An' I reckon we're all goin' with you in th' mornin'. It ain't much of a steer but it's all we got. Come in an' I'll put you to bed. I ain't feelin' very chipper myself. Maybe I'll turn in with you."

"Do," said Dual, "but first I want to ask Mr. Reich a question. Do you. Mr. Reich, perhaps know anything of a woman known as Greek Annie?"

"I do not," replied Homer, frowning. "What's she got to do with the thing?"

"That is to find out," Semi responded. "The reason I ask is that she was mentioned by a girl who sat at a table behind ours this evening. She said that Greek Annie had left town yesterday morning, with a girl."

"Left town with a girl?" Reich sat up in his chair and leaned forward. "You heard her say that? Why—then you understand Greek."

"Oh, yes," said Semi Dual.

"But a girl? "Reich began and faltered, and then went on with a rush. "Sheldon, maybe she took Lilly to Seattle."

"But how could she?" queried Sheldon sorely puzzled. "How could she get her to go? My, Lord, she couldn't handcuff her and take her. Why couldn't the girl make a holler and git help? It gits by me."

"You don't understand," said Reich almost fiercely. "That's the trouble. You don't understand. They wouldn't take her by force.

"This woman, say, would pretend to be sorry for her and be helping her to escape; then she'd get her to go with her quiet, and the next thing she knew she'd find they'd betrayed her again. Oh, they work it a dozen ways, Sheldon. I can't tell you how it was done. I'm sick. Let's go to bed."

Dual, who had seated himself at a table and drawn some sheets of paper before him, looked up and nodded.

"Do," he urged. "If we are to make an early start, rest is the best thing for you. I have some work I want to finish, but you and Sheldon had better retire."

He turned back again to his papers, yet, as he did so, swept me with his eyes.

"If it won't disturb you, I think I'll read a bit," I remarked, because in that fleeting glance it came to me that he wanted my presence.

"As you please," he assented without looking up.

"Good night," said Sheldon, and led Homer into their room, closing the door.

I sat down and reviewed the evening.

Dual busied himself with the papers before him. Once

he rose, went to the phone, and ordered a pitcher of ice-water sent up. Not once did he address me.

I fussed with a paper and smoked several cigarettes.

For the life of me I couldn't see where the drift of things was leading. Like Colonel Mac, I began to think that after all Seattle might be the one best bet, despite the fact that the information we had gathered from Paulos and Hermostyple had not impressed me as being sincere.

I twisted and turned it, and out of it I gathered the one fact that Lilly Lawton had undoubtedly been held for a time in the so-called Greek town. That was a fact I no longer doubted; nor did I doubt that she was a victim of the white-slave people.

I glanced at Dual where he sat bent slightly above the table. I wondered why he had asked me with his eyes to remain up—what possible use he might have of me.

His great head and shoulders made a dark outline between me and the little reading-lamp on the table, and recalled other times when I had watched him at work over his occult calculations, by which he peered into the destinies of souls.

Still he worked on, and my thoughts flew away and took up the police woman, Miss Foote. I felt a subtle interest in her and her work. I wondered what she, working alone, might have learned this night, and if we would see or hear from her again.

I wondered what it was about her that I rather sensed than felt, which spoke to me of a mystery in her own person, and I wondered what had got into Semi Dual.

Like Reich, he impressed even me as doing little. Never had I felt more in the dark in all my workings with him.

When he shot me that glance which had held me here on the excuse of reading I had hoped that at last we were to have one of our old-time talks in which he would point out to me the leading of at least some of the threads. But an hour had passed and he had not spoken.

I was half minded to speak to him myself when once more the telephone rang—or rather clicked, for it was a mere tapping which reached my ear.

My interest bounded on the instant.

Dual had risen and crossed to the phone, and even as he did so I realized that he must have loosened the bells to prevent their ringing at the time he had ordered the water—which I had noticed he did not touch. If he had done that, I knew he had had some vital purpose.

Even as I wondered, Dual was speaking, had hung up the receiver, and turned to me.

"Gordon," he addressed me. "I want you. Miss Foote is below, and we are going down."

I rose and followed him out of the suite and down the hall, where he rang for a cage. When it came we dropped swiftly, and I followed him out on the mezzanine floor.

Lucile Foote was waiting for us in the now deserted space. She turned and led us to chairs well away from the cages, and began to speak.

"I had to come, Mr. Dual, to keep my promise. I told you I had agents down there, and as it happens you chose the café where the cashier is in our pay. I know what those two told you, and it's all a plant. They are even suspected of being white-slave agents themselves."

"Of course. I understood that from the first," said Semi Dual.

She smiled.

"I believe you understand more than you say," she replied. "At the same time I wanted to tell you this. I also have some reason to believe that the girl was taken to San Francisco."

"By Greek Annie?" Dual inquired.

Miss Foote started slightly.

"What do you know of her?" she said quickly.

"Merely that she left town yesterday morning with a girl."

"But how did you learn?" Miss Foote seemed puzzled.

"From the girl who sat behind me. I understand Greek," Dual explained.

"I see," said Lucile. "There is a specimen of their work. That girl used to be a daughter of a family not fifty miles from this city. Well, she's going the pace. You saw. Oh, isn't it hellish, isn't it— Oh, I don't want to talk of that."

"Miss Foote," said Dual, "do you know this Greek Annie?"

"By sight, yes," she responded. "She is the wife of Paulos."

I gasped.

"Would you consider going with us to San Francisco?" Semi suggested.

Again Miss Foote smiled.

"I believe you can read minds," she made answer. "Not only will I, but if you hadn't asked me, I was going alone. I want to see this case cleared up and I want to help."

"Good. You will go with us then," said Semi.

"I used to live there," informed Lucile. "I am sure I can help you."

"I am sure you will," affirmed Dual.

"By the way," she remarked. "It seems Mr. Reich told the

truth about meeting that Stakos last week. The cashier tells me he was in there with him one evening. I understand he made quite a scene to-night."

"He's on a pretty keen edge as to nerves," I suggested.

"Can you blame him?" she answered. "Well—I'll say good night. Do I meet you here or at the train in the morning, and what road will we take?"

"The Short Line. Meet us at the depot. I'll arrange your ticket," replied Semi Dual.

"Always ready, even with an answer," she accepted lightly. "Really, Mr. Dual, I'm beginning to want to know more about you. Well, then, *au revoir* till to-morrow." Declining Semi's escort, she moved away.

I glanced at my friend and found him smiling his at times well-nigh inscrutable smile.

Even while he had talked with the woman, I had sensed a subtle understanding between the two, to which I was not admitted, nor did Dual offer me the slightest explanation as we turned and regained our rooms.

Yet the night held, as it chanced, still another surprise for my dazed lack of understanding. Hardly had we regained the parlor of our suite, with Dual gathering up his papers from the table, and I thinking of bed, when a tap fell on the door.

Impatiently I crossed the room and flung it wide.

5

A MAN OF MYSTERY
AND SYMPATHY

A UNIFORMED MESSENGER-BOY stood outside.

"Which of youse calls himself Semi Dual?" he wanted to know.

I lifted a hand and waved him to Semi at the table. He crossed and produced a telegram and receipt-book from his cap, shoving them like an automaton into Dual's hands.

Semi took the message and signed the book, slit the envelope open and gave the message one glance, turned and tossed it to me.

I caught it as it fluttered and spread it before my eyes, and then I continued to stare. It was brief and seemingly without meaning as all the other things which had been treading on each other's heels, and it consisted of merely one word of current slang:

Gotcha. Bryce.

I folded it up, put it back in its cover and walked over to the table. There I laid it down and raised my eyes to the gray ones of my friend. Deep within them I fancied I saw a faint spark of something like invitation, and I burst out in brief piqued question:

"For the Lord's sake what does it mean?"

Dual bunched his papers in his hands, folded them twice, and thrust them into his pocket.

"It means," he replied in a somewhat offhanded manner, "that we leave for San Francisco in the morning."

IF YOU ARE going to San Francisco by the northern route from Salt Lake you have to go first to Ogden, where the Short Line turns you over to the Southern Pacific. Consequently, the next morning found us steaming out of the Union Station bound north.

Lucile had met us just before we boarded the train, not a little to Homer's surprise. He eyed her with an almost antagonistic stare as she gained our side beyond the barriers, and as soon as possible made an opportunity to speak to me.

"What is that woman doing with us?" he wanted to know.

"She's going along with us, I understand," I informed him.

"What for? Why don't your friend Dual take the whole town on this hunt?" he scowled.

"She's going along to identify Greek Annie, as I understand it," I replied.

"Oh," said Reich. "Well, I hadn't thought of that."

He lapsed into silence and presently moved to a seat with Sheldon, to whom he began to talk. Meanwhile Lucile and Semi had found a seat together and were conversing in lowered tones. I leaned back in my seat and gave myself up to my own thoughts as we steamed up the valley.

I thought of Connie and wondered what she was doing. Surely Dual had been right that morning out of Grand Junction when he predicted that my honeymoon would be interrupted. I reviewed the whole matter thus far, and as before I ran up against the blind wall of Semi's reticence.

The farther we went the more I wondered at his course.

Of course I knew that he was acting from some purpose, but for the life of me I could not understand why I was shut out. I confessed that I was beginning to feel as I imagine a sailor must who moves through a blind fog under the guidance of a pilot.

I had every confidence in my pilot's ability, and with reason, and yet instinctively I wondered—where we were going, and just when we would arrive—where?

Such things held me until the train ran rumbling across a considerable river, and Dual rose and began gathering up his and Lucile's bag.

"Ogden. We change cars here," he announced.

Reich's head came around with a jerk.

"Change cars! What for? This train goes straight through to Portland," he said quickly, and I realized then that neither Semi nor I had mentioned our changed destination to either him or Sheldon. Semi did so now briefly.

"But we go to San Francisco," he replied.

"San Francisco!"

Reich almost shrieked as he sprang to his feet and confronted Dual.

"We do not. I won't do it! We're going to Seattle on this train; do you hear me, you fake sleuth—Seattle! You can come or get out if you like. You've done nothing but blunder. This is Sheldon's and my affair after all, and what we say goes. Ain't that right, Colonel Mac?"

Sheldon struggling with his own surprise cleared his throat in a visible effort to adjust himself to changed plans, before committing himself to words, and in that moment Dual spoke again.

"That is undoubtedly right in part. Colonel Sheldon, as the man who was acting as Miss Lawton's protector at the time this happened, has the *entire* right of decision in the matter. You at present, Mr. Reich, have no part in it at all save as the man who was to marry the woman.

"Colonel Sheldon asked me to take on this case, and I have done so. Throughout you have persistently raised objections. We have reached the time for a final decision. Colonel Sheldon, I advise our change of destination on the strength of things which happened after you and Mr. Reich retired last night."

"Then, by God, she goes," Sheldon decided. He turned to Reich who stood pallid with clenched hands and distorted face.

"Homer, I'm backin' Dual's play right through to the last turn, an' I'm copperin' anybody else's bet. If he says Frisco, I say Frisco, too.

"I never was stuck on that Seattle idea nohow. Now, I reckon that settles the matter even accordin' to your tell, son. Be good. We're all tryin' to help you find your girl."

Muttering under his breath, Homer seized his bag and Sheldon and I followed the others out of the car to the depot platform, as the train sighed to a stop. There was a very large unanswered question in Colonel Mac's eyes, which he managed to voice in the end passage of the car.

"What happened last night, Glace?"

"We got wise to the fact that the Greek's tip was a plant," I responded. "Lucile came up after you folks went to bed."

Sheldon whistled softly, then chuckled.

"False steer, eh?" he remarked. "Well, my Lord, that girl's a corker. It's lucky she got wise."

Reich, who preceded the colonel, turned his head but refrained from speech until he had reached the platform when he spoke directly to Lucile.

"So you're the one who advised this jaunt to Frisco, are you? I might have known it. Trust a woman to ball things up. What's there in it to you?"

"Satisfaction. I hope," she made answer. "The satisfaction of seeing justice done, Mr. Reich."

Reich snorted.

"I've a notion to go it alone and keep on to Seattle," he growled, glancing back at the car we had left.

"And I've a notion you won't," flared Sheldon. "And I've another that you'll cut out this here actin' like an unlicked cub. I'm gettin' a new line on your make-up, my boy, an' I don't like it.

"You might have sense enough to see that we're all doin' everything we kin to help you an' find Lilly, an' to jump in an' help stead of beefin' around like you do.

"Dang me if I ain't kinder glad Lilly didn't get hitched up to you no matter what's happened. Now shut up an' come along. I'm runnin' this show as it happens. Get that under your hat."

I felt like shaking the old man's hand, and telling him I agreed most fully with him. Reich's actions were becoming rather galling even to me and threatening to kill the natural sympathy by which I had at first sought to excuse them.

This last flare up of his, even though it brought a sort of ultimatum from Sheldon, at the same time served also to yet further strain the situation at a time when Heaven knows we should have all been acting in concert to the common end.

I felt that I was in accord with Sheldon in thinking Lilly Lawton was lucky to have escaped marriage with the erratic Reich.

I left him under the escort of Sheldon and joined myself to Dual and Miss Foote, and we made our way to the waiting-room, where under Semi's directions I arranged for our reservations on the limited, then nearly due.

I confess I felt much better when it came in and we took our sections and rumbled away toward the west.

At least I felt that anything Homer might do from now on would consist of nothing more overt than words, which while they might be unpleasant, could in no way militate against the final end of our trip.

However, he didn't even go that far, but contented himself with sulking in the buffet all afternoon.

Sheldon and I kept him company part of the time as the buffet seemed to rather appeal to the colonel. Dual evidently had work of his own peculiar nature to attend to as he evinced a desire to be alone, and Lucille retired to the parlor at the rear of the train and read a book.

We met again at dinner, and after it was ended I suggested to her that we go out on the rear platform and have a chat.

She assented readily enough in her frank, almost boyish

way, with the result that we presently found ourselves ensconced in a couple of chairs looking back along the twilight-blurred track.

For some time the conversation was inconsequential. I spoke of the vast stretch of sage grown, barren country across which we were flying, and Lucile compared it to the desolation of a blighted life.

The remark brought me up standing so to speak, and I shot her a swift glimpse under cover of the dusk. She was staring straight ahead of her along the dusk-shrouded rails.

"Even a desolated life may become full," I suggested.

"Yes?" She did not turn her head.

"Take Dual, for instance. Would you believe that he has known what it is to suffer?"

"I certainly would," her answer surprised me. "He is too kind not to have suffered and learned how to sympathize with others, Mr. Glace. He is the strangest, most magnetic man I ever met. Have you known him long?"

"A long time," said I.

"Tell me," she begged. "Tell about him. I want to know at least a little. He isn't like men of to-day—there is something—something I can't express—different from the rest of mankind I have met.

"He baffles me, Mr. Glace—makes me feel like a child in his presence, instead of a worldly-wise woman.

"When he looks at me I feel as though he could read my very soul. I felt that the first time I ever met him and he made that peculiar remark about my being able to sympathize. Does he read minds?"

I smiled at the question. I had known the same sensation

she mentioned, myself, as though Semi were looking clear through my head and tearing my thoughts from their beds.

"He certainly does," I made answer. "I've felt at times as if my head were glass, when he fastened his eyes upon me."

"No, but really. I am serious now, Mr. Glace." She met me fully with her eyes, and no vestige of a smile lurked in them.

"And I am serious, Miss Foote," I responded. "Dual actually does read people's thoughts. Not only when he is with them, but when at a distance."

For a time she made no comment, but sat silent while the wheels rattled and rang beneath us, then:

"Telepathy," she said.

"Yes. Miss Foote, what would you think if I were to tell you that he knew Colonel Sheldon wanted him in Gold-field and told both my wife and myself as much, before we received any message to that effect? I assure you it is so."

"I would say I believe you, strange as the thing seems," she declared. "Mr. Dual impresses me as a monster mind in a body, and it seems to me that that mind sees and knows things which are hidden to such as myself. Tell me: Can he do these things at will, or merely on occasion?"

"At will, Miss Foote."

The moon now in its full had come up and was flooding all the country with its mellow light. The girl beside me shivered slightly ere she spoke.

"What a power—to look into the human mind and read what it is thinking—to sense the thought waves it throws off. Mr. Glace, just what is your friend—a reincarnation of one of the olden Magi?"

"Do you believe in reincarnation?" I queried.

"I don't know," she said softly. "Why not? Millions of people do. Wouldn't it after all be a sort of divine justice. Should we be utterly condemned or rewarded on just one trial—one life?

"I don't know. Why shouldn't some of those old people who did believe in it—some of those ancients upon whom this same moon has shone, thousands of years ago, have had a perception of the truth as well as we of to-day?

"I think I should like to believe in it—I think I should like to live again and see if I couldn't make something better out of life.

"I don't know much of religion or God, Mr. Glace, beyond what I feel within myself, but take the case of this girl we hope to rescue. Suppose we should fail.

"Can you imagine a God who would condemn her eternally for some fate thrust upon her without her volition? Yet this life of hers must, if the worst comes upon her, be utterly ruined. Don't you think that justice demands another chance for her?"

She paused again and after a moment smiled.

"But you haven't yet told me, who or what is the man, we know as Semi Dual."

"Nor can I tell you," I answered, "save to say he is a most wonderful man, whom I have known for years. Yet since you press the question, I shall give you the valuation he once placed on himself to me. He said that he was a man who had suffered much, and studied much, and, as he hoped, learned a few of the great truths of life."

She nodded.

"That sounds like him, too. And one of the things he has learned is to read thoughts. I wonder if that was how he knew the tip on Seattle was false. Did he read those Greeks' minds?"

"I think so," I confessed.

"But how does he do it? I never really believed in it as a practical thing."

"His explanation is seemingly simple," I returned. "He begins with the theory that all life phenomena are manifestations of vibration, and that every life act depends upon and is produced by vibration. From that he says that the formation of a thought sets up vibratory waves and that a mind trained to the act can sense these waves and retranslate them into intelligible thoughts again."

"Then they must be all around us—these thought waves. Millions of people are thinking—setting them free, every minute. They fill all space like wireless currents.

"It would be odd to be able to read them. Mr. Glace, at the risk of seeming improperly curious, I am going to ask further, what he does when he works over those sheets of paper? I am both a detective and a woman, remember, and hence doubly inquisitive."

I smiled, as I made my answer.

"Miss Foote, it may seem strange to you, as it did at first to me, to find in this twentieth century a man who still consults the stars. Yet that is what Semi Dual at times does.

"He is an astrologer.

"I have seen him make some wonderful predictions from his calculations on those bits of paper, and I have seen his predictions come true. In fact the results have at times seemed almost uncanny in the foreknowledge they exhibited of what would befall. As a rule I hesitate to say such things to people because they laugh, but I believe you are sincere in your questions."

"Indeed I am," she almost whispered. "I shall not laugh. They believed these things when that old moon up there was young. I wonder—were they wiser than we?"

Suddenly she sat up in her chair and clenched her hands.

"We will win—we will win. I am sure of it now. My God, why couldn't I have known Semi Dual before!"

Her words were those of a soul in torment, and for the moment she seemed to have forgotten my presence. Yet in a minute she spoke again in her natural voice.

"Pardon me, Mr. Glace. Suppose we speak of something else."

I nodded assent. "You have lived in San Francisco," I suggested.

"I was born and raised there," said Miss Foote.

"And how long have you been a detective?"

"Three years."

"I suppose," said I, "that you have met some pretty gripping things in the line you have followed. My work is mostly with thieves and major criminal actions. Yours, I take it, has been more along sociological lines?"

"Yes." She seemed to consider for a moment before she went on.

"Would you like to hear one instance of the work of these people we are fighting at present?"

"Very much," I rejoined.

"I was thinking of that when I made my outburst a few moments ago," she explained. "It was in San Francisco that it happened, too. There was a girl—a young girl—pretty, of course.

"They don't bother with the ugly ducklings—they have to have the fairest flowers.

"Well, it doesn't matter who she was or what she was doing, does it? She was a good girl, Mr. Glace, but fond of pleasure, and the least bit headstrong, as your spoiled beauty is apt to be, but she was clean at heart as I happen to know.

"At the same time she was from people of moderate means, so that when she found employment she took it. She was employed in a photographer's shop.

"One day a man, a young man, came there to sit for a picture.

"He saw this girl and as a customer he addressed her. From that time on he made it a point to see her and gradually they became friendly. He began to show her some little attentions. He took her to places of amusement, and sometimes to dinner at a café. After a time he asked her to marry him.

"She told her mother—her father was dead—and her mother objected. There was a scene, of course. You see, I knew the people well.

"A few days later she went with the man to dinner, and he persuaded her to elope. She never came home again, and she never was married.

"This man took her to a place, and placed her in a room, telling her to wait there until he could arrange for the ceremony. Shortly after he had left her a woman came to her room and told her everything was ready and that she was to accompany her to a place where the man was waiting.

"Instead, she took her to one of the places where these people detain their victims.

"Not until she was shut in and hopelessly lost did the girl suspect. Then she decided to die rather than submit to the fate she had rushed forward to meet.

"She had some photographic proofs in an envelope in her bag, and upon the backs of these she wrote what had happened, and the name of her betrayer, sealed them up and addressed the envelope to me.

"She managed to throw this out of a window, where it was found by some one passing and sent to me. Then—then—she took the pin out of her hat, and stabbed herself straight through—the left breast."

Lucile Foote drew her kerchief and wiped her eyes.

"I ought to cut that out," she observed in a moment, "but you see I had known the girl since she was a baby, and when her mother learned of her death, the shock killed her also. And what good did it do—what end did it serve?"

"And the man?" I inquired.

"Went free as men do," said Miss Foote. "He simply disappeared. The girl had his picture in her room at her home, and we had his description of course, but he was not found.

"Yet he murdered that girl just as surely as if his hand had guided the pin instead of hers, when it pierced her heart. Don't you think a girl driven to a thing like that ought to have a chance to come back and try it over? If not, what would become of her?"

"I think," I rejoined, "that a girl forced to such a choice, who chose death to dishonor, ought to go to a little white and gold room in the very highest heaven."

Lucile Foote turned toward me and I thought that she

seemed pale in the moonlight, and that her eyes were very wide and very dark.

"Thank you, Mr. Glace," she murmured softly and turned her head away.

"But as for the man," I went on: "the one who was responsible for that pitiful ending of two other lives, even though he escaped the justice of man, he cannot escape the justice of Fate. It will trail him sooner or later to his doom."

My companion glanced back again to me.

"Do you believe that?" she whispered; "about Fate? Really?"

I nodded.

"Yes. I have seen it work out again and again—that men who had done crimes, and thought themselves safe, were overtaken by the arm of an unsuspected justice. That is one of Dual's strongest beliefs also.

"He says it *always* happens. He calls it the law of *Retributive Justice,* which demands that every person pays in full for every act he performs of evil, and is rewarded for every good deed."

"Wherefore by his good deeds one 'acquires merit' as the Orientals say," quoted Miss Foote, "Well, why not? It isn't so long ago that we so-called Christians spoke of a recording angel. If there is a life after this, why should there not be a ledger kept, with debits and credits for or against each soul?"

"Dual calls those records the Karmic Scrolls," I replied.

"You mean he believes in such a record?" inquired Miss Foote in a rather small voice.

"Indeed, yes. In fact it is through that that the law of justice works. He says that every act, every thought of a man makes its record for or against him, and that an act or a thought lives and operates until it produces its effect.

"With him all is cause and effect. The act is the cause, its effect the result.

"The sum total of a man's acts is his karma—the balance, as it were, of the things he has done, which determines what he is to do next. If he is right, and myself I believe that he is, then the man who betrayed that girl cannot escape the payment for his act. At least it is some satisfaction to think that some time, that must be."

She made no answer and I too fell into silence, watching her out of half-closed lids.

Her profile told me she was thinking and would rather not be disturbed by more words. I let my eyes wander from her face out over the moon-drenched landscape, silvered into a weird beauty.

Far off to the right a point of reddish light winked from a dark blot—a hut in the wilderness of sage. I watched it dwindle and die behind us. Lucile Foote drew a long, quivering sigh.

"You are right, Mr. Glace: that man shall pay."

A tall figure appeared in the door at our backs and I recognized Dual. He stepped out on the platform and stood behind us.

"Even now the hand of his fate is driving him into the web of the law," he remarked. "I have listened to the last part of your conversation, and Gordon has told you broadly of my belief. He is right. His fate shall overtake the betrayer of your sister."

"My sister?" Lucile repeated in surprised accents.

"We are all children of the one Father, all earthly brothers and sisters," said Semi Dual. "If we could only remember that fact! I perceive that the death of this girl has affected you deeply.

"It is for that reason that I have spoken; because after the matter of Miss Lawton shall have been brought to a close, my next act shall be to enable you to apprehend this other girl's betrayer."

Lucile lifted her eyes and gazed into his while I sat silent in the grip of the situation. Then without one word she rose and turned into the car behind us, and as she went I heard her sob in a hard, dry way.

I turned to Semi Dual.

"I wonder what is the secret of that girl's life?" I remarked.

"I think that is *her* secret, my friend," he replied.

"And you mean to take up the case of this other girl?"

"Why not?" said Semi.

"And you will be able to find the man who betrayed her?"

"Did you ever know me to fail to find a man, Gordon?" he queried with a smile.

"And how about our case?"

I ran on now that the ice was broken and he seemed all at once the old Dual I knew.

"Will we find the Lawton girl in time, Semi? Why have you shut me out as you have? What is it that makes you so different in this?"

"Necessity," he answered. "I have hurt you, haven't I, Gordon? My friend, believe me that I would not have done it, save for the vital need. In all that I do, salve your hurts with that."

"Oh, I knew there was good reason," I began with the sudden feeling that I had been childish.

Dual smiled upon me.

"Gordon," he said, "in this case—this matter of a little human fly in the web of a spider—every step of our course thus far has been fraught with a danger unrealized by you. And, my friend, it is best that you do not see, lest in your knowledge you blunder.

"Even in this half explanation my words doubtless seem cryptic, and must continue to do so, until I shall have lifted the fly from the web once more. Hence I ask you to trust me wholly, and do whatever I ask without question. In so much you can serve me, and the little human fly. Will you follow me blindly my friend?"

"Do you need ask?" I faltered. "After all you have taught me, I was a fool not to have understood. Still I am glad we had this conversation, because I think from now on you'll find me a pretty good soldier."

"And now," said Dual slowly, "I shall answer one of your questions. So far as Miss Lawton's welfare is concerned, we will be in time."

My spirits rose. It was a direct statement. Never in all my knowledge of him had I known him to make such a prediction without reason.

The night took on new beauty as I turned his assurance in my mind and felt my courage rise for the final attack in the fight we were waging. Rather than break the mood I rose and held out my hand.

Dual took it with a smile of understanding and I said good night.

The next day passed with little of incident to record.

Reich and Sheldon stuck pretty close. Dual, Miss Foote, and I passed the morning on the observation platform, and in the afternoon I joined Reich and the colonel in the buffet.

Evening came and brought us into the valley of the Sacramento, down which we fled toward Oakland. A gradual chill and the tang of salt air crept into the breeze as we rushed onward, until at length we ran under a long steel shed and stopped.

Some time after that I stood on the front of a ferry and gazed across a stretch of black water toward the illuminated face of a clock in a tower, and rows on rows of twinkling lights which rose back and beyond it, and other pin points of red and green and yellow, which threw trembling reflections into the bay.

It was my first sight of the phoenix of the Golden Gate—San Francisco, decked like a queen, in a scintillating diadem of light.

6

TO THE GOLDEN GATE

IT WAS EIGHT by the clock in the tower of the slip when we docked on the San Francisco side.

Dual took instant control and hurried us to the street front, where he bundled us into a taxi and cried to the driver for haste.

My first impression of the city was of a long street paved in asphalt, lined by massive structures of granite and steel, brick and concrete, lighted by a million points of sparkling light, coursed by a thousand gorgon-eyed motors and a hundred clanging trolleys, where blue-coated traffic men checked us or waved us onward in undisputed direction, under a dimly misty atmosphere, which I subconsciously knew was fog.

Out of this we presently turned into a quieter street, stormed up a hill and stopped before the arched and pillared entrance to a massive white building, from whose doors charged a squad of pages, who seized on our bags and escorted us across a yellow marble foyer to a yellow marble desk, where we inscribed our names in a massive tome, lettered Hotel St. Francis at the top of each page.

Such was the beginning of a rather eventful night.

Dual took a suite with three bedrooms and parlor; two

pages staggered to the elevators with our baggage and led us to our rooms, unlocked the doors, piled our bags, pulled up one blind and lowered another, chased an imaginary fly from a table, accepted their largess and left.

Sheldon cast an eye about the apartment.

"Swell dump, all right!" he announced, nodding. "I reckon I'll unpack my war-bag and turn in."

"Not just yet, colonel," replied Dual. "I fear that you must wait some hours for that. I want to close this affair to-night."

I think we were all more or less surprised at his words. I know I was, and Colonel Mac fairly gaped as he whirled toward him and repeated the one word, "To-night?" in a way which showed he was far from convinced.

But it was on Reich that the words had the most marked effect. He actually swayed on his feet and his face seemed to me to grow almost ghastly like that of one who has received an unexpected shock.

"To-night," he faltered. "But, my God! how can you? What can we do to-night?"

"It is of that we must speak," said Semi Dual. "First"— he turned to Miss Foote—"will you, Miss Lucile, take one of the hotel's taxis, go to the proper place and establish our standing with the San Francisco police? As soon as you have done so, request them to place a detective at our disposal and return with him here."

Lucile, who had not removed her hat, nodded and left the suite without a word.

Dual turned back to us.

"Suppose we sit down," he remarked. "From now on I

wish it distinctly understood that I am in control, because from now on we must work and work fast."

"Bully!" cried Sheldon, slapping a hand on his knee. "Now maybe we'll git action. I kin jest nacherally live on that. What do I do?"

"I was coming to that," said Semi Dual. "Colonel, I want you to listen closely and do what I ask, no matter what you yourself may think of the request.

"You can see for yourself that Mr. Reich is unstrung. This experience has completely shattered his usual control. You as the one of us who knows him best, I am going to ask to constitute yourself his companion for this evening.

"His mental condition is such that he may say or do something at a time when it would have very serious results unless he has an older head to watch him, and it is that duty to which I now assign you. In your own way of speaking, *'stick to him,'* colonel!"

"I don't need a guard or a nurse," Reich protested. But his words even to me lacked force. "If you think I'm likely to interfere with your plans leave me here—put me to bed. I won't kick."

"Mr. Reich," Dual addressed him, "you also come under my mandate of complete obedience. For reasons of my own I do not wish you to remain here in your present mental state.

"It is harder to wait than to lie on the field of action. I do not wish to condemn you to that. I merely want to provide in advance against any contretemps which a sudden outburst on your part might occasion. For the rest, let me advise that you control yourself to the best of your ability and await the end."

"But I don't see—I don't see how you can end things to-night. How can you? You've just got here— How—" Reich spoke in a manner half dazed.

"It is not necessary that you should," said Semi. "You may remember that in Goldfield you said it was results you wanted, and that I promised that you should have them. In a few hours I shall redeem that promise. At the same time I told you that my methods were peculiar and there is now no time for explanations. After the matter is ended I shall explain everything to you."

"But what are you going to do? Why keep us all in the dark?" complained Reich.

"I work in my own manner," said Dual. "Gordon, are you armed?"

I nodded.

Dual turned his eyes on Sheldon.

"And you, colonel?"

"Me? Am I heeled? Well, rather!"

Colonel Mac rose and walked to the piled-up luggage, dragged out his bag, unlocked it, and put in his hand. In a minute he withdrew it, clutching the butt of a long barreled .45 revolver.

"I fotched along my old 'lamb's leg,'" he went on, holding up the weapon. "I've shot off the head of more'n one chicken an' rattler with this here, an' I reckon I ain't forgot her balance. All you got to do is lead me to it. I ain't pulled trigger for a right smart spell." He lifted his vest, thrust the revolver inside the band of his trousers, replaced the vest above it, and resumed his chair.

"You got a gun, Homer?" he remarked.

Reich nodded. "Automatic," he said.

"All right," grinned Sheldon. "Only you want ter be careful how you pull it. I guess then we're all heeled, Mr. Dual."

"There remains then but to wait for Miss Foote's return," advised Semi. He leaned back in his chair, closed his eyes and folded his hands. For the time he seemed to slip away into a field of unconscious relaxation which none of us sought to disturb.

Reich, too, sat hunched in a padded armchair. Sheldon lighted one of his series of panetelas, and I sat silent.

So we waited. The noises of the outer street came faintly to us; the clang of a passing trolley, the clack of horses' hoofs. Through a partly opened window a cool damp breeze crept in and brought with it the odor of the fog.

I looked out over the night-shrouded city, where the twin rows of lights outlined the far-flung streets.

From the water front drifted the mournful hoot of a ferry boat's siren like the voice of a soul in torment—a lost soul drifting through a world of night and fog. Subtly it came to me that it was like the hopeless cry of the soul of the woman who somewhere out under those twinkling lights was held in a pitiless bondage.

I turned my eyes back to the room and the figure of Dual. He had not moved from his position.

Only the slow rise and fall of his chest told that he lived, and I wondered what was passing back of his broad brows, inside his strange brain. Would he, I questioned, heed that cry of the lost and follow it to bring again the light of freedom from bondage and danger, and even as I wondered, I chid myself for asking the question.

Footsteps passed down the hallway outside our door.

A voice spoke and was answered; a woman laughed—the door of an elevator clanged softly.

I glanced at Sheldon. The old man sat stolidly smoking, yet a change had crept into his face. The lips which held his cigar seemed to me to have grown thinner and firmer, with almost a tension at their corners, and the set of his fighting chin had, too, taken on a new angle.

Under their heavy brows his gray eyes brooded. He looked like a grizzled veteran waiting the call to action which he knew was about to come.

From him my eyes traveled to Reich—almost with a feeling of pity.

After all, I thought, the lad had lost far more than any of us who judged his erratic temper, and his protests against what must have seemed to his youth like inaction.

And surely he seemed to have suffered. He was worn, his face pallid, drawn, almost haggard, and there were darkening circles beneath his eyes. I noticed that the hand on the arm of the chair in which he sat twitched now and then as against his volition.

His brows were knit in brooding thought, his chin sunk on his breast.

Sheldon rose and walked to a window, standing there with his hands clasped behind him, gazing out over the lights of the city. I crossed and joined him where he stood chewing upon his cigar which had gone dead.

"She's some city," he muttered, nodding his grizzled head at the miles of lights. "Some city to go out into an' find one leetle gal tucked away to keep folks from findin'. But I reckon Dual kin do it, an' if he does, he's a wizard. My Lord, I'll be glad to see Lilly again!"

"He will do it," I whispered assurance.

"I ain't doubtin' it, son," he made answer. "When that Lucile girl gets back I reckon the fireworks will begin to sizzle. I reckon you an' I know Semi Dual."

Well, his was the faith of the soldier in the general who had sent him to victorious action. I thrilled at his words, and laid a hand on his shoulder. He turned, and his lips twitched into a slow, grim smile.

Again footsteps sounded from the passage. The door opened and Miss Foote entered in company with a man.

He was a small and somewhat shabby person in a sack coat of brown tweeds and trousers to match. His face was thin, nervous, and incisive; his hair, when he took off his derby hat, was a dark and close-cut auburn, and he walked with a shuffling stoop.

We all turned to face him on his entrance, and in so doing looked into a pair of cool blue eyes.

"Gentlemen," said Miss Lucile, "this is Mr. McKabe, of the Chinatown plain clothes squad."

McKabe nodded his head and perched himself on the edge of a chair fiddling with his battered derby.

"Th' young lady has given me the lay," he began. "Now just what'jer want to do?"

Dual, who had lifted himself to attention, upon the entrance of the detective, immediately answered:

"We want to find this girl and assure her safety, and we want the assistance of your people, and as time is an important factor, we want to act at once. If you already know the main details, you can suggest the proper moves."

McKabe frowned, placed his hat on a table close beside him and locked his wiry fingers about one knee.

"From what Miss Foote told me I reckon the best bet would be to try and glimpse this Greek Annie, whom you think brought the girl from Salt Lake. If we can cross her trail most like it will strike some wheres pretty close to the girl. There's just two places where I think we'd be most likely to pick her up—one is the Pacific Avenue dumps—what most folks call the Barbary Coast, an' the other is the Chinatown District.

"The last is the best, because right now most of the avenue places is pretty quiet, an' they ain't pullin' much rough stuff over there. But the chinks always have kep' us guessin', an' I guess they always will. Lately these white slave people have been makin' a good deal of use of them, too. Only last summer we dug out six girls what a chink was holdin', an' sent them back to their people, an' at that we couldn't git a conviction. The chink brought a dozen witnesses to prove the girls was boardin' with him, an' we couldn't prove it wasn't so. Of course we knew all right, just as we did when we grabbed three girls a feller was shippin' out to China offen a vessel. That's the way they work it. Girls what lays down easy they keep here and send out over the country. Them as won't they're beginnin' to send out of the country."

"But how do they git by with that sort of thing right under your eyes?" inquired Colonel Mac.

"Under our feet would be a better way to say it, my friend," said McKabe. "We're wise it's goin' on, but stoppin' it's like the old recipe for rabbit stew—first catch your rabbit. An' they're just like rabbits. Folks will tell you that the new Chinatown is a sort of model settlement with the worst features of the old one left out—a sort of expurgated edition, but that's 'cause they don't know. When they rebuilt they was told to cut out all them underground passages an' dives an' that sort of thing—but did they? I'm askin' you, an' the answer is: they done what they pleased.

"There's miles of them runways under them houses up there, an' they're worse than any rabbit-burrow. They can git a girl or a dozen down there an' then you try an' find them. Everything is snarled up like a puzzle picture. They can move them girls ten feet, an' anybody huntin' them will be as far off as they would in New York, so far as findin' them goes. Oh, it's a sweet game!

"Of course we have dug some of them out, but God knows how many we missed! Still we kin try. That's why they sent me. I know Chinktown pretty well, an' I understand a bit of their lingo. I spend a lot of time up there, an' most folks think I'm just a professional guide. That's my lay, an' I ain't been uncovered yet. So if you'll take my advice, I'd say, let's cover the town, an' maybe we can fasten on this Salt Lake agent."

He reached into a pocket, drew out the badge of a Chinatown guide and pinned it on the breast of his coat.

"I quite agree with you, Mr. McKabe," Dual assented. "In keeping with your suggestion I would advise that we go as a party, seemingly, of tourists under your leadership. Miss Foote must go along, at all events, to identify the woman when we meet her, and Colonel Sheldon and Mr. Reich know the girl."

McKabe rose.

"You're runnin' the show," he remarked. "We may as well set out."

"And I suppose," sneered Reich, "that you think this

woman you're hunting is going to walk up and let us see her. Do you?" He turned to Dual.

"That is exactly what I do suppose," Semi replied. "As to her volition in the matter, that is a different affair. At present, however, she has no reason to believe that we are in the city, and will feel no special need for keeping concealed. Now I think we are ready. Come!"

He moved toward the door.

We left the hotel, and McKabe led us through Union Square, where the tall shaft holds the flying "Victory" aloft. It came to me in that moment that to one superstitious it might seem like an augury of fortune to us who were setting out under a fog-streaked sky to fight a battle for the freedom of a human victim.

Late as it was more than one person still sat on the benches of the little park as we passed. They glanced up and probably judged us as the party of sightseers we seemed. One of them even spoke to McKabe and received a nod in turn.

Our guide turned at Stockton and Sutter and led us down to Grant, turned again and led us straight along the latter up a gradually rising course toward our destination.

It was nearly ten, with a sky overcast and hidden by the streamers of fog, through which the moon sought to shine and only succeeded in throwing a sort of silver sheen.

The very air seemed damp, as though full of an impalpable mist, so that the sidewalks glistened with a faint moisture as we advanced up the hill. After a time we came to the top and the edge of Chinatown itself.

It stretched before us with its strange appeal of something hybrid—a strange blending of East and West, with a thousand foreign noises and a thousand unaccustomed smells.

Electric arcs and incandescents threw their light over its garish night life. Painted lanterns bloomed like dream poppies before the doors of some of its shops and restaurants, and the facades of a joss-house swinging blobs of color in the night breeze. Painted ideographs flaunted on crimson banners from a balcony, half-hazed by the streamers of fog.

Stretches of plate-glass in some modern pagoda roofed and towered business emporium gave glimpses of displays of beauty, things of wondrous workmanship, toiled out with what must have been indescribable patience by fingers of other lands.

Sandwiched beside them, murky lights of swinging incandescents gave views of dimly lighted squalor, and round Oriental faces, stolid, world-wearied, as it seemed.

Its pavements were full of a varied and polyglot life. Slant-eyed Orientals in flowing blouse and trousers and wide white-soled shoes, shuffled past with their more modern brothers in Occidental sack coat and pants.

Now and then a woman, stooped slightly, her dark hair coiled on her head, thrust through with jeweled pins, her limbs clad in twin tubes of silk, teetered along, turning her dark eyes out of heavy lids like wax.

Here and there a child toddled, staring at you out of beady points of darkness set in the midst of round faces, for all the world like dolls from a toy store come to life and clinging to the skirts of their mother's blouse. Groups of Eastern tourists in the trail of a guide passed us now and then, treating the denizens of the place with open stares of curious interest.

Through and among it the night-owls flitted, creatures of the dark, men—and even women—with the thin pallor of slaves of the poppy, slinking out of their lairs into the night life, passing you with a furtive glance and a twitching of pallid lips, bits of human flotsam cast into this backwater of world-old life.

And withal it was strangely without sound. Unlike an American crowd, its people moved with few words, little outcry, spoke in a low singsong, which carried little beyond the speaker. The squeak of a fiddle as we passed a doorway was a noise in that place. And I do not remember that we spoke to any extent as we moved.

In fact, it all came to seem like the strange phantasmagoria of a dream to me as we followed McKabe's shuffling lead. The lights, the crowds, the weird changing, shifting life, the damp kiss of the fog, the odd pungent odors, the cool night wind fanning my face took on the unreality of a subconscious rather than of an objective something, so that I turned my head and picked up Sheldon and Reich, Lucile Foote and Semi Dual, and lastly McKabe, in order to break from the spell which had gripped me and forced me into a waking dream.

And so I noticed Dual. He was walking straight forward in the wake of our guide, and I saw that Lucile, at his side, was gazing up at his face with an almost puzzled expression on her own. Semi was walking straight onward, with his face to the front, and on his features was the look of a dog when it dreams of the chase.

I don't know how else to describe the expression. His

clean features had grown tense, acquisitive, with a set as of one seeking a thing elusive. His lids were almost drooping, his lips drawn slightly at the corners. His nostrils swelled slightly, and could it be said of a man, I would have sworn his ears were pricked. I would have said that he was listening with all his being for a something so faintly perceptive as to be almost beyond the range of perception.

Yet I was not surprised. Perhaps it was the odd mood into which I, myself, had fallen, but it seemed to me that I understood. It came to me in that moment that in the same way he had sensed Sheldon's call on the platform at Salida—so now Semi Dual was seeking to pick up some subtle thread of leading which should bring us to the object of our search.

As if to prove me right he spoke:

"Wait, Mr. McKabe. We have come too far."

The little guide stopped in surprise.

"What do you mean?" he inquired. "Too far for what? Do you know this district?"

Dual shook his head and smiled slightly.

"No. I have never been here."

Then as we all gathered closely about him he went on:

"It is my opinion that the party we seek would most likely frequent some restaurant in this section, if she came out of quarters to-night. Presuming that she would wish to meet some confederate or a dealer, or an agent, she would in all likelihood appoint a meeting in some such place, I would advise that we visit some resort of that nature."

McKabe nodded slowly. He had been eying Dual with fresh interest since Semi's interruption of our course. Now he spoke:

"Maybe it wouldn't be a bad notion. I've run onto more'n one party I was after in such places as that. I was thinkin' of something the same myself, an' I thought we'd go to the last in the line an' work back. Shall we go on?"

Dual shook his head.

"Not on—but back. As I said, we have come too far."

"Too far?" McKabe seemed a bit puzzled. "How do you know we've come too far?"

"Let us go back and prove it," said Semi. "There is no time to explain."

McKabe frowned slightly and took the back track.

"I guess it's your case," he mumbled, "an' I hope you know what you're doing. I don't."

We retraced our steps—and once more I noticed the odd trailing expression settled over Dual's features. Lucile glanced back at me as in question, and I nodded to her without words.

We walked on. Behind us I heard Reich speaking to Colonel Mac. Dual spoke again:

"Stop! This is the place."

We had come to the front of a building where many lanterns of great size swayed in the breeze from a balcony lined with flowers, above a doorway painted red and lettered with ideographs of gilt.

McKabe stopped.

"This joint?" he asked. "Well, all right. This is the swellest place in the town. All the big men give their parties and banquets here. For a man who's never been here before you're a good picker, Mr. Dual."

He grinned slightly and turned toward the door of the place.

I started to follow after Lucile and Semi. Reich and Sheldon were behind me, and Homer burst out into objections.

"This is all piffling nonsense, I tell you! I don't want to eat chop suey—I want to find Lilly. Come on, Sheldon, let's slip this bunch and do something. It's been dinners and tea parties ever since we started. I can't see—"

I turned back, just as Sheldon seized his companion by the arm and literally ran him up the steps.

"I know you can't see, son," he rumbled, "an' neither can I. I ain't tryin' to any more. But Dual's wise an' he told me to stop your tryin' to kick over the traces, an' I'm on the job. Shut up an' come on. I don't like tea any better than you do."

The thing was ludicrous, and I found myself grinning as I resumed my progress after the others.

We came into an entry where was a counter, a modern cash register, and a Chinese cashier wearing a pair of very large shell-rimmed glasses. He nodded us toward a stairs, and we began to mount.

Above us I heard the climbing feet of Dual and McKabe and Lucile, and I ran up after.

At the top we turned and mounted yet another flight of stairs and emerged into a passage before an arched entrance into a room set out with Oriental trappings.

We went in and sat down at a table.

I gazed around. Beyond me were the windows opening onto the balcony of flowers. Around me were embroidered screens and screens of lacquer with birds and flowers of ivory carving strewn across them. Curtains of bamboo painted and gilded swung from the ceilings.

Teak-wood tables and chairs, quaintly carved, were scattered all over the room. At a far table a party of Chinese—men and women—were dining.

A waiter came up and took our order.

"Chicken chop suey," said Lucile. "I haven't had any for years—and I'm hungry."

McKabe smiled.

"You talk like a native daughter, Miss Foote," he remarked.

Lucile returned his smile and replied quite frankly:

"I am."

The detective nodded.

"You look it," he told her, and turned to the waiter. "Double that for mine, Charlie."

Dual and I and Sheldon ordered tea, and Reich, after a moment of indecision, ordered noodles.

The waiter smiled and shuffled away.

McKabe nodded at his retreating back.

"They're an odd bunch," he observed. "Now you wouldn't think it, but Charlie there is a graduate of the University of California, and yet he's a waiter in a chow shop. He speaks four languages, too—Chinese, Japanese, English, and Spanish. He's a pretty nice chink."

I glanced at Dual. "How about you, Semi?" I inquired.

"Not yet," he returned slowly. "Yet before this night is over I shall show you something more appalling than that."

"You ought to show us something," said Reich out of a sulky silence. "I can't stand this waiting-game much longer. You might have a little pity on a man's feelings. You haven't lost anything, of course, and aren't liable to, but try to imagine how a man in my position must feel. Do you think I want to sit here eating and drinking when I don't know what's going to happen. Oh, for God's sake, say what you're going to do?"

He broke off to glance somewhat wildly about the room.

"The waiting is almost over, Mr. Reich," said Semi. "As for pity, perhaps I pity you, in my own way, and for reasons of my own."

"And that's another thing," complained Homer. "Every time you say something the thing's got two meanings. Why don't you say what you mean?"

"At least," Dual responded, "I always mean what I say, Mr. Reich."

Charlie came back and served our order and a quantity of sweetmeats filling the triangular compartments of a circular tray.

Lucile drew her steaming bowl of chop-suey before her, picked up her chop-sticks as one accustomed and gave proof of the assertion that she was hungry.

Sheldon eyed her performance upon the mixture of chicken, ham, rice sprouts, and mushrooms, with unconcealed interest.

"You act like you liked it," he grinned.

Lucile nodded and smiled. "I do," she admitted. "Here, taste it. Open your mouth."

She deftly fished up a ball of shredded chicken and sprouts in her sticks, and as Colonel Mac separated his jaws, dropped it lightly on his tongue.

The colonel chewed in a ruminative fashion. "Sorter like chewin' on a bunch of string, ain't it?" he observed dryly.

"You old fraud, I believe you like it," accused Miss Foote. "If you think this stringy what about Mr. Reich's order?"

Sheldon glanced at Homer, deftly consuming noodles, and chuckled.

"I reckon they charge for them things by the yard, don't they?" he suggested with eyes which twinkled.

The old feeling of non-understanding crept upon me again as I listened. Here we sat eating and drinking and chaffing. To hear us one would have thought us a party of tourists as we seemed.

Yet under the surface of the seeming we were bent on a quest as vital as one of life and death. It was odd, grotesque, outre, as bizarre as the setting in which it was staged.

Yet through it all like a basal note ran Dual's calm assurance of an ending ere long. I glanced at him where he sat, nibbling at a rice-cake and sipping tea. Lucile and Sheldon still ran on with their banter. Homer finished his noodles and sat staring straight down into the bowl before him. McKabe was eating in an impassive content.

Other guests had entered and found seats while my thoughts had held me. They came in by parties and alone from time to time. It was after one such arrival that Miss Foote's actions caught my attention.

From no apparent reason she shortened her chop-sticks and using their butts, tapped McKabe lightly on the hand.

"In about a minute, lamp the dame at the corner table— the one in black with the willow plume," she whispered, and turned back to her eating and Colonel Mac.

I let my eyes wander where she had directed, and I saw a short, heavy-set woman, with a heavy featured face, and dark hair; a woman of such a type in fact as one meets with among the Italians, and the people of southern France.

She sat at a small table and seemed to be giving an order

to Charlie. I brought my glance back and saw that McKabe had found an opportunity to sweep the room with his gaze.

For a moment his eyes ran over the place, now here, now there, with no apparent object, came back and dropped to a tea bowl in his hand. He nodded. "All right. I've mapped her. What about her?" he questioned softly.

Miss Foote smiled brightly and nodded, fished a portion of mushroom out of her bowl and thrust it between her lips.

"*She's Greek Annie,*" she said.

7

THE WEB'S CENTER

"GREE—"

Reich started and burst into sudden exclamation, drowned in a splintering crash of china as Lucile's bowl of chop-suey struck the floor.

The girl sprang to her feet in simulated consternation and hissed at Colonel Sheldon.

"Get him out of here quick or shut him up. He hasn't any sense."

Sheldon's hand fell on Homer's shoulder.

"Shut up, you darned fool!" he rumbled. "Dual oughter told me to gag you. A man can't tell when you're goin' to shoot off your face."

He rose and towered above the youth, blanketing his pale face and twitching features with his bulk.

Dual, too, had risen and moved to Sheldon's side. Now he spoke.

"I think we had better be going. As I predicted, our companion is not exactly himself, and had best be removed. Come."

With Colonel Mac leading Homer and we others following after, we made our way from the room, down the two flights of stairs and paused while Dual settled our score, adding the price of the broken bowl.

Sheldon's features wore a scowl, and the hand on Homer's arm gripped pretty firmly; so firmly in fact that Reich complained:

"You don't need to break my arm. You're hurting. Let go."

He twitched at the grasp of the fingers, seeking to pull away.

"You oughter be hurt," growled Sheldon. "Ain't you got no sense at all. We come here to twig that she wolf, an' when we spot her you start to squall. What sort of an addled egg do you use for a brain? For two bits I'd slap yer face off. Go put on skirts if you want to have hysterics. Oh, hell!"

He caught sight of Lucile and flushed.

"I beg your pardon, Miss. I'm a leetle bit riled."

"Don't apologize to me," Miss Foote responded. "I think I agree with the sentiments you expressed."

"I didn't think," began Reich, in a whimper of explanation.

"I reckon not," gritted Sheldon.

"I didn't see why Dual wanted me to wet nurse you this evening, at first, but I guess I'm wise now."

"Come," said Semi Dual.

We passed out of the entrance into the street and stopped. Dual went on. "You saw that woman, Mr. McKabe. She is the one who brought Miss Lawton from Salt Lake. She is in this house at present; but she will leave here. In my belief, when she does, she will return to the place where her captive is kept. You, as one conversant with this place, are the best qualified to follow, and see where she goes."

McKabe nodded.

"I'll shadow that wren, if she comes out," he declared. "But what will the rest of you do?"

"Follow you in our own fashion," Dual replied.

"But *will* she come out?" queried Lucile, with a glance of contempt at Reich.

"Did she get wise to our crowd. Tipping that bowl wasn't the best play, but it was all I could think of at the moment."

McKabe shook his head.

"You had to think quick," he replied, "an' I think you did the right thing. Smashed dishes always make a bit of a tear up in a feed store. I don't think the jane got wise. I was slanting that way, an' she was still talkin' to Charlie. She slid a gleam our direction an' went right on talkin'. You an' Sheldon cloaked this kid pretty well, an' I reckon she thought we was just a bunch of trippers, who'd tipped over our order.

"Anyway, I'll find that out. I'm goin' back in an' slip up to the next floor, an' lay doggo. There's a back stair to this place from there, an' I can get to her whichever way she goes, when she comes out. If I ain't out in a half hour let Miss Foote come up an' if I'm there I'll spot her. If I ain't I've gone out back on this dame's trail, an' you can go back to the hotel—or no, hold on—you go down in front of the telephone exchange on Washington Street an' stick around until I come. Just drift around in that section—see?"

We agreed and saw his stooped figure shuffle back into the building. Then we turned and walked slowly up the street, looking idly into the windows of shops and saying little or nothing. Dual had taken place beside Reich and Sheldon, and that left me with Lucile.

She nodded at Semi's back.

"How does he do it?" she whispered. "How did he know that we would meet that woman in that place? Why did he say we had gone too far, and then say this was the place? What told him?"

"His soul," said I.

"Don't," she laughed shortly, putting a hand on my arm. "I am like Reich. So many of Mr. Dual's remarks have a possible double meaning. Please, Mr. Glace, don't you begin to speak in riddles."

"I'm not," I protested. "I mean just that. If you don't like the word soul, call it the subjective self. You noticed Dual's expression while you walked beside him this evening. I saw you study his face. Didn't you realize that you were walking beside a man whose objective intelligence was for the time asleep?"

"Merciful Heavens!" cried Miss Foote. "Do you mean that he was making his subjective mind lead him to the place where that woman would come?"

"Precisely, Miss Foote."

"But how could his subjective mind know?"

"That I can't tell you, save that Dual says that from the subliminal self nothing is hidden."

I sensed that she trembled.

"Are you cold?" I questioned, because the fog had thickened and dripped from the awnings at times as we passed.

For a moment she made no answer, then:

"No—unless it is my subjective self that shivered. The idea you expressed made me feel oddly, that was all."

Again she laughed nervously.

"Do you know, this whole affair is having an odd effect on me, Mr. Glace. Some way I feel as if we were all moving in the midst of such a fog as lies over the city to-night and that, after all, Mr. Dual was the only one among us who saw clearly where we were going. Ah, little one?"

She paused and glanced down at a beady-eyed baby which had toddled across the pavement and thrown itself against her, clasping her limb in its pudgy arms and gazing up toward her face.

She stooped and drew its pudgy hands into hers and all the time it never winked from its stare. Back of it in the door of a shop a man sat smoking a pipe.

He looked on and smiled slightly.

Lucile shook gravely one of the little hands, as she glanced at the man.

"How'ye do, baby? Your baby?" she asked.

The Chinaman nodded.

"Yeh," he replied withdrawing the stem of his pipe and smiling in a sort of sheepish friendliness of manner.

"Him wan' be fliendly—say how do. Alla time him do alle same that way"

He broke off and spoke in Chinese to the child.

Very gravely it extended its hand again to Lucile. She laughed, shook it and fumbled in her purse for a coin, pressing it into the warm, little palm. We turned away.

"Good-by," said the man.

"Cute little tyke," Lucile spoke to me.

"Do you like babies?" I questioned.

"Love 'em," she smiled. "Being a police woman, without any home, I naturally would.

Dual, Sheldon, and Reich turned back to retrace our steps.

We fell in behind them once more, and so again we

passed the door of the shop and saw the yellow baby cuddled in its father's arms, under his long-stemmed pipe. He saw us, nodded and smiled.

We walked on, back toward the gaudy lanterns of the restaurant, behind which Greek Annie, and the police agent lurked. Again as all along, we were waiting. It seemed to me as we walked down that fog-dampened street that throughout all the days we had waited, and that our progress had been rather a species of drifting upon a slow current than one of volitional advance.

And all about us, as we drifted, other strange currents of purpose had flowed with us, crossing and twisting and weaving about us, to bring us at last to this strange street of a foreign quarter where still other currents had seized us and swept us along.

And there had been times when I had glimpsed some of those other currents. There was the something in the life of the woman beside me, which whispered of a tragedy untold: there was Reich's constant and almost insane outbursts which had threatened to throw us upon the shoals of unsuccess; there was Semi Dual's speech to me, which told me that he acted alone, because necessity forced it, and Lucile's remark that if not with us, then she would come to San Francisco alone.

Why, I asked myself, should she have felt so keen an interest in this one case, over and above others she had doubtless handled. Oh, it was a very maelstrom of cross currents, cross purposes as it seemed, on which we drifted on a fog-clouded night. Even the fog seemed in keeping with the rest of the affair, as Lucile had said.

We had nearly reached the red and gilt entrance. Dual

swung his companions up to a window, where costly trea-
sures of the Orient lay behind the glass. Lucile and I, too,
turned in beside them, and we stood gazing through the
thin barrier which shut us out.

Then I heard the girl at my elbow catch her breath in
a gasp of quickened attention. I followed her eyes as she
turned them.

A figure had come to the entrance of the restaurant and
stood for a moment, gathering up its skirts. It was short
and heavy, clad plainly in black, and above it quivered and
nodded a hat crowned with waving willow plumes.

The woman glanced up and down the street, stepped
down and turned directly past us. I swung back to the
window and gave it my attention.

I heard the click of her heels as she passed, and swung
away from my forced inspection, in time to see a stooping
figure emerge from the doorway she had left, and shuffle
after. McKabe was on the trail.

Not until he was well past did Semi give the signal
which turned us from the window and started us on the
heels of the detective along the street.

Himself, he forged slightly ahead of Sheldon and Reich,
walking with a long stride, his head thrust slightly forward,
his eyes never, as I believe, losing sight of the shuffling
figure of McKabe.

The woman went straight on. So far as her actions
showed she was without suspicion of the man who dogged
her footsteps, but at that she observed the axiom, that the
longest way round is the safest way home.

She walked slowly up Grant toward Clay, passed that
and continued to Sacramento, swung up that partially

darkened thoroughfare toward Stockton, and so brought McKabe to a pause. He was waiting as we came up.

"She's foxy," he muttered. "I don't believe she's on to my follow, but she know's somethin' could happen, so she leads us clean out of the 'town' an' ducks west along here. You can glimpse her around the corner, an' if we was to start after, she'd spot us too quick. You folks wait here for a while an' then come round in a body. Now I'm goin' ahead, I reckon."

He broke off and peered up the street in the direction Greek Annie had taken, looked back and nodded and was gone. We stood huddled together and waited, and presently we, too, were off again on the trail.

Two-thirds through the block we could see a shadowy figure trotting forward in a slouching gait. We quickened our own pace to keep it in sight. We forged up the slope at something like a dog-trot. Lucile's hand struck against mine and I took it into my fingers.

She gripped mine in turn and we ran on. I glowed as we ran. This was something more like it. At last we were on the track of something. And I smiled as I asked myself if ever there was a hunt just like this. Literally we ran in a pack to the chase.

McKabe's figure slid around the corner of Stockton, going north, and as we followed it sank back out of sight. We slowed and went forward boldly, waiting for his reappearance. Midway of the block he stepped from a doorway.

"Hurry up," he panted. "She stopped on the corner and I ducked." He set off running, darted around on to Clay going east, and ran forward, with us at his heels.

Thus it came that at the corner of Grant when we had completely circled the block, and McKabe started to cross and continue along Clay still east, Reich once more attempted interference.

"Where are you going?" he snapped, springing forward and laying a hand on McKabe's arm. "What are you going down there for. She went up this street. I saw her."

He waved a hand along Grant.

McKabe shook off his hand. "Not much you didn't," he retorted. "She went straight down Clay here, toward Kearny. You mind your own business and don't try to teach me my own tricks."

"I'm not trying to teach you a thing," Reich persisted. "I tell you the woman went the other way. You just didn't happen to see her. Come on. Don't stand here talking about it or she'll slip away."

"That's right, too," said McKabe. "Mr. Sheldon, call off your cub here, he's foggin' the game."

"Go ahead, McKabe," advised Sheldon, stepping up beside Homer. "Cut it out, son, can't you?"

But Reich appeared to have thrown discretion to the winds. "Oh, you fools, you fools," he stormed wildly. "Had the game in your hands and lost it. All right, go your own way if you want to. I'm done. I quit. From now on I go it alone."

Before Sheldon could lift a hand he had turned and ran along Grant in the direction he alleged Greek Annie had taken.

For one instant the colonel stood as if frozen to the pavement, then with a wordless bellow, turned and bolted after the flying figure, at a most surprising pace for one of his age.

Not until then did Semi Dual speak, and his words were
but a direction.

"Go on now, Mr. McKabe."

McKabe shook his head.

"If we can," he suggested. "Anyway, she went down this
way. Let's try to follow, I reckon she hit through the square,
here. Well, come on."

We set off down the street, and midway of the square the
buildings on our left fell away and showed the dark blot of
a shrub and bush grown little park, checkered by light and
shadow from the street lights.

"Portsmouth Square," said McKabe, turning across the
pavement in its direction. "I've a hunch she struck through
here, because I had her in plain sight till that feller butted
in, an' when I turned around she was gone. She either cut
across the square or along this street here." He indicated a
narrow thoroughfare which bounded the parking on the
west.

"Now I tell you," he went on. "You, Mr. Dual, go along
this street straight through to the next one. Miss Foote, you
take Glace and take a stroll through the square, an' I'll run
down to the foot of the street and go around to the upper
corner an' meet Dual. That's the best I can think of. We'll
all meet at that place. All right."

He started off down the street, and Dual, without
comment, began to walk along the alleylike course of the
street to the west. Lucile and I plunged into the shadows
of the little park and threaded its paths, slowly scanning
every bench and seat as we went.

It was growing late, and the fog had evidently driven

the loungers to cover. We found the place deserted as we walked through its length and breadth.

We passed the spot where bowered in trees stands the monument to Stevenson, with its little bronze ship in full sail. Lucile waved her hand toward it. "There," said she, "was another man, in many ways like your friend Semi Dual, I think."

We moved up the path from the monument toward the northwest corner of the square.

"Do you think she suspected?" I asked.

Lucile shook her head. "I hardly think so. Why should she? We are here pretty close on her heels. I don't think she'd expect us this soon. They tried to steer us off to Seattle in Salt Lake, as you saw.

"That Greek, Paulos, is her husband, and he may have wired her about us, probably did; but as we left Salt Lake on the Portland and Seattle train, and Mr. Dual bought tickets straight through and changed them at Ogden, as you know, he probably thinks that we went there, unless he had a spy at Ogden, and I didn't notice any.

"No. I believe she thinks herself safe yet, but she is going home by a roundabout way as a matter of principle. These people, like foxes, rarely run straight to cover. They double."

"If only she'd double back this way," I remarked in rather rueful tones. "I wonder if Sheldon caught up with Reich?"

"From the rate at which he started he should have," Miss Foote rejoined.

We could see Dual's figure standing at the corner, from where we were, and hastened forward to join him. Yet, before we had recovered the ground, McKabe shuffled up, spoke to Semi, and went on west along the street.

A moment later we came up, and I addressed Dual.

"Not a trace, Semi."

He smiled slightly.

"Probably not," he returned. "McKabe just followed her off. She passed on the other side a moment ago, and, just after, our guide came along. We had better follow."

"Then she did double back!" I exclaimed.

Lucile nodded.

"Kismet," she said. "It is fate. To call it luck would be an insult to the goddess of chance. Now I feel sure we will win out yet. She's probably running to cover right now."

We moved up the street in the wake of McKabe, whom we could see at times, dodging back and forth through the scattered pedestrians on the pavement.

Dual, still silent and introspective, walked beside us as we mounted the hill toward the street we had first traversed this evening.

Greek Annie, wherever her destination might lie, had led us around several city squares and then turned and back-tracked toward her objective point.

I agreed with Miss Foote that it seemed as though her fate must have driven her back into our hands after Reich's interruption had caused us to lose her.

At the same time I prayed that that fate might hold until McKabe should be able to locate the point of her ultimate disappearance.

Glancing ahead, I realized that the detective was no longer in sight. The fact brought me out of my mental straying, into active question. Where, I wondered, had he gone now?

I glanced at Semi, and found him still moving forward

without hesitation, and decided that the best thing I could do was to follow his lead. At the same time I called Miss Foote's attention to McKabe's disappearance.

"Can you see McKabe?" I asked.

She shook her head.

"No. I did a minute ago, but he seems to have turned in somewhere. Let's see, where are we? Oh, yes, we're pretty close to the native theater now."

Hardly had she spoken when we saw our missing companion shuffling toward us. He came up and met us and began speaking at once.

"She went into the theater here. I followed her clear to the steps and saw her go inside; then I went up and bought tickets. Come on."

He led us to a wide front and up some steps to the entrance. A slant-eyed Chinese took our tickets, and we passed into the barnlike structure where the native Thespians portray the Oriental form of drama, the play running on in an unbroken stretch from night to night, at times for weeks before the denouement is reached.

Before us as we came in stretched a sea of heads, occupying the pit of the house. A low balcony roofed the rear portion of the auditorium and was plainly reached by a stairs from one side of the entrance.

Everything was in a half light from the stage illumination, but even so I could see that there was little attempt at ornamentation in the hall. Evidently with these people gathered before us the play was the thing of interest.

And the play was in progress on a stage which reached across the major portion of the end of the room. To the Occidental it would have lacked in setting. There was a surprising lack of scenery or stage properties about it. Things appeared to me to be indicated rather than portrayed in the presentation.

There appeared to be a sort of symbolism about it, rather than any representation of actual every-day affairs. At the same time the costumes were gaudy and rich at one and the same time, and made a scintillating bit of color and life upon which the audience gazed in rapt attention.

They took their pleasure silently, but with seemingly sincere relish.

On one side a set of wooden steps led up from a side passage running back along the seats of the pit, and reached the level of the stage through a wooden door in the foot of a wall between the auditorium and that portion of the house usually designated "behind" by actors and stage johnnies.

All this I saw as my eyes roved about the place searching for a glimpse of a heavy-set figure and a feather-crowned hat. I didn't see it, however, and I saw by their faces that McKabe and Lucile had met with a similar lack of success.

We had taken places at the back of the audience, not sitting down, but standing behind the last row of seats, from which point we could sweep all before us.

"Wait a minute," McKabe counseled and turned away up the balcony stairs. In a moment he was back with a disappointed face.

"She ain't up there either, so far as I can see," he announced.

"You're sure she came in here?" I suggested.

"Sure," he answered shortly. "Wait a bit. It's just a chance, and yet it might be."

He knit his brows and in a moment began again to speak.

"About a month ago we raided this joint on suspicion. I was tellin' you tonight, if you remember, that there was a lot of underground runways under this part of town. Well, when we come in here we found the start of one all right. It goes down from back there on the stage, and just where it goes after that I don't know, for I didn't see it; but the boys was tellin' me it didn't seem to end nowhere.

"Anyway, they said there was a lot of little rooms down there and a lot of passages leadin' by and to 'em. Now, supposin' this here dame came in here an' ducked straight back onto the stage an' down there. Maybe the girl might be stowed away in a place like that. It would be like them and by the lord Harry I believe that's the answer."

"Mr. McKabe," said Dual, "I am inclined to believe that you are right."

"Think so?" McKabe made eager query. "Well, then, see here—here's what we'll do: You folks stay here an' I'll go out an' get a bunch of the boys an' come back here, an' we'll pull off another raid. If she's down there an' we have luck, we'll get her. I won't be long."

"Oh, go to the devil! I haven't any ticket, but I'm coming in. Get out of the way."

The sound of a protesting singsong was followed by an involuntary exclamation, and a figure came through the entrance with a rush.

Without pausing, it turned and ran along back of the seats to the side passage which led forward, turned again and dashed down this, mounted the steps and dragged open the door in the wall, at the end of the stage, sprang through, and pulled the door shut.

It happened quickly—so quickly that it left barely more than a fleeting impression, and that of a frantic, an almost desperate haste. Yet because of our position at the rear, the man had been forced to dash past us as he ran; and, in the instant of his passage, we had looked into a white, open-lipped, drawn and distorted face.

Now, as we turned and faced one another, there was one thought in the minds of each. Lucile was the first to voice it.

Her hand went out and gripped the arm of Dual, and her words were a sibilant whisper of something like dismay.

"Reich! Did you see him? That was Reich!"

8

THE UNDERGROUND WEB

DUAL NODDED.

"Yes, it was Reich," said he.

"You bet it was Reich," snapped McKabe. "Well, that settles the thing. You saw where he went? He's caught on to something. I didn't think he had it in him, but he must have spotted this Annie some way, and he ain't wise to the chance he's taking. We've got to follow, and we've got to do it quick or they'll get him. Now, see here—"

But he was interrupted. Breaking into his words there came again the sound of an altercation from the street-front, a voice raised in protest and the sound of a snarling bellow, like that of an animal suddenly brought to bay. Out of it broke words, short, panting, as of one impatient of restraint.

"Let go of me, you yellow fool. Let go, I tell you! Get out of the way. Oh, for the Lord's sake, I'm in a hurry!"

Followed then a scuffle, a shrill outcry and another, and a huddled jumble of figures pushed its way inward to resolve into that of Colonel McDonahue Sheldon, striding doggedly forward between two of the theater's attachés, who clung frantically to his clothing and did their very best to trip him up.

"Let go!" he bellowed. "Let go, you darned shirt-washing runts. Git out from under my feet!"

McKabe sprang forward and so did I.

"Sheldon!" I cried.

With the same sort of motion a dog uses in shaking itself free of water, Sheldon shed his clinging human burs, who sprawled grotesquely on the boards of the floor.

"Glace," he exclaimed loudly. "Say, did you see him? He come in here. I seen him. The danged fool's been runnin' around like he was bughouse, an' I thought he'd give me the slip. Then I seen him come up these steps an' I follered. Dual told me to stick to him, an' I done it: but it's been one sweet job."

"He came in here. We were just going after him when you came," I told him.

"You all here?" he queried, and drew his sleeve across a sweat-dampened brow.

The two Chinamen who had vainly sought to hold him had risen, and stood half minded to resume the attack. McKabe addressed them in hurried singsong, and they drew back scowling. The detective turned to us and rushed into advice and direction:

"There ain't no time to go get a squad now. If we're going to save a killin' we've got to move. That fool's gone down there alone, from the looks. Miss Foote, you go outside. Take care you ain't followed, too. Grab the first harness man you see an' tell him about this. Tell him Mac said to get a bunch an' come back here, an' take the first door under the stairs to the actors' rooms. Now hurry. The rest of us'll try to follow Reich an' see where he's gone, an' pull him out fore it's too late. Come on, the rest of you."

He set off at a run toward the side passage.

Lucile darted out of the front door, and Dual, Sheldon, and I followed McKabe. He led us straight down the passage at the side of the house to the stairs at the end, leaped up them and wrenched open the door. In a crowding rush the rest of us followed, and I closed the door behind me. We stood in a space to one end of the stage, with its occupants plainly visible through some cheaply painted wings.

Before us stretched a narrow passage, midway of which a wooden stairway ran upward. McKabe darted straight for this.

But instead of mounting he ran around it to a small door half hidden in shadows, set into what appeared to be a closet built in under the slant of the stairs. A spring-lock held it shut. McKabe twisted back the latch and dragged it open. The interior yawned empty of anything save shadows, as it seemed.

The detective drew a pocket-flash and swept it inside, along the walls, and over the floor. There at our feet the light showed a metal ring and a square of boards, which, unlike the rest of the floor, were free from dust.

"Here we are," he exclaimed, and stooped down, grasping the ring and dragging up the trap-door to expose a yawning hole like the mouth of a mine-shaft, and the dimly lighted upper rungs of what appeared to be a vertical ladder.

"Come on," he directed shortly.

Letting the trap-door fall back on its hinges out of the way, he lowered himself upon the ladder and began to descend. Dual went second and Sheldon third, and I came last.

I had to admire the nerve of the little plain-clothes man as I crept down the ladder. Here he was advancing into an admittedly unknown region of tangled passages and alleys dug beneath the city as calmly as he might have walked its streets. He was a cool little pickle all right, was McKabe.

I reached bottom in a moment or two and joined the others.

It was dark down there as the tomb, the only light the brilliant point of McKabe's flash as he threw it over the floor and walls. And it was foul, indescribably foul, with an odor of decomposition, and a smell of sewers and rotting life. I felt my feet sink into a spongy surface which I sensed was soggy earth, sour from lack of sunlight. The beam of the searchlight showed walls shining damply with moisture and a ceiling stained with the damp, from which dropped down the bulb of an electric lamp.

"There's a light," said McKabe's voice, "but blessed if I know where the switch is. Probably up-stairs."

He swept the light to the ground at our feet and showed it black, and blotched with patches and streaks of white.

"When they were in here last month the boys made 'em throw lime around," the detective continued. "Thought maybe it would sweeten the smell. If it did, I don't quite sense it. Hello! Look here!"

He dropped the light close to the floor, and bending forward we saw the outline of feet pressed into the wet earth of the passage. Not only that, but they were the marks of shod feet, and, judging from their size, those of a man.

"Reich's, for a guess," declared McKabe. "Where's his

next one? Oh, here. Good ways off. He was still runnin'. Well, we got to chance it. We'll follow these tracks. Come on."

We started onward. A second light sprang up, and I realized that Dual had drawn a pocket-torch also, and was advancing side by side with McKabe.

So we went forward down the passage, following the tracks.

The walls seemed to me to be of brick, covered with a thin coating of whitewash, now smeared and streaked and stained with the underground seepage. There was no sound save our stifled breathing and the drip, drip of water from the roof.

The ground grew more soggy, even muddy at times, beneath our feet. The wavering points of light from the flashes showed side passages leading off from the one we followed on either hand at every conceivable degree and angle.

Save for the line of footprints we would have been utterly confused as to direction, for so far as I could see there was no way to distinguish one tunnel from another. One not acquainted with the anglings and turnings of that place would have been hopelessly lost inside of five minutes.

It was a labyrinth, a maze, a literal web in the bowels of the hill.

Dual and McKabe paused and brought us to a halt. The passage angled now and split into three new tunnels, more narrow and not quite so high, and close by the right-hand passage our companions were bending above some new object of interest. Pressing forward we saw that it was another print, smaller and but faintly pressed into the earth, save at the back where the heel had cut and torn the surface of the floor.

"I guess Annie must have made that," said McKabe quickly. "It's fresh if you notice. She turned here an' threw her weight on this foot as she went around. It's a right shoe, you can see. Well, they're ahead of us all right. Reich must have spotted this mark for he's followed—that is, if he made these other tracks, which I think he did."

"But, great cats!" rumbled Sheldon. "How could he see anything a-tall in this place? How'd he follow her this far?"

"Speak softly, colonel," warned Semi Dual. "Mr. Reich or some man did follow. We must go on."

Just beyond the turning of the right-hand passage was a door set into the wall. McKabe's light fell upon its boards and he paused to try it. It swung open and showed a tiny room not bigger than a closet, which held a filthy cot covered by a moldy blanket, on which lay a bamboo pipe. After a glance McKabe swung the door shut, and we went on.

I heard Sheldon breathing at my elbow, like one seeking to suppress his feelings. Then he broke into whispers as we walked.

"My Lord, Glace, do you reckon anybody lives down in this here cellar? Why, what would be the use of livin' at all in a place like this? A man might as well be buried alive."

"Yet some of them do," I replied.

"My Lord!" he repeated softly, and lapsed silent, padding along at my side.

Presently he spoke again.

"An' McKabe thinks they've brung Lilly down here. Poor leetle gal."

We went on. More doors appeared in the wall, loosely built barriers before the cell-like cubicles they closed. But McKabe gave them no further attention.

Bent forward like a hound straining on a leash he followed the footprints in the damp earth as they led us on through the branching alleys. Abruptly the roof of the passage we followed came down till we stooped as we walked, and ended at a little arch like the door of a kennel.

We went to our knees before it, and found the marks of other knees before us. Crawling on hands and knees we advanced. As we passed, the spotlights of the flashes showed the chipped surface of water-soaked concrete. Plainly we were passing through the foundation of some building to gain the other side.

Beyond it the passage widened and lifted again, and we rose once more to our feet. To each hand and ahead the tunnels continued. Dual's light picked up the steps turning to the left. The floor sloped sharply and led us downhill. We ran forward now and came to a blind end, beyond which there was nothing but solid earth.

I heard McKabe exclaim softly. He swung around and began searching the floor more closely. The footsteps led quite to the end wall and stopped, turned back and stopped again in front of a little door not over three feet high.

"Huh!" growled McKabe and fell upon it.

It swung outward, and without hesitation he ducked through, with his light swinging before him.

"Come on," he called deeply, and waited while we followed.

We stood in a little room, floored with rotting boards. On one side a steep wooden stairway ran up, and beyond us was yet another door. The detective nodded to the stairs.

"One way out," he observed dryly; "but Reich seems to have gone straight on."

He dropped his light upon a bit of damp lime lying beside the opposite door, crossed the room and pushed the door before him.

We emerged into a passage so low that we walked with a stoop. It was lined on either side by little doors not over two feet high. They were just about large enough to admit a human body, creeping.

It seemed almost inconceivable that they had been designed as even a temporary abode for human beings.

We crept along it, still led by the prints of shod feet, sometimes now of a man, sometimes of a woman, sometimes of both.

I heard McKabe whispering to Dual, and pricked my ears to listen.

"I've an idea that if they brought the girl in here they'd stick her into one of these cribs," declared the detective. "It would be just about impossible for any one not wise to the place to get this far in. If it wasn't for the trail we've had we couldn't have done it in a thousand years.

"What gets me is how the fellow who made it ever done it unless he followed the marks of the woman and blotted them with his own. At that he must have had a light.

"Well, all I can say is, he had his nerve. I'd hate like sin to try it alone myself. They could grab a man an' croak him like a rat down here, an' nobody'd ever know. See here. He was walkin' along here. He'd quit runnin'. We'd better go slow."

His whisper died away and the silence came back.

The passage turned at right angles and ran both ways. We crept to the end and the trail led down-hill. On the instant the lights in the hands of McKabe and Semi died.

I glanced forward and found the cause.

There before us, as we crouched under the low, pressing roof, for the first time in all our searching, was light. It shot from one of the kennellike doors and streamed across the tunnel, striking in an oblong blot on the opposite wall.

It was faint, like the glow of a candle, yet in the gloom of the passage it struck out distinctly, and as we watched it wavered and paled and brightened as though from a flickering flame.

We crouched and listened with every nerve drawn tense. As we turned toward the light, we had seen that the footsteps we had followed ran directly toward it.

Whether they passed the light beam or stopped we did not know, but I think we all asked ourselves what had happened in or in front of that lighted room.

Had we come too late after all?

Had the man Reich rushed blindly to his death in this underground burrow?

Had some one sprung upon him and sunk a knife into his body?

Was he even now perhaps lying there in the shadows beyond the wall of light?

Yet there was nothing to answer. No sound filled the low walls save our own beating hearts and slow breathing. After a moment of painful waiting Dual began to move forward. McKabe joined him, and Sheldon and I followed.

So we came to the light and bent down to peer inside of the little door.

It was merely a cell, with a board cot and a box on which stood a little glass lamp with a flaming wick. McKabe thrust in his head and shoulders and crawled through, and on the instant he spoke.

"Come on in here, quick."

There was suppressed excitement in his tone, and as quickly as the space would permit we obeyed. The room heightened beyond the door to an ordinary height, and we rose to find McKabe standing beside the cot holding a crumpled woman's kimono in his hands. He turned with this to Sheldon, shaking it out before him.

"Do you know it?" he asked.

Colonel Mac seized it, scanned it for a moment, and nodded slowly.

"It's hers—Lilly's," he made answer. "She's been here. They brought her down here. I've seen her wear that there wrapper."

He paused, and, glancing at him, I saw a tear roll slowly down his cheek. Suddenly he bunched the kimomo and hurled it to the floor, lifted his hands, and broke into hoarse vituperation.

"They've got her, damn 'em, got her! They had her in this room, an' now they got Reich. But I'll get 'em—so help me God I'll get 'em if I have to follow to hell!"

He dropped to his knees and flung himself out to the passage.

"Quickly," said Semi Dual, and bent to follow. His shoulders filled the door, and I heard him speak sharply.

"Sheldon. Wait. Don't try to run in the dark."

McKabe and I joined the others, and we bent to examine the floor. I heard Sheldon breathing as one under the grip of an overmastering emotion.

McKabe's flash showed the footprints of a man and what seemed like two women running off along the passage beyond the beam of light from the door. We rose and ran in the direction they pointed.

Again we came to a blind end and a low arch in a foundation wall. Without a word we crawled through and rose and ran on up a slanting floor which seemed to lead back the way we had come.

It came over me now that we must be getting close. It seemed that they must have left the room behind us in a hurry, not to have put out the light. That would mean that perhaps they had even heard our advance and slipped out just before we turned the last corner beyond the room.

Yet why, I asked, should Reich have gone along as he seemed to have done, and the thought came that perhaps he had compelled Greek Annie to lead him out some shorter way than the back track would have been.

We came to yet another lighted room, far larger than any of the others we had seen. As we ran past I caught a glimpse of its interior through the half-opened door.

It was furnished, and well furnished at that. It looked like a comfortable apartment. I wondered at it and ran on.

Another angle led us off at a slant, continued for perhaps fifty feet, and divided again.

McKabe bent to follow the prints with his light, and I heard him grunt and speak quickly to Dual.

"One of the women went up here," he said, pointing with his torch, "and the man turned off up this way." He dropped the light on the larger tracks which led into the other passage.

Sheldon swore.

"They're wise to us, an' they're tryin' to fool us," he growled, and quite without warning cried out loudly:

"Lilly! Oh, Lilly! It's Colonel Mac, Honey! Leetle gal!"

His voice woke the echoes of the place and rang weirdly through the passage.

McKabe straightened and whirled upon him.

"Quit it!" he rasped, and stiffened into surprised attention.

Muffled, choked, distorted, yet clearly perceptible to our ears, a woman's voice had screamed.

Its shrill appeal rang thin and eery in the darkness, thrilled us once and died in a gurgle, and it seemed to me that there came the sounds of a scuffle somewhere beyond us.

McKabe leaped into the passage marked by the larger track and ran forward.

We followed with what speed we could gather in the dark.

"Lilly!" cried Sheldon again as we ran. "Lilly! Reich! We're comin'! Wait!"

Quite abruptly a voice spoke out of the gloom before us.

"That you, Sheldon?"

"Thank God!" gasped the colonel, even before he answered. "Sure, Homer! Where are you, you darned lucky fool?"

"Here," answered Reich. "Stop where you are. I can see your light."

We paused and waited. Dual's and McKabe's flashes

came up and pointed in the direction of the voice. They met and focused beyond us in a blot like the spot of a theater's light, and into their beam stepped the figure of Reich, half supporting a woman who leaned on his arm.

"Lilly! Thank God!" whispered Sheldon hoarsely at my elbow.

It was a gripping tableau. The slender, tawny youth, his hat gone, his fair hair awry, his pale face, with wide eyes blinking in the brilliant light, and the girl, brown-haired, sweet-faced yet haggard, clinging to him for support and protection.

I felt my own heart swell and throb with emotion and thanksgiving as I gazed upon them in that night-soaked passage where we stood.

Homer advanced and joined us while the light played upon him.

"Why didn't you call sooner?" he questioned. "We've been running away for the last fifteen minutes, and then Annie gave us the slip back there."

"Never mind. We've met up now," said Sheldon. "Oh, Lilly girl, I'm sure glad to see you. We all been most crazy about you, honey. How air ye, anyway?"

"All right," murmured the girl. "Oh, it was good of you to come to hunt me. Homer has told me all about it. I'm so glad."

McKabe cut in.

"Just how did you get onto this dump?" he asked.

Reich grinned as the detective turned the light once more on his face.

"Don't feel sore. We ain't out yet, McKabe," he replied. "My getting in here was just fool luck after all. After I left you to-night I followed the woman I thought was Annie, and pretty soon I found out I'd been wrong and you were right.

"Sheldon had come up, and when I was sure I'd followed the wrong woman I was just about dippy. I couldn't think what to do, so I ran back to where I'd left you, but you were gone. Then I began to run around anywhere I could think of to see if I could find her, and some way I lost Sheldon, too, in the crowds.

"Then I met a guide, and asked him if he knew the woman; but he didn't, and I told him part of my trouble. It was that fellow told me about this theater being over a lot of underground places, and he said maybe Annie would hit for here. I thought it was a chance, so I came down, and after a bit I saw her go in. Then I knew where she was, and I began to hunt for you folks again, but I must have missed you.

"When I was sure I could not find you and was just about desperate, I decided to chance it alone. I ran into the theater and came down here and followed some footsteps and came to a room where Annie had Lilly shut up, and—"

"Just a minute," McKabe interrupted. "How did you follow those footsteps?"

"With a light, of course," returned Reich. "I had a pocket-light like what you fellows use, but I dropped it back there somewhere when Annie broke away. Well, Annie was in a little room with Lilly, and I made her promise to take us out of here quick. I told you I had a gun, and we were getting along all right when all of a sudden she ducked into a passage back there and knocked my light out of my hand as she did it. Then I heard you people behind us, and we ran up here, and then you yelled. Lilly screamed, and I was so surprised I grabbed her and dragged her into a side passage up there, and that's about all. Let's get out."

"Good boy!" exclaimed Sheldon. "I reckon this has got a dime novel skinned to death. Where'd that she-wolf go to anyway?"

"I don't know," said Reich. "There's about a million of these and she ran off in the dark. But I guess we can follow her tracks back with your lights."

"Listen!" Dual commanded.

We obeyed on the instant, and it seemed that somewhere feet were running. Their echo came in dull, thudding falls through the darkness, not one but many, as of a body of people trotting forward together somewhere within the alleys which honeycombed the hill.

"Back," hissed McKabe. "Beat it. Stick together."

"Stand where you are," said Dual.

On the word light filled the blackness.

Overhead, before and beyond us, the swinging incandescents grew luminous and glowed at the bidding of a hand unseen. All the tunnel's length grew visible in the glare, and into its sweep, springing out of the mouth of a passage, came a woman's form.

It was still clad in black, but its hat was gone, and the tumbled hair on its head hung in tendrils and strands above a face distorted by every savage emotion. She leaped out and turned toward us, and at her back ran a pack of yellow wolves.

My heart bounded and seemed to stop as I gazed upon them racing to the attack. The light struck upon their yellow faces, their glaring eyes, and snarling lips.

Some of them ran in flapping garments, some of them half naked as they had sprung up from sleep. Their naked torsos glistened under the lamps as they strained forward behind their leader.

Light was flashing from the gleaming blades of knives clutched fast in bony fingers and shone on yellow teeth in half opened animal mouths. They boiled out of the mouth of the passage like a yellow wave, and turned down upon us where we stood.

Greek Annie pointed to us. Her voice rose in a scream.

"Kill them. They're stealing the girl. Slay them and spare not. Kill! Kill!"

McKabe sprang past me, drawing his police weapon. I reached for my own. My glance fell on Sheldon at the moment.

The old fighter had lost his hat somewhere in the tunnels, and his hair glowed grizzled in the light of the incandescent over his head. Beneath it his face was set into a snarl of a creature at bay; his lips drawn back, his eyes staring.

He had drawn his revolver and was swinging it loosely in his hand in the manner of the gunman of old, ready to lift it and fire swiftly from the hip. I thought with a sense of satisfaction that he would give a good account of himself, and that before the commands of the woman heading the yellow pack could be fulfilled, some of her wolves would die. I even resolved somewhat grimly that I would add to the score myself.

I looked for Reich. He stood somewhat to the rear of the others, close beside Lilly Lawton, who had sunk down in a huddled heap and hidden her face in her arms.

Dual, too. I noticed had drawn out an automatic and was holding it ready.

So much I thought in an instant of time, while Greek Annie led her pack into the tunnel and turned toward us, still leading the charge.

One thinks fast at such times, and I glanced back to find that some twenty feet still separated us from the yellow horde. In that moment I lifted my weapon, my finger went to the trigger, and then—

"Stop!"

The word boomed out in irresistible command, with a subtle power such as only Dual could have given to it at such a time. For it was calm, positive, arresting in its intonation. Under its sudden, whiplike demand the onrushing mob faltered and wavered, and lost headway.

For the first time, perhaps, they sensed that we were armed and would fight, and that some one beside ourselves would die; and perhaps it was all in the power of that word and the way it was uttered which reached their coolie brains and demanded obedience to one who spoke like that.

They paused and huddled in a restless, ragged front before us, with the dark, wild figure of Greek Annie between us and them.

And it was then that McKabe took action. I have said he was a nervy little man, and he proved it then. Even as her followers checked their advance he sprang forward, seized the woman by an arm, and dragged her back to our sides.

"Call off your dogs!" he gritted hoarsely. "Call 'em off or, so help me, I'll drop you. You ain't a woman, you're a she-wolf, an' I got you. If they rush us, I'll drill you if it's the last thing I do. Call 'em off!"

"No!" she hissed at him shrilly. "No!"

Dual spoke again.

His voice rang out against the crowding figures like that of a master to slaves. Not that I understood one word that he said. It was the intonation, the subtle meaning which lay in accent and gesture.

He advanced slightly as he spoke until he stood almost midway between us and them. His figure towered like something majestic, and his words poured forth upon them in a steady stream of sibilant, almost musical rhythm, which rose and fell and ran on and on in variant gradations of sound.

And as he spoke, it came upon me that this man I had known for so long was speaking to them in their own language; addressing them as a ruler of their country, as a mandarin of highest caste might have hurled contempt and contumely upon them.

For they cowered away before the things he said. Like culprits before an implacable judge they shuffled and cast down their eyes, and drew back as though each might be seeking to escape too prominent observation.

Dual raised his arms and swept them forward as though driving them before him, and they retreated. He lifted one arm and pointed and they fell back. And even as he ceased, came the shrilling of whistles from behind, and I knew the police had arrived.

They came storming around the angle where we had turned at Lilly's cry and charged down upon us. Their blue coats and glinting brass filled the passage from side to side. With them ran Lucile. I gave them one glance, and turned my eyes back to Dual and beyond him.

The passage was clearing. Like rats into their holes the yellow men of this underground world were leaping and darting in an effort at escape. Not one stood his ground against this menace of the force they feared and yet defied.

Without a word or a cry, or a sound save the pad of their feet, they turned in frantic flight, and left Greek Annie still in the hands of the grinning McKabe.

Upon her, Reich advanced with a scowl and a threatening hand.

Staring into her face he spoke swiftly some words I did not understand.

Without any apparent reason Greek Annie laughed in his face.

Lucile had bent and lifted Lilly Lawton to her feet. McKabe snapped a pair of handcuffs on Annie's wrists and surrendered her to two of the policemen. We turned back along the underground tunnels to the room where the stairway ran up, mounted it, and came out in the back room of the squalid shop.

No one sought to bar our passage, and our sudden advent seemed to bring consternation to the proprietor of the place. He stood silent and staring while we made our way through to the street.

McKabe glanced up and down the thoroughfare and broke into a chuckle.

"Washington," he said. "Well, that's some tunnel. We came under one street and ran around in the half of a circle. Come on and we'll close this business up."

9

RETRIBUTION

THE HALL OF Justice stands at the corner of Washington and Kearney. A great gray sandstone oblong, its massive walls and deep-set windows give it an appearance as immovable, as mighty, as unswayed and unswayable by any transient condition as the justice it was built to house, and as somber as the penalty of sin dealt out within its walls.

Here McKabe led us when once the underground passage had given us back to the upper air, and here was played out the last chapter in the tangled web of events which had led us to its doors.

He straightened as we passed beneath its portals, and the stoop went out of his shoulders until he seemed to have gained a couple of inches in height.

At the same time the shuffle fell from his feet, and he walked with a jaunty step. He scarcely seemed like the same man who had led us on our strange adventure, and he saw I noticed the change and grinned.

"Whew!" he whistled. "It's good to get rid of the stoop and the shuffle, Glace, and stand up straight again. Exit the Chinatown guide. It's a good part, but tiring sometimes."

He broke off and spoke to a man coming down the hall.

"Captain Connel still here?"

"I think so," replied the other and saluted. "Shall I see?"

"If you will," said McKabe. "Tell him Mac's here. He'll understand."

We stood in a group and waited while the man retraced his steps down the hall and rapped on the door of a room. In a moment he stuck his head through the doorway, stood so for a moment, and withdrew it to beckon us to advance.

We went down the corridor and turned through the door which the officer held open.

Directly before us sat a heavy-set, florid man, well past the middle-age mark, of an almost military erectness and set of shoulders. He swept his eyes over the party and nodded at McKabe.

"Back so soon, Mac?" he questioned. "What luck?"

"The best captain. We found the girl and we've got the woman who trapped her." He waved a hand at Annie. "The rest are the friends of Miss Lawton," he continued and introduced us in turn.

Captain of Detectives Connel made his acknowledgments shortly and turned to Dual.

"I understand that you have conducted this case until this evening, according to Miss Foote," he remarked. "I suppose you wish to make a formal charge against the woman?"

"Of course," replied Semi. "But before we proceed would it be too great a trouble to ask you to ascertain if a message addressed to me in care of the department has been received here to-day?"

"Addressed how?" asked Connel.

"To Semi Dual."

The captain nodded and picked up a phone at his elbow; spoke briefly and turned back to Dual.

"They've got it," he announced. "They'll send it up at once."

Dual bowed and sank into a chair.

"I desire to see it before making my complaint," he advised.

Reich had found a seat beside Lilly. Sheldon and Lucile and I sat together. Annie sat alone, rigidly upright and defiant. McKabe was perched on the arm of a chair.

"Good work, Mac," the captain addressed him.

"More likely to have been a funeral too but for Mr. Dual here," returned McKabe. "This dame," he glanced at Annie, "tried to have a bunch of China boys rush us."

Captain Connel's eyes narrowed.

"So? Went as far as that did you?" he queried. "Well, now you can travel a different road farther."

"I'll have company maybe," she sniffed.

A rap came on the door and a patrolman entered with an official, yellow envelope in his hand, Connel waved him with it to Dual. Semi took it and ripping it open scanned it once, smiled faintly as in satisfaction and placed it in his pocket.

"And now, captain. I want you to listen to Miss Lawton's story," he remarked.

Connel nodded and Semi spoke to Lilly.

"Tell us all about it, my child," he directed.

The girl shivered, straightened herself slightly and began:

"I guess you all know about the message telling me Homer here was hurt and not expected to live. Colonel Mac would tell you that of course, I suppose."

Her eyes ran among us and Sheldon nodded.

"I told 'em," he said.

"Well, then," Miss Lawton continued. "When I got to Salt Lake a little dark-complexioned man met me. He looked something like an Italian, and he came up and asked me if I was Miss Lawton, and I said I was, and he said he was Dr. Morehouse. Then he told me Homer was dead."

She paused and put out a hand to lay it upon Reich's.

"It was an awful shock, and I began to cry. He told me to try not to, and asked me where I was going to stop. I told him, I'd see Homer, anyway, and then go back home, and he said he would fix it for me to see the body at an undertaker's, and that in the mean time he would take me to the house of a friend of his and ask the lady there to let me lie down till I felt better."

She sobbed; then went on:

"Well, he did and he took me to what looked like a sort of cheap hotel and took me in, and told a woman there about me, and asked her to let me lie down. She took me to a room and told me to lie down on a bed, and the doctor said he'd give me something to settle my nerves, and he fixed something and made me drink it.

"I guess I must have gone to sleep, because the next thing I knew it was dark, and I got up and I felt sick and dizzy, and when I tried to go out of the room the door was locked. I called and pounded on the door, and after a time, a heavy set, dark man came and threatened me if I didn't keep quiet. I was dreadfully scared and I didn't know what to do, so I went back to the bed and sat down and tried to think.

"Then after a bit this woman here," she pointed to

Annie, "came and unlocked the door. She was dressed like a servant and brought me some supper. I asked her what they meant to do with me, and she told me that I had been captured by the white-slave people, and that they'd sell me after a bit. I offered her money to get me out and help me escape, and she just laughed and said it was as much as her life was worth, and went away.

"I didn't sleep that night. I couldn't. I cried and I thought and I prayed, and I tried to get out of the window, but it was nailed down and I was afraid they'd hear me if I tried to break it open. Then the next day this woman came back and told me that she'd been thinking and that she was sorry for me and that she'd try to help me get away, and I gave her what money I had and told her I knew Colonel Sheldon would give her more if we got away. I thought that would surely make her help me, if she thought she'd get more out of it later. She said all right, and that I should keep quiet and she'd watch for a chance.

"Then one morning she came in and said that the man and woman had gone out for an hour, and now was our chance. So we got out of the house and ran through the block and got on an electric train and went to Ogden, and went to a lodging-house close to the depot. I wanted her to let me send a message from there, but she said no, that it was too close, and that when they missed us they'd have their agents watch the telegraph office and that we must come here, because they'd think first that we'd started back to Goldfield, and wouldn't think of our coming here till later. And that afternoon we took a train and came here, and they took me up where you found me, and down to that underground room, and shut me in and took my clothes away, all but a kimono.

"Then, to-night, she came to me just a little while before Homer came and told me that a Chinaman was going to buy me, maybe, and made me dress, and then Homer came running up and spoke to her and made her lead us away from there, and we went along a lot of passages, and finally she broke away from Homer and ran off, and he dropped his light, and we went on, and then I heard Colonel Sheldon call to me, and I screamed.

"Homer didn't think I'd heard anything, and he told me to be still and pulled me into another passage, and then we saw your lights and heard you call again, and Homer spoke to you, and you know the rest. But you can't know what I suffered—what I felt—what I feared—or how I resolved to find some way—to die."

She broke off, her voice choked with an emotion beyond words to express.

Lucile moved to her side and drew her into her arms with a gesture of protection. Sheldon spoke.

"Never you mind, Lilly girl. It's all over now, I reckon, an' you kin come straight home again an' fergit all about it."

Captain Connel nodded.

"Miss Foote, do you know this woman?" he inquired.

"She is Mrs. Annie Paulos, wife of a man in Salt Lake whom we have suspected of this sort of thing for some time," said Lucile.

"That's sufficient. We'll hold her," Connel decided.

"I would also request that you permit Miss Foote to wire the Salt Lake authorities to arrest the woman's husband and his associate, a man known as Hermostyple, whom she arranged to have kept under surveillance before we came on here," said Dual.

"Be glad to. You're making quite a clean up, ain't you," Connel agreed, smiling. "And now I want to add my congratulations to you all on the lucky outcome of this matter. It was clean work. I fancy, though I, of course, don't just know how it was done."

Dual shifted his position slightly.

"That is what I want to tell you," he remarked, as Connel paused. "But first I must ask you for Mr. Reich's arrest."

Lilly Lawton screamed sharply and struggled to free herself from Lucile's arms. Sheldon stared in speechless amazement, and all at once I saw a blinding mental illumination in my brain.

As for Reich he sprang to his feet and whirled upon Semi.

"What do you mean? Have me arrested?" he cried out and stood swaying slightly.

I saw the muscles of his throat contract in a spasmodic manner, and he swallowed as though choking and unable to go on.

At the same time I saw an expression of lightning comprehension sweep McKabe's face. He swung slightly toward Homer and answered for Dual.

"I've an idea he wants you *pinched*," he remarked.

The words broke the spell. Reich rushed into speech.

"You cowardly fakir, that's how you play even is it? Ever since you were called into this thing you've been bluffing and loafing. What did you do? Nothing. You sat around and drank tea and scribbled on pieces of paper, and told what you were *going* to do, and said we must wait.

"Well, we waited, till it was most too late, and then I beat you to it. I went down into that place alone and got this girl at the risk of my life, and now you're trying to make me trouble. You're a shine detective, and you're a shine as a man. But you can't make it stick. I loved the girl and I saved her. And what did you do? You just trailed along and talked.

"What have you got on me? Not a thing? You're jealous and you want to get hunk. Rats! You can't do it. And all the time you were talking so big, this is what you were. A fakir. Your talk was all lies—things which meant two things at once. You talked with a double tongue. You're a cowardly hypocrite and sneak."

"Homer," roared Sheldon "Homer, shut your trap!"

McKabe came over and took the raging youth by the shoulder.

"Quite right, Homer. Close up," he said.

"But where's his case?" stammered Reich. "Where's he got anything on me?"

"Maybe he'll tell you, if you let him," McKabe suggested. "Anyway, you're grabbed. Sit down." He forced him into a seat.

All eyes turned to Dual. He spoke:

"Mr. Reich, wherein have I lied to you? In what have I played the hypocrite's part? What have I said to you in any instance which has not been the literal truth? In nothing. To-night you asked me why I did not say what I meant, and I told you that I would explain to you later. I am about to do so now.

"You say that all I have done in this case has been to advise waiting—and scribble on bits of paper. I admit that to you that may appear to be correct, and I will also say that that was practically all I needed to do, for the simple reason that I knew you would lead me to the place where they held the woman you had betrayed."

He lifted his eyes and swept them over our staring faces.

"To-night I told you that I would show you something more appalling than any of the human paradoxes you mentioned. This is it: A man who has used the sacred passion of a woman's love to work her ruin.

"Mr. Reich, I told you that my methods were peculiar and unlike those of the police. They embrace the use of forces not recognized by even the bulk of mankind, yet in this case they have succeeded. If I tell you that the reason I seemingly waited and did nothing was that I had read your mind and knew you guilty, and used you to guide me to your victim, even while you tried to mislead me. You will doubtless sneer, but I shall allow the result to constitute the proof and explain my acts.

"Shortly after I met you in Goldfield I perceived the true character of your nature. Thereafter I used you to your own undoing. To read a man's mind it is first necessary to fasten it firmly on the thing it wants to conceal. That I did by speaking and acting in a manner which destroyed your mental quiet, and kept you in a state of uncertainty as to my meaning and actions. For the rest it was merely necessary to wait, while you betrayed yourself."

Reich laughed with a sneer.

"And you base your accusation on that? Just what do you accuse me of, too? You haven't said."

"I accuse you," said Semi, "of being an associate of the white slave people, and specifically of having betrayed Miss Lawton into their hands."

"On that evidence? Mind-reading. What is this—a joke?"

"Oh, no!" said Semi Dual. "I was merely explaining how I worked so that you would understand. At the same time I am aware that such evidence would be worthless at law. Therefore I obtained more substantial facts to support my complaint.

"First, let me call your attention to the fact that before I arrived in Goldfield you sent several messages to Salt Lake. One of them was addressed to Mrs. Annie Paul. I saw that message, and it was so worded that it might be either a request for information about Miss Lawton or a warning to the ones who held her.

"Further, there is only the difference of two letters—'o' and 's'—between the address of the telegram you sent and Mrs. Annie Paulos, now under arrest. That you really filed the message is proven by the fact that it was in your handwriting as shown by another sample of your chirography upon the back of a photograph of yourself, found in Miss Lawton's room.

"Also, while at Goldfield, you received a letter, missent from Denver, the envelope of which contained a return post-office box number in the Denver office. As you remember, I saw that letter, and I noted the number of the box.

"When I reached Salt Lake I wired Mr. Glace's partner—a man by the name of Bryce—asking him to ascertain the name of the party holding that Denver box; and later I wired him from Winnemucca to send his answer here.

"Now, Mr. Reich, you claim to have loved Miss Lawton, and admitted that you had offered her marriage. Let me read Mr. Bryce's reply to my message which you saw me receive a few moments ago."

He drew the telegram from his pocket and read:

P.O. Box No. —. Denver, held by Mrs. Ada Richmond, wife of Harold Richmond, *alias* Homer Richmond, alias Harold Reichman. Disappeared from Denver some two months ago. Alleged destination Salt Lake. Present name under which he is operating unknown. Homer Reich—quite probably correct.

"Mr. Reich, you are a married man and incapable of offering honorable marriage to any other woman. Now to proceed. When we reached Salt Lake you made an excuse of impatience of my methods and arranged a meeting between Mr. Glace, Colonel Sheldon, and myself, and a Greek named Paulos and his friend Hermostyple. Both of them were suspected of being white slave agents, and one we now know was the husband of Annie Paulos who brought the girl to San Francisco.

"In a very flimsy story they posed as detectives, and told us the girl had gone to Seattle, which information you sought to enforce by your remarks. I allowed you to think I was deceived until we reached Ogden, and I announced that we would come on here. To-night after you broke away from us you went to the underground tunnels where the girl was kept—after you had, as you thought, lost Colonel Sheldon, and you went directly to the place where this woman was with the girl, and you warned her to remove her, because we were on the track.

"And in proof of the fact that you knew her, we have

your attempt in the restaurant to cry out and warn her after
Miss Foote had identified her to Mr. McKabe, and later
still, the fact that after her arrest you spoke to her in Italian
and asked her not to betray your connection in the case. As
it happens, I heard you and I understand Italian as well as
Greek. Besides that, we still have the message addressed to
her assumed name in Salt Lake, which conclusively shows
that you knew the address, which Miss Foote tells me is
that of the wife of Paulos, and presumably the house where
Miss Lawton was held while in Salt Lake."

Reich sat pale and shaken while Dual was speaking—
his eyes fastened on the floor. At the end he heaved a long
tremulous sigh and lifted a haggard face.

"But," he began, grasping vainly at a technical straw, "but
you haven't proven that I am married. You haven't proven
that I am not Homer Reich. You haven't proven that I am
this Richmond or that—"

"Wait, Mr Reich," said Dual. "Wait till you know of
what I accuse you. It is this: I accuse you first of being an
associate of these people—of going to Goldfield and meeting Miss Lawton and deciding to betray her; of winning
her affection and making her an offer of marriage, and of
establishing your position in that place by a pretended
intention to buy an interest in a moving-picture house. I
allege that after she had given her promise to wed you, you
came to Salt Lake and met Stakos and Paulos, of which
meeting we have proof, and of plotting the girl's capture.

"You so timed your return to Goldfield that you arrived
too late for her to be intercepted by a warning on the train
she had taken, and you returned to Goldfield solely as you
believed to clear yourself from any suspicion of complicity

in the case. In that you blundered, because after you went to Colonel Sheldon he kept you with him, so that you had no opportunity to disappear. Later, after I came into the case, you sought to mislead me, but failed, for the simple reason that you were combating a force you did not understand, which demoralized your self-control and robbed your efforts of power.

"The uncertainty of your position made your actions either to warn your confederates or make your own escape futile. Quite without your volition you were caught in a web from which you were unable to free yourself, and so—"

With a twitching face Reich came to his feet.

"You fiend," he cried hoarsely. "You fiend! You're right! Yes, I was caught in a web—a web of your spinning! I hadn't known you fifteen minutes before I felt something about you I couldn't understand. You played with me—played with me for days, damn you—like a cat with a mouse! I was afraid to stay with you and afraid to leave. Once or twice I had a chance to leave, but my nerve failed me. That night I went to see Paulos I wanted to make a run for it, and they persuaded me not to. They said I ought to stick and keep an eye on you and tip off your hand.

"Well, I tried, and there wasn't a chance. I only had one chance after that—one real chance I might have sent a wire from the train, but Sheldon stuck to me all the time and I was rattled. I kept waiting and trying to make up my mind and I couldn't. I was afraid—afraid. I thought after we got here I could find a chance sure, but you acted too quick.

"Well, it's all over. You've got me—and I'm glad. These last days have been hell! I couldn't say a thing. I couldn't do a thing that you didn't seem to block almost as soon as I thought it. I guess you did read my mind as you say. You must have. You couldn't have acted like you did if you hadn't. I thought I could fool you, but I've been the fool, and you've broke me—broke me—I'm sick—sick—my nerves are in rags.

"But it's over. They'll take me away—somewhere. I don't care where—so long as it's away from you—you smiling devil! Take your eyes off of me—take 'em off—*take 'em off, I say—I cant stand 'em, Sheldon—make him quit looking at me. I— Oh—*" He sank panting into his seat and buried his face in his hands.

Greek Annie laughed in the silence which followed.

"You poor simp! I guess there wasn't no need of my squealing," she said.

"My Lord!" muttered Sheldon.

Lilly Lawton wept, with her face buried on Lucile's breast. I don't think her faith had faltered until Reich's own words had spelled his guilt. Then—and only then—she accepted the awful truth and turned, moaning to the older woman at her side.

"And so," said Dual, "you stand self-confessed as the vilest of human creatures, lost to decency and to shame; a despoiler of youth and innocence and virtue; a betrayer of the holiest of human passions: a befouler of the fount of life itself; a modern vampire preying on your fellows; a menace to the social fabric, more loathsome, more to be shunned and blotted out than any foul disease; a creature beyond the pale of any charity or mercy; an insult to the name of man."

Connel nodded slowly and cleared his throat.

Dual spoke again:

"And now, Miss Foote."

Very gently Lucile disengaged the arms of the weeping girl and led her across to Sheldon, who took her hand and patted it softly in an awkward effort to comfort.

Miss Foote turned back. Her hand darted inside the neck of her waist and drew forth an old-fashioned locket of silver. With her eyes fastened on Reich, she pried it open, extended it in her hand, and thrust it before him.

"Do you know her?" she hissed.

Reich gave one glance at what she held and drew back as from a threatened menace.

His eyes started from their sockets, and he shrank with a peculiar cringing motion, as though confronted by a ghost! If ever a man's face held the stamp of guilt, his did at that moment. Yet he said no word.

Lucile laughed harshly.

"No need to answer," she began, speaking in fierce, gloating accents. "Your face is enough to condemn you. No need for you to say that you recognize the face of little Laura Foote, of San Francisco, whom you betrayed to her death three years ago; of little Laura Foote, whom you taught to love you, as you did this girl, and betrayed as you did her; of the little woman you trapped and turned over to your companions after you had won the faith and trust of her heart—Homer Richmond; of the same little heart she stabbed when she found out that she was lost; of the little girl who died rather than meet the fate to which you had led her, even as this girl said to-night that she meant to die.

"You say that we don't know you are not Homer Reich. It doesn't matter. I know you are the man who betrayed this girl here three years ago, and were then known as

Homer Richmond. I knew you the minute I saw you in the hotel at Salt Lake three days ago. I knew you after the whole three years—because—I'd been hunting you all the time—hunting you and praying that I might find you— praying every night that I might find you, since the day I leaned over the cold, white face of my little dead sister, and swore to Almighty God that I'd find you, if He gave me life and strength!

"And the other day I found you and spoke to you and you never suspected. Then I knew that God had heard my prayer and given you into my hands. Since then I have played my part and watched the coils of the web as they gathered about you. And I gloated. Great God, how I gloated while I waited! And I waited in order that your latest victim might be saved before I struck.

"You, Homer Richmond, or Reich, or whatever you call yourself, sent my sister to her death, but you left behind you a picture upon which you had written a message of love to her in your own hand. The very same words you wrote on the picture you gave to this little girl who sits here now—'Your loving Homer!' Do you remember? You wrote them on Laura's picture of you, and you wrote them on the one you gave to Lilly Lawton and the writing is the same. There is the last link of the chain to bind you—and prove you the man you are.

"It's taken a long time, Homer, but my hour has come— after three years! Your action robbed me of my sister and made me the woman I am. Your action put me into the business I've followed for the last three years. They've been a long three years full of hardship and horror and hope deferred, but they're past, and to-night is worth all they have cost—because at last I have you as I've prayed to get you! After three years—after three years—*I've kept my oath!*"

Her voice rose to something approaching a scream—and broke. For a minute she stood with clenched hands, gasping. Then, by an effort controlled her emotions and drew a long breath.

"That was the page in my past of which I spoke, Mr. Dual," she said quite calmly. "There is no doubt that this man is the Harold Richmond mentioned in your despatch."

Reich sat utterly collapsed—a pitiful object—beside McKabe. Not once since Lucile had thrust the picture of her sister before him had he moved or attempted to speak. Utterly cowed—utterly beaten down by the tearing away of the veil from his soul—he half sat, half lay in his seat, his chest heaving in short, shallow panting—all vestige of resistence wiped from his being; utterly bound in the web of fate into which he had so unwittingly cast himself.

Sheldon gave him a glance and turned to me.

"He fooled me—fooled me silly!" he said in a tone of complaint. "He fooled me an' Green an' Lilly, *but by the Lord, he didn't fool Semi Dual!* That man's a wonder! My hat's off to him! Thar, thar, little gal, don't cry. Good Lord, but you're lucky, after all!"

Connel broke in, addressing Reich:

"Richmond, have you anything you want to say?"

Homer made no response, and the captain spoke to McKabe:

"I fancy we hold him on about two counts. Take him and the woman away."

"Come on!" said McKabe, tapping Homer on the shoulder. He beckoned to Annie and led them both from the room. The woman walked defiantly erect with a fling of her figure; the man stooped forward, slouching, with eyes downcast and never a glance for the woman whose life he had sought to despoil.

We shook hands with Connel and departed. As we were leaving the building we met McKabe and said good night to him as well. Dual had telephoned to the hotel for a taxi, and it waited in the street below.

As we came out the fog had cleared away, and the moon rode high, flooding all the sleeping city with a soft, clear light.

We entered the cab, and Lucile drew Lilly into her arms, where she nestled with the sigh of one utterly tired.

I sank back against the cushions beside Semi, and gave myself to my thoughts.

And as we rolled back through the streets it came into my mind that the incident of the spider at Salida had, as Dual had predicted, set the parallel of all which followed, and that even as then, he had put out his hand and freed the unwitting fly.

ABOUT THE AUTHOR: DR. J.U. GIESY

BORN NEAR CHILLICOTHE, Ohio, August 6, 1877. That makes me a Buckeye, and some people have suggested that I was a nut. Of my actual birth I have no recollection. So this is mere hearsay evidence. When I was eight months of age my parents removed to southeastern Kansas and took me with them, as I was still unable to shift for myself.

When I was thirteen we again removed to Utah, where I received my common school education in common with other youngsters of a similar age. In 1895, I entered the Starling Medical College, Columbus, Ohio, and received my medical degree from that institution in 1898.

Returning to Salt Lake, I served an internship in a local hospital and have practiced medicine in that city ever since, with the exception of the time I spent in the United States service during the World War as a captain in the Medical Corps. As regards the Army, I am still a major in the Reserve, attached to the Division Surgeon's Office of the 104th Division. In 1916 I was instrumental in organizing the first Plattsburg camp ever held in the State, starting the movement and acting as secretary of the general committee which put it over.

I began to write in 1910. Unlike many well known writers, I have had rejections since. At the same time, I've found a lot of editors who liked my work. I have written as an avocation ever since. At present I am associate editor for Utah on the staff of *California and Western Medicine,* and the staff of the *Archives of Physical Therapy X-Ray and Radium.* Because of the latter fact I am a member of the American Medical Editors Association.

I am also a member of the Salt Lake Chamber of Commerce, and a life member of the American College of Physical Therapy, which I have served as an officer for several years. My ancestors made me a Son of the American Revolution, and I have made myself more or less of a nuisance to a lot of people all by myself.

I was married in San Francisco, to Juliet Galena Conwell, in December, 1904, and the marriage took. Personally I think they did better work along those lines, that long ago. Anyway we're still living in the same apartment, with no intentions of divorce.

Just why the editor should want to print this confession I really can't imagine. But that's his business. He's asked for it and here it is!

ABOUT THE AUTHOR: JUNIUS B. SMITH

I WAS BORN at Salt Lake City, Utah, September 29, 1883, at approximately 3:55:27 P.M., right ascension of the mid-heaven (for the benefit of my astrological readers) 16 hrs. 27 min. 57 sec., or 246° 59' 15"; position of planets, Neptune 20° 45' ret. Taurus, Saturn 10° 6' ret. Gemini, Mars 22° 10' Cancer, Jupiter 0° 26' Leo, Moon 22° 24' Virgo, Uranus 24° 34' Virgo, Sun 6° 27' 23" Libra, Venus 8° 52' Libra, Mercury 20° 31' ret. Libra. Declinations: Sun 2° 34' south, Moon 0° 7' south, Neptune 16° 13' north, Uranus 2° 50' north, Saturn 20° 2' north, Jupiter 20° 18' north, Mars 22° 25' north, Venus 2° 20' south, Mercury 11° 17' south.

With this meager astronomical data, the astrologians will know more about me than I could write in a volume.

For the benefit of you other readers:

I am an attorney at law and practiced for many years, paying my office expenses in the lean years by writing. I never had the bitter experience of having to write years before anything sold. At the beginning of my writing career, Dr. J.U. Giesy and I joined intellectual forces, and our first joint effort was submitted to *Argosy* way back in 1911. It sold, first time out. Rapidly we "dashed" off more and they sold also. We each write separately as well as jointly, at such times as we cannot get together.

Early in life I took up astrology as a hobby and lived to see it recognized in judicial decisions as a science. That I have helped, in some measure, to brush away the misconceptions in the minds of many people regarding this much maligned subject is perhaps testified to by my election to Fellowship in the American Academy of Astrologians, an organization that one can't get into for the asking.

I've wasted enough time playing checkers to have built one of the Egyptian pyramids single-handed. Another hobby is shorthand, which has fascinated me for thirty years. I understand several systems. I can sling a wicked toe on the dance floor, but only dance when my weight crowds two hundred. One year I spent the summer on the desert drying out, where my own cooking, plus the heat, effected a material reduction. But I come honestly by it: my father weighed two hundred and sixty in athletic condition—three hundred when not.

And speaking of ancestors: My grandfather was a brother of Joseph Smith, who founded the Mormon Church, which probably explains why I was born in Utah.